They Called Her
Jewgirl

They Called Her
Jewgirl

A novel by
Kurt Meyer

Pentland Press, Inc.
England • USA • Scotland

Also by Kurt Meyer
Bitches, Bastards and Lovers (1982)

PUBLISHED BY PENTLAND PRESS, INC.
5122 Bur Oak Circle, Raleigh, North Carolina 27612
United States of America
(919)782-0281

ISBN: 1-57197-158-0
Library of Congress Catalog Card Number 99-070096

Copyright © 1999 Kurt Meyer
All rights reserved, which includes the right to reproduce this book or portions thereof in any form whatsoever except as provided by the U.S. Copyright Law.

Printed in the United States of America

To Freda, my wife who inspired me
To Susan Rabiner who guided me

Although most of the characters and narrative are based on real persons and actual events, this book is entirely a work of fiction. Many scenes and characters have sprung from my own imagination and most dialogue is of my own presumption. Nothing in this book should be construed as a comment on or criticism of what really happened.

Man no more knows his own time than fish taken in the fatal net, or birds trapped in the snare; like these the children of men are caught when the evil time falls suddenly upon them.

Ecclesiastes 9:12

Chapter 1

November 1932

As Karl started up the old, steel-arched bridge, the *Hohenzollernbrücke* that crossed the Rhine River, the lambent glow of gaslights danced feverishly on the rain-streaked windshield of his Opel, blinding him except for the quarter circle that the solitary wiper kept clear. Driving cautiously, he eased his way down the bridge. He held carefully to his right past the main railroad station, its ready locomotives venting their blazing, Stygian smoke into the foul night. To his left, the soot-blackened *Dom*, Cologne's mighty, twin-towered cathedral, completed in 1880 after six long centuries and only ten years before he was born, loomed like a giant, boundless shadow.

As he looked right above him, his eyes caught the bluish, neon sparkle of the new "Eau de Cologne" sign. Konrad Adenauer, mayor of Cologne, had derided the sign as *furchtbarer Kitsch*. Yes, it was in bad taste, one of the many vulgar pretensions so rampant now.

God, nothing was real any longer! Nothing in his life! Not his marriage, not his family! Nothing at all! All of it was a big, huge sham! All of it was full of cheap, vulgar pretensions! The whole world was a like speeding, silent movie, its images flashing by, its captions but a blur.

Suddenly his eyes glassed over, his cheeks hollowed, and his throat snapped close as if he had been caught in a chokehold. He bit his lips until they ached. There was only one answer. There really was no other way. "Reggie," he said, taking a deep breath, delivering his words as if he were in a court of law, "I have decided to leave you!"

He had finally uttered the words. But they were hardly adequate. She'd only laugh at him—like she always laughed at him. Laugh at him with that sly, lustful laugh of hers.

He felt for the gash. The gash of shrapnel cut deep into his cheek. Yes, it was true: all of his dreams were still mired in the trenches of the Marne. Mired in those swampy, dungy urinals. Lost there! Lost there forever! Many years ago! Way back! Way back in 1916! That's when his dreams were still real. Or, maybe, that's when his only reality were his dreams. His dreams of a home, a wife, children. The whole megillah.

Whatever happened to all of his dreams?

Yes, Kitty was all that was left in his life. Sitting at the Steinweg, her tiny fingers reaching for the far keys, her brown eyes fixed on him, waiting for him to give the nod.

God Almighty, how she had whacked those little fingers. "Your little darling Kitty, your sweet little pet," Reggie had complained to him, "peed in her pants at Cafe Wien. Mind you, an eight-year-old! Right in front of all of my friends. To embarrass me." She had whacked her little fingers until they were raw, wet with blood. Yes, it was her way of getting even with him. So his little girl couldn't make music with him.

What in the world would happen to her?

He drove on mechanically, cautiously, finding his passage through the narrow, winding lanes of the old quarter. He crossed the *Ring*, the broad half-circle boulevard that encompassed the inner city and passed the great opera house. It was only last month that he had heard pudgy, big-voiced Henny NeumannKnapp sing the role of frail, consumptive Mimi in *La*

Bohème. He grinned. Opera could be such a farce. So damned melodramatic, so damned preposterous, so laughable. The tragic characters brought down by their own foolish passions, their own flaws, never by a downturn in business or events over which they had no control. The way most mortals are brought down.

Yes, Mimi! That's the kind of woman he should have married! Whatever had attracted him to Reggie anyhow?

Ah, the competition he had had! Better men than he. Early on, he had decided to seduce her into choosing him. He had wined and dined her lavishly, had taken her dancing, to the opera, to concerts, to every event at which a beautiful young woman like Reggie would want to be seen. He had always taken her to the best! It had been his way of telling her that he could afford her.

What a fool he had been! What a goddamned, idiotic fool!

When Karl finally arrived at his *stattliche Residenz*—really an elegant townhouse, which so far he had been able to hold on to—he got out of the car and opened the front gate. It had stopped raining. But the night was still pitch-black, filled with the seeping, chilled air from the North Sea. Only a lonely lantern, peering over the wall of the front garden, flickered a weak and eerie challenge to the portentous darkness.

Still, nothing in the world could have prepared him for the events that awaited him. Like a chaste, unsuspecting lamb going to slaughter, to be cut down, skinned and quartered, he had no premonition of the coming doom, no sense of the hopeless reality of his situation. No sense that his future was bereft of any of his conventional expectations. No inkling that the scythe of death was already hanging over him. No sense either of how the tragic impact of the coming moments would consume his Kitty for the rest of her life.

Stroking his bald skull, he grabbed for the railing. Yes, he must steady himself. He must try to relax. Slow down his breathing, slow down his heart.

It was moments later that Karl, rooted to the doorway of the salon, stared at them both: Reggie, his wife, and Fritz, that old chum of hers, a fellow cast member of a small stage production of *The Merry Widow*. Why not say it? He was her boyfriend. No, that wasn't true. He was really her lover. That's what he was. His wife, Reggie, was sitting there on the couch, acting so demure, even guileless. She was behaving as if it were the most natural thing in the world for a married woman to entertain her boyfriend in her home while her husband was away on business.

His blood was surging, his temples pulsating, a knife twisting in his stomach.

Yes, he was entitled to some answers!

Of course, Reggie would only deflect his questions. She would accuse him instead. "What do you expect me to do?" she'd say. "You're gone all the time. You're gone for weeks, even months." Yes, he knew her exact words. "I'm still a young woman, a sociable person. I get lonely. Don't you think I need some civilized adult company once in a while? But you, you with your dirty, little mind, you always suspect the worst." Then her eyes would drop in a self-effacing gesture, so false it was almost laughable. That's all it was with her, a game, and he, her husband, was the object of her sport.

"Reggie!" He avoided looking at Fritz.

"Yes, Karl." Showing her teeth, she allowed the slight smirk to remain on her face. "So you're home!"

Yes, there it was again—that icy smirk of hers, pregnant with scorn, which always reminded him of a beast of prey, of a large cat with slit pupils, a stoic maw and a blank, impenetrable bearing. Even in all of her nudity, in their few private moments, she was always defiant, mocking, that inscrutable smirk on her face, inching her snarling stare across his sagging flesh, pointing her nipples like thorns, keeping her thighs locked in prissy denial. Forswearing any interest in physical intimacy. Denying him any recognition of his manhood. Amusing herself with her defenseless prey.

Biting his lips, he buried his feelings for the moment and walked over to her. "I'd like a word with you." He said it quietly, trying his best to sound resolute.

"Go right ahead." Reggie looked up from the couch, her lips twisted into a wry smile.

He kept staring at her. God, how her calm elegance had captivated him at first, how her beauty, more German than Semitic, had always been her secret weapon, had instilled an arrogance in her, in all of her dealings with him. For she ranked high in the day's beauty hierarchy: fair skin, blue eyes, and a fine nose, all among the highest requisites for a good-looking woman or man. It had always caused such deep self-hate in him.

Even if he felt the lesser for her beauty, he would be man enough to stand up to her tonight. "Not here!" he said, his eyes indicating Fritz sitting next to her.

"Why not?" Her tone was short, sarcastic, the contempt on her haughty face communicating just what she thought of him.

He could hear her words. You're a nebbish if there ever was one! A big-nosed failure that calls itself a man. Still, he insisted, "It's a private matter."

Fritz got up.

Reggie grabbed his arm. "Sit down!" she commanded. Then she turned back to her husband. "You're telling *me* what to do? *Me*?" He didn't answer her. "Whatever you've got to say, you can say it right here, right here in front of Fritz."

For a short moment, Karl's mind quivered with all the bitterness of his shame, smarting as though an old wound had been reopened. Yes, of course, that was it. She knew too much about him. Yes, he had been a total failure! Not only had he lost his business, but he had lost it disastrously. A business failure that had turned into a personal calamity. Reggie reminded him so often—the really sharp fellows came out of their bankruptcies in good enough shape to start again in something else, having cached a stake to bankroll another go at the brass ring.

He stared at her, pursing his lips. His breathing quickened. "What I have to say is a family matter." His voice had firmed. "It's private! I'd like to speak to you alone."

She tossed her head, her slender lips set in yet another smirk. "What if I don't want to?" Her steel-blue eyes stared icily back at him, while her nostrils flared. "It's all over, Karl! It's time you faced it."

Over or not, she was still spending what little of his money was left. She had used two thousand marks of his money and spent it on that Oriental rug. As if she were unaware that Germany was immersed in a depression, with more than seven million out of work. As if everything were his fault. Not giving a damn about anything except the fact that life had become inconvenient for her.

This time his voice was stronger but still contained. "I'm telling you for the last time. I'd like to talk to you alone!"

She looked up at him, holding back a big grin. "Go ahead! Make me! You're such a fool!"

"All right!"

He grabbed her arm and yanked her from the couch. Immediately, Reggie jerked herself free, the smirk still on her face. The thought that she was enjoying it all was just too much for him. He grabbed her hair and pulled her back. He'd force her to hear what he had to say.

She quickly wheeled around and, before he could gather his wits, kicked him in his shin and dug her razor-sharp nails into his cheeks, not letting go until blood oozed from his puffed cheeks. The pain forced him to release her.

He caught her triumphant grin.

Once more he grabbed for her arm. She easily twisted away. But, as she broke free from him, she suddenly staggered. When she finally regained her balance, she appeared so stunned by his unexpected aggressiveness that she momentarily froze in place. Reacting instinctively to the scorn he saw in her eyes, he smacked her hard across the face, causing her to stumble, lose her balance, and finally, tumbling backwards, fall on her back. At once, he threw himself on top of her and, grabbing her neck, he started to choke her, tossing her head back and forth. "What do you think you're doing?" he screamed at her, losing all control.

Fritz had rushed over and, grasping both of Karl's arms, tried to loosen his grip on Reggie's throat. "Let her be," he said. "Karl, that's enough! Let her be."

Karl pushed him away. "Mind your own damned business, you damn ass," he screamed at Fritz, beside himself with rage.

Struggling to free Reggie from Karl's grip, Fritz appealed to him once more. "Let her be, Karl. It's no good this way."

Suddenly Karl let go of his wife's neck, rose and, turning on Fritz, pushed him backward. "Mind your own damned business," he screamed at him. "This is *my home!*"

As Karl shoved him backwards, Fritz suddenly landed a hard punch to Karl's stomach. With courage that seemed to emanate from all of his rage, Karl quickly recovered and landed his own closefisted punch to the younger man's face. It was the first time he had delivered such a wild blow since his boyhood.

While the two men threw themselves clumsily around the room, grappling, striking at each other again and again, Reggie rose from the floor and looked about for a weapon to finish the battle. She spied a large Chinese vase. Filled with all the hatred her disappointment in her husband could engender, with all the reckless abandon her contempt for him made possible, she grasped the vase with both hands and raised it high above Karl. There was only the briefest moment of hesitation before she brought it down on his head.

He fell immediately.

He did not move. He lay on his stomach, a deep gash to the side of his head.

Reggie and Fritz stared at the crumpled body with vacant eyes. Karl was out cold.

From where she was, Kitty, kneeling on the landing halfway down the stairs, her curly head squeezed between the balusters of the stairway like a book wedged onto a crowded shelf, had observed most of what had been going on in the salon. She had heard the loud voices, had watched the scuffle, and had seen her mother grab the vase and bring it down on her father.

In the violence of the confrontation, nobody had noticed her wide, dark brown eyes taking it all in.

She was terrified. "What are they doing to you, Papa?" The cry echoed in her head.

Chock-full of the hidden qualms of childhood, Kitty trembled and shook, overcome by a deep nausea. She was afraid to cry. Why couldn't she cry? How she wished she still could cry! Like in those days, when she had heard Bubi's woeful wail from the street. That time when she carried her little white schnauzer up to her room, his eyes gazing at her helplessly, blood oozing from his snout, spilling all over her dress. When, flushed with the ache of Bubi's pain, her warm, salty tears still came so easily.

Ruth appeared on the second-floor landing, looking over the railing. "They're at it again?" she asked.

Kitty nodded.

Ruth, nearly a head taller than her sister Kitty, barely changed her expression. "Why can't he leave her alone?"

She couldn't understand Ruth always taking her mother's side. Played up to Fritz, when she knew that Fritz didn't really belong here. But she played up to him anyhow. She even smiled at him—that is, when she tossed her hair to the side, like she always did when she was with boys.

"But he's our Papa!" Kitty looked up at her sister.

But Ruth had already turned away. When she heard Kitty, she quickly turned back. "Yeah, Papa! You mean, your Papa!" She raised her eyebrows. "Whenever he happens to be around."

"Papa's working hard."

Ruth's narrow lips twisted into a wry smirk, just like her mother's. "Papa's a fool! You know he is!" She waited for her sister's reaction. Then she added. "Papa hasn't made a living for years."

"That isn't true." Ruth upset her so much. She always talked like that about Papa.

But Ruth had already disappeared.

It was always the same. Her sister taking her mother's side. No matter what. It was always her mother and Ruth. She liked Ruth better than she liked her. Ruth was like Mother. She was more like Papa.

Kitty was still watching when her mother left the salon and returned with a pitcher of water. When she splashed it on Papa, the wetness soaked his shirt until you could see through it. Finally, Fritz, bending over her father, held up his wrist and said, "I think he's going to be all right."

Only then did Kitty return to her room. It was all over. "Everything has an ending." That's what Papa always said. Maybe, after all, everything would be all right.

Reggie watched as Fritz turned Karl on his back and grabbed him under the arms. "Give me a hand." He indicated to Reggie that she should take the legs.

They both carried him to the upstairs bedroom. Fritz turned to Reggie. "Maybe we better call a doctor."

Reggie wasn't listening. She was deep in her own thoughts. That idiot! That idiot husband of hers! Hadn't made a living since '29. Since he left Berlin and those blasted *Philharmoniker*. Yes, he was a musician of sorts. He played the fiddle. Said he was going to go into business and make a killing. Some killing he had made. He had nearly killed his wife and family. She could spit in his face. Even right now! He and his goddamn pet, his Kitty! Paying for those expensive piano lessons they couldn't afford. He had this showdown coming for a long time.

"We should have finished him off," she said quietly, more to herself than to Fritz.

Fritz shook his head. "You can't be serious?"

In the end none of it really mattered. Karl died the next day. It could have been that he died from the blow to his head or some other injury suffered in the fight. Or, perhaps he died from the weight of his regret and the realization that he could no longer reverse his life.

One could only guess. In point of fact, not one person of all those who came to the funeral inquired about the cause of Karl's death. But everyone wondered. They knew about the failing marriage. They knew about the boyfriend. There was a lot of talk, especially among Karl's friends. At the afternoon coffees at the Monopole Cafe they talked about his death for days. "What did he die from?" they asked each other. Was it really pneumonia—a deadly disease in those days—as they had been told? Why had he been left to die without a physician?

No one really wanted to question Reggie. They said that Reggie was made of steel and malice.

Only Kitty asked to see him on the last day of his life. That encounter would eventually lead to more tensions with her mother and help create more guilt than any young child could handle.

"All right! I'll let you see him. But don't you dare talk to him," her mother warned her. "Not a single word out of you!"

So Kitty was allowed to see her father one last time.

Sitting next to him in the dark bedroom, the little eight-year-old tried to understand what was happening. Of course, she knew already how despised he was—a foolish, incompetent man, her mother had said—but she really did not understand how this could be. To her, still so young, still so innocent, he had only been a loving father, her *Papa*.

For a long time she sat quietly next to him. She stared at him with those melancholy, vulnerable eyes of hers, like a young basset waiting for its master's command. She waited and waited. Finally, sensing her presence, Karl's eyes widened, his lips parted and, employing great effort, he turned his head and gazed at his young daughter.

For some odd reason, at that moment, when she met her Papa's eyes, Kitty found new hope. She folded her little hands as in prayer and whispered. "I'll take care of you, Papa! I promise I will!"

He gave a faint, distant nod. Then, suddenly, he reached for her hand and placed it into his. As she felt him straining to squeeze it, she closed her eyes and, with tears flooding down her cheeks, her little heart overflowed with all the love she had for her father. "Papa, I love you so much!"

There was but a hint of a smile on his tired face.

"Oh Papa," she sighed, staring into his white eyes, "when you get better, will you take me to a concert?"

Haltingly, he placed her little hand upon his chest, took what seemed like a very slow, shallow breath, and spoke in a coarse whisper, "When I get better . . ."

Kitty remained with him for a long time, her little hand resting on his chest. He didn't speak another word.

That's all Kitty remembered about her father's death. Even that faint memory—those images of wide-open eyes and drained, fallen lips—faded with the years like a desert trail that disappears with the twirling winds of time.

Except that later on her mother blamed her for Papa's death. "You talked to him," she proclaimed to Kitty, "even though I forbade it. You upset him!" And then, as if her face had suddenly been shrouded by a black shadow, she spoke in a low, icy voice, a voice pregnant with doom. "*You killed him!*"

Chapter 2

May 1933

On 30 January 1933, Adolf Hitler ascended to power as *Reichskanzler*, chancellor of Germany.

The immediate effect of this change was negligible. Yes, the street fights between Communists and Nazis ended almost immediately. Except for diehard Nazis, most people did not have much hope that Hitler could lift Germany out of its depression. There was no consensus on what the future held and much doubt about Hitler's intentions, even though he had earlier published a clear battle plan in his widely distributed book *Mein Kampf*.

Cologne in the 1930s was a typical European city. Over its two-thousand-year history, its *Altstadt* (the old town), had expanded in ever wider concentric circles, not at all like the grid patterns of most American cities. Beyond the *Ring*, which half-circled the old town between the north and south shores of the Rhine, were the few linear thoroughfares of the city, radiating like star beams out to the suburbs.

One of these was *Aachenerstrasse*, which, starting at the *Hahnentor* (the old city gate), passed by the great opera house and reached the townhouse where Reggie, now a widow, lived with her two daughters.

Almost immediately after Karl's death, Reggie opened a millinery shop in an elegant section of Cologne, quite near the Dom. There had been no money left to her by Karl. Just one more indication of his total ineptitude, she thought, and the insignificance of his life. Luckily she had found herself with several offers of financial advice and assistance from the men at the *Jüdischer Kegelklub* (the Jewish bowling league), where she was the only woman bowler. The only condition these benefactors attached to their gifts was that their help remain secret.

These men greatly admired Reggie, not only for her beauty—which some of them said was as close to perfection as that of the classical Aphrodite—but also for her seductive playfulness, which added some spice to their dreary lives. It was one of her fellow bowlers who gave her a nickname based on her appearance in the title role of Franz Lehar's operetta that would stick with her the rest of her life: *Die Lustige Witwe (The Merry Widow)*. It was a most appropriate title. Not that any of her fellow bowlers ever asked more of her than an occasional wink, a knowing chuckle, or to share an occasional lusty guffaw. In those days in Cologne, where all the Jews knew each other's business, husbands were careful not to seek or accept, or even appear to seek or accept, sexual favors from those within their own community.

Reggie enjoyed her new freedom. Yet, as often happens when circumstances change, with the advent of Hitler's coming to power her liaison with Fritz was interrupted by the politics of the day.

Six months had now passed since her father's death, since Kitty had sat silently next to her sister Ruth while the sounds of men praying had drifted in from the next room and the hushed chatter of their wives had filtered in from the kitchen.

To Kitty, the eight-year-old, her father's death was inconceivable. The concept of a finality was still beyond her grasp, making sense solely as another form of going away. To her it seemed inevitable that in the fullness of time he'd be standing again at her bedroom door. That he'd take her up into his arms.

That he'd hold her, that he'd kiss her and rest her head upon his shoulder. That he'd whisper once more those happy words that she'd never forget in all of her life, "*Mein liebes Goldkindchen!* (My darling, golden child!)"

These thoughts made her ache with hope.

Still, as the months passed and he didn't reappear, her fantasies became more like the flick of a passing shadow and they afforded less and less consolation to her anguished longings. That's when Kitty perceived a connection between her mother and her Papa's dying. It wasn't that she remembered the events surrounding her father's death. But she began to defy Reggie. Whatever prompted her to defy her mother had to do with the eight-year-old's understanding of evil. Something was wrong here. Papa shouldn't have died.

Whenever her mother scolded her or hit her and, finally, whenever she did not get her way, she stamped her feet or held her breath. This was her way. This was her way of expressing what she couldn't say in so many words. That something was wrong. That something was a lie.

There wasn't another child in all of Cologne who could hold her breath as long as Kitty could. To Kitty there was no threatened consequence or punishment that could hurt her more than she had been hurt already.

As time went on, Reggie wondered what could be done about her younger daughter's strange behavior. Of course, she concluded, Kitty's father had caused it all. He had spoiled her. Yes, it had always been left to her to scold the child, to punish her. He had never done it, no, not him. He would never raise a hand to his precious child or do anything that might make her think less of him. Of course, he was not around to deal with the predictable consequences of those lenient ways of his.

Over time, Reggie became ever more impatient with Kitty. Her younger daughter took too many things for granted. There were never any words of thanks from her. These were difficult times and she was a lonely widow. "Don't you think I have enough on my hands," she said to the child, "trying to be both father and mother to you without having to put up with your damned fits?"

But Kitty's answer would only be more stamping of her feet and holding of her breath. The former enraged her, but the breath-holding seemed to confound her.

Reggie would question her friends about her daughter's perversity. "What can I do with her?" she'd ask them, her eyes choked with tears. She was a poor widow burdened with what she called *mein Missgeschick* (my misfortune). "Some of us are made to grace this world with a pleasant personality. Others are born headstrong, obstinate, and willful. As for myself, I have always preferred an even-tempered child like Ruth."

No, Kitty was not at all like her sister Ruth, who, although barely three years older, helped her mother daily in the millinery shop after school. Ruth, with that fair skin, those sparkling blue eyes, and that fine, Grecian nose. If it hadn't been for Ruth's help, she'd be in the poorhouse. Surely, when you have two daughters so different, isn't it only reasonable, even proper, to reward the more helpful one with a greater degree of affection?

At times, Kitty's behavior was so embarrassing to Reggie that she no longer bothered to correct her younger daughter. "Go, do whatever you want," she would say to her. It was a total resignation. She accepted that Kitty was the way she was and that nothing in the world would ever change her. That's when she began to avoid her. She talked to her as little as possible. She no longer picked her up from school. She justified herself to Kitty. "You don't appreciate the way I struggle to provide for you, to keep us all going in these difficult times."

There was one person in Kitty's life who brought her solace from the void she had felt since her father's death. It was Alfred Schweitzer, one of her late father's friends, a musician of the first rank, a star violinist of the *Philharmoniker*. They had been colleagues in Berlin, Alfred the concert master, Karl a member of the string section. After Karl had left the profession, they remained close friends. Just before Karl's death, the changing ambiance in Prussian Berlin caused Alfred to leave the *Berliner Philharmoniker* and join the Cologne Opera Orchestra.

Alfred saw to it that Kitty continued her piano lessons at the Cologne Conservatory of Music. Her father would have wanted him to do that, he told Kitty. There, in the conservatory, Kitty and Alfred met secretly.

"How are you doing, sweetheart?"

Holding her school satchel under her arm, Kitty gave a faint nod. "Fine."

He pointed to the wooden bench. "Sit down with me for a minute."

Kitty sat down next to Alfred.

"You're getting much Czerny?"

"Yes." She really hated those practice pieces.

"Good! What else are you playing?"

"Mendelssohn! Spring Song! Venetian Boat Song! Schubert's Impromptus!"

"Yes, of course, I know. And, your mother?"

"Yes?"

"Does she know yet?"

Kitty shook her head.

"You're not going to tell her?"

She shook her head again.

Alfred's jaw dropped. It was beyond his comprehension that a nine-year-old would have to sneak out of the house to take her music lessons. In his confusion he sought confirmation of the rectitude of what he was doing from the child herself. Putting his hand to Kitty's cheek, he asked her, "You do believe that you are doing the right thing, yes? That your father would have wanted it this way? Why don't you speak with your mother? Or, if you prefer, I'll be happy to speak to her for you."

Kitty shook her head violently. It was too frightening to think of the scene that would result if her mother learned of her deceit.

Alfred could only shake his head. He sighed deeply. Then, suddenly, he drew Kitty's head close to him, hugging the little girl for whom he felt such compassion. There was something wrong with this world.

But Kitty, being embraced by her father's friend, taking her back to the time when she still felt safe in her father's arms, could no longer cry. She didn't yet understand what kept her from crying.

Of course her mother found out. One day she opened Kitty's satchel and found the instruction notes. "So you're getting lessons?" she said.

Kitty bit her lip.

Reggie took a deep breath. "What do you think you're going to do with that?"

Kitty shook her head.

"Make a living? Like your father did?"

Kitty shook her head again.

"Figuring on supporting me with your damned music?"

"No."

"So, what the hell are you doing it for?"

"I don't know."

"Is Alfred paying for the lessons?"

Kitty nodded.

"That old fool! He's the one who stood in your father's way until he was a big nothing! A dreamer, that's what Alfred is, always was. 'Serve the arts, serve mankind,' that's what he used to say. A lot of good it did him. Maybe your father should have stayed the mediocre musician that he was. At least he got a paycheck most weeks, small though they usually were. That's all your father was good for. I should have faced that sooner, a small regular paycheck. On his own, he fell flat on his face. Never one for figuring out what it takes to make it in this world." She glared at Kitty. "So you want to be a musician like him?"

Kitty gave a faint nod.

"Lovely! Just lovely! Alfred Schweitzer is doing it to me all over again. Same old baloney!"

Kitty's look was fixed.

"I don't give a damn! Do whatever you want. See where it gets you. Go and see Alfred. See what good it will do you. But don't you ever ask me for a penny. I won't spend a penny on that damned stuff. Do whatever you want. Just don't ever come to me for help."

Kitty looked up at her mother. "I won't."

The dreaded encounter had gone better than she could have hoped for. Alfred Schweitzer was paying, and she didn't need her mother's help. Oh my God, she couldn't believe her luck! She could continue with her music.

Kitty sat at the beautiful Steinweg grand in the salon. That's all that was left from the days when her father was still alive. She did not look to her right, for that's where her father would have been sitting. Instead she stared out the window, her lips pressed together. Oh, how she missed him! He shouldn't have died. God, why did you let him die? She gave a deep sigh. The sigh didn't clear her mind.

She could still hear Papa's voice. "The man who has no music in him, let no such man be trusted." His charge to her. His gift. A gift that would last her forever.

She played Czerny. Practice runs to make her fingers move, to make her bend the knuckles, to keep the back of her hands steady. But also to help her play the notes in even sequence, with no delay when turning the thumb. Speed it up. Find a better tone and a clearer sequence.

"For heaven's sake! What are you doing?" Ruth was standing next to her.

Kitty stopped playing and looked up at her sister. "Practicing."

"Practicing?" Ruth cocked her nose as if she got a whiff of a noxious stench. "Is that what you've been doing?"

Kitty nodded.

"Why don't you forget it?"

Kitty stared at the keys.

"It won't get you anywhere, I promise you."

"It doesn't matter." Kitty's eyes remained on the keys.

"Well, you know what you want. It's your business. But, if I were you..."

Suddenly Kitty looked up at her sister. "Yes?"

"I'd forget it."

Kitty bit her lips. Ruth didn't understand. Everyone was against her. Her mother, her sister, everyone. "I won't! Never!"

"You'll find out," Ruth added.

Kitty stared out the window. She didn't want to hear any more. Why didn't they leave her alone?

"So you really want to be like him?" Ruth shook her head.

Kitty nodded. *Oh God, why did you have to leave me, Papa?*

Ruth sighed. "You're foolish to fight Mother. Causing yourself all that trouble. And what are you doing it for? For the love of a dead father? For the love of a father who never amounted to anything?"

"That's not true!"

"You're making a mistake! A big mistake!"

When Ruth walked away, Kitty's fingers were still on the keys, ready to practice. She was still staring out the window, her lips pressed together. He would have wanted her to play. Yes, he would have. He had always said so.

Chapter 3

March 1936

Cologne of the mid-1930s had no ghettos. Its nearly twenty thousand Jews, many of them small businessmen or in the professions, lived throughout the city. They regarded themselves as Germans by nationality, and as Jews by religion. They also felt a strong affinity for their region, the Rhineland, with its gay, lighthearted life, so much influenced by Catholicism and the proximity of its French neighbor. Their special city, Cologne, exemplified the wider, more worldly aspect of German culture, as opposed to the pinched Prussian outlook. The Jews of this area still saw Nazism as a national phenomenon with little local relevance.

On national holidays, Reggie, like many of her fellow Jews, displayed the flag of the *Kaiser* from her balcony. Not the swastika, of course, and not the forbidden flag of the Republic. Among the sea of swastikas, it was ironic that the Imperial flag would be the flag of the Jews. It was a symbol of their insistence on identifying with the country of their birth, of their culture.

It seems that by 1936 the Jews of the Rhineland should have known that Nazi anti-Semitism was much more than a transient political passion, that there was no future for them in the new

Germany Hitler and his cronies were fashioning. Yet many had great difficulty accepting the enormity of the change that had already been wrought—that the centuries-old process of Jewish assimilation into German culture had not only been stopped, but reversed. After only three years of Nazi rule, marked by public Jew-baiting and incessant anti-Semitic rhetoric, Germans of the Jewish faith were now segregated from the rest of the German population by the Nuremberg laws. Their relationships with old friends and neighbors were made untenable through a campaign of political intimidation directed at Jews and non-Jews alike.

The arts, an arena where the universal brotherhood of man tends to be articulated, were closed to Jews. No more symphony halls or opera houses for them. The signs next to the entrances read: "*Juden unerwünscht!* (Jews not wanted!)"

Forcibly excluded from participation with fellow Germans in the enjoyment of the arts, yet unwilling to accept exclusion, Germany's Jewish elite created their own cultural sanctum, *Der Kulturbund* (the Cultural Alliance), an organization that was able to showcase for its nearly one hundred thousand subscribers an array of talent so exceptional that at almost any other time it would have earned praise as an important national contribution to the arts. Big names like Richard Tauber, the great tenor, Bruno Walter, the conductor, and Max Reinhardt, the director, had already left Germany, but more than enough talent was left behind to provide monthly programs for the Jews of most of Germany's larger cities. There was the great basso, Alexander Kipnis, the famous blackout staging of Paul Ehrlich, and a full symphonic orchestra gathered together from the dismissed non-"Aryan" artists of Germany's major orchestras.

When the Cologne Conservatory of Music was closed to Jews early in 1936, Alfred found Kitty a teacher within walking distance of her home. Herr Eisenstadt, a former student of Schoenberg, had also left the hectic life of Berlin to teach in Cologne.

Alfred introduced her. "This is my Kitty," he said to Herr Eisenstadt as he shook his hand.

Kitty curtsied.

Herr Eisenstadt cupped her chin and gazed at the little girl. "I've heard a lot about you."

Kitty blushed, averting his eyes.

"Alfred thinks so highly of you."

She was uncomfortable with praise.

He smiled at her. "I knew your father."

Kitty looked down. She felt the pain.

He nodded. "A wonderful artist."

His words rang in her mind as if she had spoken them herself.

"Alfred tells me that you already play Liszt, Rachmaninoff."

Kitty bit her lips. She barely nodded.

He raised his eyebrows. "Well, we'll have to see. It's a little early for Rachmaninoff."

Early? She didn't understand.

"Alfred tells me that there is much of your father in you."

Kitty blushed. He was comparing her to her father.

"Well, we'll have to see." He walked over to the grand. "Play something for me."

Kitty played Beethoven's Minuet in G. It was an easy piece. She knew it well.

When Alfred left with her, he looked at his protégé and smiled. "You're so very lucky. You're so very lucky that he came to Cologne."

Under this new teacher Kitty, now twelve years old, made even better progress than she had been making at the conservatory. Under Herr Eisenstadt's special attention she developed an extraordinary mastery of the keyboard. What especially surprised her new teacher was the rich variety of shadings she brought to her playing, not at all suggested by her sullen disposition. The interpretive maturity of her playing in so young a student astounded Alfred as well, who told Herr Eisenstadt that he had seldom seen such a lucid musical instinct for expressing life's joys and pains. After consulting with Alfred,

Herr Eisenstadt arranged for Kitty to perform at one of the *Kulturbund* concerts to be given at Cologne's great synagogue, an imposing temple that held nearly twelve hundred congregants.

On the night of Kitty's performance in May 1936, the temple was packed. Jewish mothers, usually confined to the balcony of the synagogue, sat with their husbands and men friends as equals, delighting in their new privilege. Reggie was seated next to Alfred, a proximity she did not cherish, although she gave no hint of her real feelings for this friend of her late husband who had insinuated himself into her daughter's affections.

The orchestra, nearly ninety men, was spread across the wide podium in front of the arc, an area customarily reserved for the cantor, the rabbi, and the elders of the congregation. When the conductor finally appeared, a hush fell over the audience. He started the program with the "Triumphal March" from Verdi's *Aida*.

Kitty was next. In spite of his earlier misgivings, Herr Eisenstadt had chosen for her first public appearance the Adagio of Rachmaninoff's famous Piano Concerto No. 2 in C Minor. The concerto is a formidable piece, often chosen for piano competitions among the most confident of young talents. Her teacher saw the Adagio, the second movement of the concerto, though a presentation of less than ten minutes, as sufficiently demanding to show off the maturing virtuosity of his pupil.

Kitty was dressed rather plainly that night. She wore a white blouse and a straight-cut black skirt. Her chestnut hair was parted unevenly. As she stepped up to the podium and seated herself at the grand, she felt out of her element among all the tuxedoed musicians. The audience, possibly sensing her unease, welcomed her with generous applause. She was embarrassed by all this sudden attention. At once she nodded to the conductor that she was ready to play. He raised his baton and waited until there was complete silence.

Her eyes remained glued on the conductor as he brought forth the opening chords of the movement. After a few bars by the strings, Kitty came in on cue, playing in measured, brooding tones, counterpointed by a plaintive oboe. Her rendition was faultless, but not much more. Yet gradually, as if she had suddenly recognized not only the grammar of the phrasing but also the special idiom of Rachmaninoff's musical language, she spoke in more vigorous tones. Soon she was pounding the broadening minor chords, leading her reading into a more incisive, yet still gloomy, crescendo. She struck the keys as if her very insides, glowing with the passion of the piece, were suddenly bursting with the agony of her own life.

Before long one noticed a phenomenon usually seen only when great virtuosi perform. Many in the audience averted their eyes from the artist, some lowering their vision, others looking off into space, as if watching the talented child directly might detract from what they were hearing. Some closed their eyes altogether.

All the vulgar realities this particular audience would have to face when the sun came up again the next morning were suspended. For this one brief moment their heavy burdens ceased to weigh upon them. Yes, it was an escape of sorts, an escape into their past, into a dreamy, shadowy vision of all that had once been for this proud people. It was also an escape into the future. If their history had put this much of all that was good into their children, how could the Creator deny them some measure of protection from the Philistines who now clamored for their destruction?

In the brooding melancholy of the music, Kitty seemed to speak for all of them. She played the music of the lost, of the diminished, as Rachmaninoff must have intended it to be played, as if he had long ago recognized the wringing anguish of the oppressed and had set their hopes to music.

Almost imperceptibly, the high intensity of the playing made its transition to resolution. Kitty raised her eyes and, looking into the distance, played on in simpler tones, letting the world come back into view. With the stroke of the last key, it was suddenly all over. She had done it. She had spoken. Without words. Spoken about her own grief, as well as the collective grief of her audience.

First there was silence from the audience as the last of her notes hung suspended under the massive dome of the great temple. Then, when the last sounds died, someone clapped, then another, then all at once. The applause was wild acclaim, people coming to their feet and raising their accolades to this young talent. Everybody knew. This had been more than music. There were few dry eyes. The applause wouldn't end. Kitty curtsied. She curtsied again and again. She even broke into a smile. This wasn't really happening to her.

Someone later commented that Kitty had spoken of the ultimate sadness that is life, the tears of things, and the nobility of the human spirit in the face of all its grim disillusions.

Her mother bathed in her success. When Reggie came backstage after the concert, she squeezed Kitty's shoulders. "You showed 'em," she said. "You showed 'em what you're made of."

Kitty, who always tried to avoid her mother's eyes, looked up at her. Her mother hadn't understood her playing. She was certain of that. Though Reggie had starred in a couple of summer stock operettas, including *The Merry Widow*, she had never appreciated classical music. "Where are the words?" she used to say, claiming that without words nothing can really be said.

"How much did they pay you?"

Kitty shook her head. "I didn't get paid."

"No?"

"We're all volunteering."

"I see." But Reggie didn't see. Only a fool would work for free.

Three weeks after the concert Alfred died, and with him a part of Kitty died. He had never replaced her father, but Alfred had been the next best thing in the child's life—a truly caring adult. He had believed in her. Not just in her talent, but in her as a child, as a person.

She didn't tell her mother about Alfred's death. What was the point of it? She was afraid of what her mother might say.

"Alfred, that fool?" She knew all of her words. "Learn something that will earn you a decent living and you won't die poor." Her mother would nod to herself, and she would know what she was thinking—that Alfred was just like Papa.

Chapter 4

May 1936

On a late afternoon in May 1936 Reggie stood on the balcony of her townhouse overlooking *Aachenerstrasse,* waiting for Kitty to come home. It was extraordinary. Most times she was busy at the store. But Ruth was old enough now to relieve her.

What a capable daughter she had in Ruth!

One after another, the streetcars arriving from the city ground to a screeching halt, their clanging bells resounding loudly as the unloading was completed. But Kitty wasn't on any of them, even though school had been over for more than three hours.

Finally she spotted her, trudging along in the distance, her head lowered as usual, her steps halting, one might even say graceless. She shook her head in quiet, almost cynical desperation. How often had she told Kitty to straighten up, to walk the way her mother did or, at least, like her sister Ruth did. Ruth walked purposefully, with pride in her bearing. But Kitty never listened. She never learned to keep her head up. It was as if she wanted to defy her mother.

No one knew better than she, her mother, about the ways of the world. *"Wie man kommt gegangen, so wird man auch empfangen!*" It was her dictum for life: "The way you're perceived is the way you're received!"

God Almighty, how many daughters were as lucky as Kitty, with the best of mothers as a model! A mother who was full of confidence, who knew all about the ways of the world, who was *lebensfroh*, happy to cherish the few pleasures that life brought her. A mother who was an example any daughter should be happy to imitate.

When Kitty finally opened the door, she stared at her mother and didn't say a word.

"Where have you been?" she demanded.

The child only pursed her lips and remained silent.

Reggie, who until only minutes before had been so concerned about Kitty's safety, who had been so worried about what might have happened to her, who still had hopes that one day her daughter would understand and correct the tragic flaw of her ways, now stared at her child, brimming with anger. Nothing fazes her, she thought, judging her silence as defiance. She didn't even come forth with an excuse! "Damn you, child," she screamed at her, "don't you hear me?" She waited for Kitty to answer her. "I'm asking you for the last time. *Where have you been?*"

Instinctively Kitty covered her face.

As if to demonstrate the futility of her defense, Reggie grabbed Kitty's hair, shook her head, and slapped her. She slapped her so violently that Kitty's head spun around. Any other child would have screamed in pain, would have begged for relief from her mother's rage, would have promised to try to do better in the future. Instead, Kitty stared at her defiantly, even, one could say, loathingly. "I was at the Jewish Orphans' Home."

"You were where?"

The fear of punishment no longer seemed to faze Kitty. "At the Jewish Orphans' Home," she repeated rather boldly.

"What were you doing there?"

"Visiting."

"Visiting?"

"Yes, visiting."

Yes, she had been at the Orphans' Home. At the Orphans' Home where no one ever hollered at her. Where no one ever slapped her.

"You were visiting who?" Reggie didn't let up.

"My friend Rachel." When Rachel's widowed mother had passed away, no one had wanted her. It had reminded her of herself. Except that *her* mother was still alive.

"Rachel who?"

"Rachel . . ." Kitty shook her head, "I don't know." Rachel was an orphan. She had no last name, at least none that she knew of.

"I insist on knowing what you were doing there."

"Nothing."

"What do you mean, 'nothing'?"

"Nothing."

"I want to know why you were there."

"Visiting."

"I'm asking you for the last time. Why were you there and not at home?"

"Because . . . I like it there."

But Reggie knew her daughter. Noticing that Kitty had dropped her hands, she gave her another hard smack. "There!" she threw at her triumphantly. "That's for lying."

Kitty only stared back at her mother with greater contempt, even hate. "I didn't lie."

How the times are a dimension of the place. In Reggie's Germany, there was no room for dissent. From times immemorial, long before the Nazis, cultural correctness was an absolute imperative. In her mind, children were to be taught to behave correctly, *"wie erwartet"* (as expected). They were supposed to hold their tongues when ordered to do so. When an elder spoke to them, Jew or gentile, they were to answer respectfully, no matter how inane or offensive the comment to which they were responding. What children felt as human beings counted for little. Kitty, rebelling the way she did—and visiting the orphanage was part of that rebellion—by following in her father's footsteps and by "wasting her time with music," just added to what Reggie saw as total defiance. Slapping Kitty ferociously, the way she had, was therefore quite an ordinary event in the Germany of the 1930s.

Reggie wouldn't let Kitty off. "I insist you tell me why you didn't come home from school!" That deserved another hard slap. Kitty had to learn who was in charge. "If I have to beat the living daylights out of you, you'll tell me!" Reggie, hearing her own words, realized that she was nearly out of control. That was the effect Kitty always had on her.

When Kitty looked down, trying to avoid another challenge to her mother that might set off more violence, Reggie mistook her discretion for disdain. The insolence of that child! The unbridled disrespect! It drove her absolutely wild! That's when she gave her daughter another slap, this one harder than all the rest.

"I forbid you to ever again set foot in the Orphans' Home. You have a home. You're very lucky. Your home is right here."

In the face of her mother's growing rage and the futility of defying her any longer, Kitty finally gave up. She lost all control. Another child might have started to whimper or wail or cry wildly, but Kitty, without being aware of it, shifted into a set of gulping, convulsive gasps, her body surrendering to a slight tremble, like a misfiring engine choking on its final spin.

Sensing that she had finally breached Kitty's defiance, Reggie shifted gears and asked in a gentler voice. "What is it?"

It was a skillful game that Reggie played in breaking Kitty down. She knew the formula for success: how much rage, how much kindness to keep her daughter off balance, and how much sternness before finding the proper moment to invite complete submission.

Finally Kitty's tears started to flow. "Look at me when I talk to you!" She jerked Kitty's chin upward so her eyes would not avoid the message Reggie's own eyes were delivering. Stern, totally in command, but now with less rage. That was Kitty's reward for accepting her mother's authority. Her mother would now rein in her rage. A harbinger of things to come.

"Please, Ma!"

"Tell me!"

Suddenly Kitty twisted loose and ran to her room. Reggie was right behind her. She knew that she had Kitty in the palm of her hand. This was the time to follow through.

Kitty flung herself on the bed and dug her face into the pillow. Reggie stood right over her. "Enough already! I've heard enough of your lies!" She turned Kitty's head so Kitty would have to look at her mother. "What happened in school? What beautiful story did you tell 'em this time? You know that I'll find out sooner or later."

She was convinced that her suspicions were right—there was trouble in school. Only a few weeks earlier she had been called before the principal. "Your daughter is not well," he had told her. "I'm not saying this to you because her grades are poor. Neither am I saying it because she doesn't do her homework. We all feel that your daughter is troubled, Mrs. Korten," he had said to her. "When she is called upon, she does not seem to hear her teacher. She appears dazed. When she finally replies, she seems to suffocate in the middle of her sentence, gasping for air, as if she were choking on some fearful thought. There is something wrong with your daughter, something seriously wrong, Mrs. Korten. She should be given a mental examination. You must take her to a psychiatrist."

A psychiatrist! he had said to her. A doctor for crazy people, for hypochondriacs! He was out of his mind! She had decided to pay no attention to this nonsense. Kitty was to see a psychiatrist? What a laugh that was! What total idiocy!

Now, as Reggie sat down on the edge of the bed, her voice became gentle once more, her strategy for getting to the bottom of it all. She did not want to be called on the carpet again by that presumptuous principal.

"Damn you, child, I don't deserve all this! I've done my best to give you a good home since your father died." The damned ingratitude of that child, she thought. "It hasn't been easy. But, of course, you wouldn't know about that. You don't *want* to know about that." She waited for Kitty to look at her but when she didn't, she continued. "I had many chances to marry again. But what did I do?" She waited, letting her question define the obvious answer. "I didn't!" The clear logic of her words escalated her anger. "And why didn't I?" Her tone grew more insistent. "Because my first concern was for you and your sister. Yes, that's right. I wanted to take care of my girls. Even though you have caused me only trouble. Maybe I should have married anyhow. At least I would have had someone to discipline you. That's what you need." She caught her breath. "Would you have wanted that?" She waited again for a word from Kitty. "Of course not!"

Reggie bit her lip. "I've done my best. The best I could. Me, a poor, lonely widow, fighting her battles in these difficult times." She shook her head, feeling sorry for herself. "All the time you seem to forget that *I am your parent.* Even though you let me know at every turn that you don't like me, I do deserve your respect."

Reacting to the brief respite from her mother's ranting, Kitty looked up at her and ventured, "They told me not to come back."

"They told you not to come back?"

"Yes."

"They did what?"

"Not to come back to school."

"What?"

"To school."

"To school?"

"Yes. I must see a doctor first."

"They told you that? All because of your damned playacting? Because of your goddam laziness? They're telling me what I must do with my own daughter?"

In spite of her protestations, Reggie was really up against it and she knew it. In the Germany of the day one did not lightly defy authority, one did not protest directives that came from above. This was a place and a time when the words of those in charge counted for a great deal. A school principal, with the prestige of a doctorate to back him up, was entitled to the presumption of being right in all matters having to do with the school and its students. Especially now. With the Nazis in power and daily publishing their canons that all citizens must sacrifice themselves to the national destiny, a school principal was charged with the awesome responsibility of educating the nation's next generation. He would not take lightly objections from a stubborn parent who presumed to know more than he did. Especially not from a parent who was a Jew.

Didn't she have enough troubles already? What with keeping up the big townhouse? What with having to provide for two growing girls and herself in a world where women couldn't function the way men could? What about a world that was in turmoil, where one never knew what new restrictive decrees tomorrow would bring?

She could only shake her head.

A psychiatrist, he had said? Really? For a child who didn't do her homework? For a child who seemed dazed when she was called upon? For a child who pretended to have asthmatic attacks? They had found something wrong with her that could not be explained. What a laugh! She'd explain it to them. She knew better. She had known the answer for a long time—it was Kitty's way of punishing her! For Kitty hated her! Kitty was determined to ruin her life! But why?

The answer to this question was so horrifying to Reggie that she would not even try to uncover it. She would not even think about it. It had to do with her own shame before her daughter. It had to do with her fear that her daughter knew a terrible secret.

The next morning Reggie called her attorney, Egon Weiss. Throughout the years, especially since Karl's death, he had been her personal advisor. She told him about her troubles. She told him about Kitty's expulsion from school. That she was at the end of her rope. That she could no longer deal with her daughter. That something needed to be done.

Egon arrived late that evening. "All this has been too much for me," she said as an opening entreaty, "more than I can handle. I mean, I'm only a woman, a widow left to struggle in this world, alone, with two young daughters to take care of."

"Of course! I understand." Egon nodded. "I often think about your determination, in these difficult times, alone, with no man in the house, the Nazis at your doorstep, making do, surviving."

Oh, what compliments can do. He had hit the right button. Tears started to spill from Reggie's eyes, like from a dam with opened floodgates. Suddenly, she was overwhelmed by emotions, as well as redeemed, for this educated man had so clearly seen the truth of her struggles. "I just can't take it any more," she said to him. "It's beyond me. My nerves can't bear the strain any longer. First Karl and now my daughter. Don't you think I deserve better?"

"Now, now, my dear," he said, shaking his head, "you are a strong woman. I know that these years have not been easy, but you have managed well. Besides, even though Karl is gone, you are doing better than when he was alive, which to my mind is admirable. I should congratulate you."

Reggie didn't know what to make of this. Of course, she had done well. After all, how much did it take to surpass incompetence?

She told Egon about the problem at hand, bursting into a detailed account of all that she had been forced to endure. "I tried to warn Kitty," she said to him, "but you cannot imagine how difficult this child has been. She still stamps her feet. She habitually gazes at the floor. She still wets her bed at night. Can you believe it, a child of twelve? I have warned her about her poor grades and the lack of doing her homework. And now I'm supposed to take her to a doctor—a psychiatrist! What utter nonsense!"

"I know what is wrong with her. It's all plain laziness. They don't know what they're talking about. Besides, who would pay for all this? Oh, Egon," she said finally. "No one knows what I've been through. A woman my age, still so young, still so full of life, burdened by this child the way I have been. I've often thought about marrying again. But who would have me? With a daughter like Kitty," she shook her head, "with this burden."

For only a short moment, Egon lifted his eyebrows. Then his countenance sobered again. "May I only say that any man would be proud to have you as a wife, with or without your daughter."

Egon's words, a harmless compliment offered in kindness, offended her because they were spoken by a man Reggie would never consider in marriage. A man so ugly, so misshapen, so unmanly, so altogether too "Jewish-looking," that the thought of a relationship with him simply offended her. But she hid her antipathy well, skilled as she was in the social graces, for she knew that at this moment she needed him.

Egon continued. "But these thoughts do not offer any solution to the problem at hand." He chewed on his thumb, reverting to the matter-of-fact, detached air of a lawyer. "How about a private school? I know of a school that specializes in handling difficult children."

She was so completely shocked by the suggestion that for a long moment, she didn't know what to say. An expensive private school for Kitty? Never! Was he crazy? How could he ever come up with such an idea?

But Reggie weighed her words carefully before she spoke again. "It would be imprudent to sacrifice my small income so that Kitty could have the privilege of going to a boarding school," she said, speaking calmly at first. Soon her anger got the better of her again. "I cannot live in the same house with her any longer," she added. "I'll go crazy! I'll put her into an institution before I put her into a private school."

The sound of her own strong words frightened her but also propelled her to continue. Egon had set her off with this stupid talk of a boarding school. "I'm still young. Much too young to have a child destroy my life," she went on. "I won't allow it! Never!"

Egon gave a slight nod. It was hard to tell what he was thinking.

She stared at him, bidding him to answer her. "Don't you agree with me, Egon?"

Egon Weiss looked away from her. Finally, he spoke. "You want to put her into an *Irrenanstalt* (asylum). Lindenburg, I presume? Is that where you want to put her?"

It wasn't a question but a confirmation of what she was clearly saying to him—that she simply didn't want the child around any longer. That she wanted to toss her overboard! Yes, it was painful indeed for him to hear a Jewish mother plan to dispose of her child like this, especially in these times. But he was here to give legal, not moral, advice. He was not her rabbi. Still, he had to be sure that he was actually hearing what he seemed to be hearing. "That is not an institution for children," he warned.

Reggie just sat there, hands folded in her lap. She did not say anything in response.

"What about her piano?" he asked. "She's so talented."

"Her piano?" Reggie asked, incredulous that he would have raised the point. "Do you really think she'll ever make any money with it?" Didn't Egon realize what he was saying? Didn't he know that there was Karl's blood in Kitty? Didn't he know that Kitty had chosen the piano because she knew how difficult it was to make any money out of a career in music?

As the conversation went on, Reggie realized that her fears about Egon were unnecessary. He was not up to arguing with her. He had finally understood her. He had understood how determined she was.

"Well, as long as you don't want her to see a psychiatrist," he said, watching her face closely, still hoping for some sign that she might stop him, "and you don't want to send her to a private school, I'll try to get her admitted to the Lindenburg Asylum."

She did not stop him. He had to know what she wanted. She had made that clear. Egon was only a lawyer, a lawyer who needed to be told what to do, what arrangements to make. Damn you, Egon! Looking at her as he did, finding her attractive. You better move on this!

Egon advised her that he would draw up the necessary papers for a commitment. She would hear from him in a few days.

When Egon left, Reggie sank back into her chair. She had done it. Finally, she could start her own life. The kind of life she deserved. A life without Kitty.

Within a week, Kitty was picked up. She made a terrible scene, screaming, struggling to free herself from the two attendants who had been sent to collect her. She didn't know what was happening. She didn't know why she was being strapped into a harness. But she was only a young girl. She understood that her fight was hopeless, and in the end, she succumbed. It was a primer of things to come, a conditioner for future coercions, a coloring of future restraints upon her freedom. Kitty was moving another step along her path, struggling in vain against forces much greater than any she could muster in her own defense.

Neighbors alerted by Kitty's screams peered out from narrow partings in their curtains. For a few short moments, while they were dragging Kitty out of the house and into the street, Reggie was overcome with shame. Her neighbors would all know her family's business, know exactly what had happened this afternoon. What would they think of her? How could they ever understand the thousand ways in which she had been driven to take this action?

When it was all over, she breathed a sigh of relief. She had done it. She was free. Kitty was out of her life.

By the time Kitty arrived at the asylum, she had quieted. The next day proved to be not so bad after all. The doctors were pleasant, and several elderly ladies fussed over her. She received a lot of attention. She was the only young girl at the institution.

The doctors saw her frequently. They talked to her in private, something they rarely did with the other patients. They asked her many questions about her home, her school, her father, her mother. They were very much concerned about her.

Within six days Reggie received a phone call asking her to come pick up Kitty. Though a troubled child, Kitty did not belong in their institution, the doctor said. When Reggie did not express enthusiasm at the finding, the caller did not go into it any further. He could not understand that she didn't give a damn about the cheerful prognosis he was trying to relate. It was her freedom that she was thinking about—her freedom from Kitty, which had lasted exactly seven days.

Chapter 5

August 1936

Reggie regarded Kitty's return from the asylum as a total disaster, for, in her mind, it was bound to provide a month's gossip for the *Kaffee Klatch* (the afternoon teas), at which her friends passed on news about those not present.

"Reggie will never escape the Nazis and make it out of Germany with a daughter like that," one of her friends exclaimed. "She'll never find a husband either," said another. "Any man worth his salt, when he finds out about Kitty, he'll turn and run."

Even though Kitty's musical talent was well known to these women, being expelled from school, being sent to an *Irrenanstalt* (an asylum for the insane), disgraced both child and family. There were also others who commiserated with Reggie, agreed with her action—to them undisciplined behavior was the ultimate sin—and defended Reggie, quoting from the Old Testament, "Rod and reproof give wisdom."

Within a few weeks of Kitty's return everybody stopped talking about Reggie. There were too many other, more serious problems to occupy them, problems so grave they trivialized the widow Korten's difficulties with her "crazy" daughter.

As Germany was drawn into what they considered "a total madness," the Jews of Cologne just shook their heads. This was not turning out the way their elders had said it would. Most of the wise old heads had expressed confidence that Germany, their homeland, one of the most sophisticated and respectable societies on the European continent, would never accept the leadership of a vulgar drifter like Adolf Hitler, a man with no formal education, no credentials in any field, a Viennese lowlife who fancied himself a world leader. Now they had to face the fact that they had been proven wrong.

They watched in fear and confusion as support for the Nazis grew all around them. Each new success with the German masses bred a new level of arrogance among the Nazis. The voice of official Germany became more strident, its threats more outrageous, its laws more restrictive, its rule more brutal.

As the paralysis of the Western democracies in the face of Hitler's mad rantings became apparent, hope for the Jews of Cologne waned. The decision was unmistakable: they had to leave their beloved city and their homeland. They had to leave Cologne and Germany.

Reggie traveled to the American consulate in Stuttgart and applied for visas for herself and her two daughters. She was assigned a number and told that she had to wait her turn. If the predictions proved right, they would be able to leave Germany within two years. While she waited, she had to hope that she and her family would remain safe until their turn came.

Kitty had grown into an early maturity. Hard times do such things. The changing political climate that promised so little protection demanded an independence, a self-reliance, even of the young.

The parent-child relationship was undergoing further distancing from Reggie's end as well. When concern about the basic needs of survival become so pressing, parenting becomes a secondary chore. Reggie paid little attention to her younger daughter.

After her return from the asylum Kitty found a job as a tailor's apprentice. Finding a job for herself—nobody cared any longer whether or not she finished her schooling—forged a new self-confidence in her. Still, she visited the orphanage regularly, probably less now to defy her mother's tyranny than to keep up the friendships she had made with some of the orphans.

Kitty had matured in other ways as well. Her rounded cheeks had hollowed delicately, her brown eyes had darkened and steadied, her taut lips had ripened and mellowed. Overnight, one might say, the child had grown into a beautiful adolescent girl. With a pleated, black skirt falling just below her knees, with budding breasts demurely hidden beneath the white blouse, her appearance suggested the kind of prim feminism that was so acceptable then. Her walk, though still indecisive—she more often looked downward than forward—gave her an air of vulnerability. This was a form of seduction that many German girls of the time, Jewish and non-Jewish alike, cultivated in order to subtly appeal to their young men. Their modesty suggested that they were prepared to subjugate their own needs to those of their male counterparts.

Riding the streetcar home from work, Kitty noticed that a student who regularly managed to stand right next to her, always left the streetcar with her, only to go off in a different direction. It was not surprising, then, that after a week of standing next to each other, he would nod to her. It took only a few more days before he helped her off the streetcar. Still, the only words that came out of him as he escorted her to the curb were *"Auf Wiedersehn!"*

The following day, though, he used the opportunity of their daily nods to speak to her. "How's it going?"

"Fine," Kitty replied.

After this bland opening, there was a long silence. He looked away from her, apparently trying to find the courage to follow up. Finally, he turned to her again. "What's your name?"

"Kitty," she answered. She was blushing. Then, deciding to disregard her agitation, to encourage the contact, she ventured to ask, "What's yours?"

"Robert."

She could tell by the color of his school cap—boys attending the more prestigious high schools in the city wore their grade caps with much pride—that he was probably seventeen, much older than she.

For a while, they both stared out the window. They had nothing more to say. Finally, he turned to her again. "You're from *Kaiserin-Augusta-Lyzeum?*" he said, naming a local high school for girls.

"No," she said, and wanting no deception between them, she added, "I'm working."

He nodded. She couldn't tell whether he was approving or disapproving. Apparently it didn't matter to him. "You're working! Doing what?"

"Dressmaking," she said quickly, "but I'm still an apprentice."

"I see."

"And you?"

"In school. Still going to school. High school, of course."

When they arrived at their stop, he helped her off the streetcar and, holding her elbow, walked her to the curb. Then he turned to her once more. "I'd like to meet you."

All Kitty could do was nod.

"How about right here in about an hour?"

"An hour?"

"Yes, an hour. All right?"

"Yes."

He smiled.

Why would he smile at her? Why would anyone smile at her? Was he really that happy to have finally spoken to *her*? To have spoken to her, *Kitty*, who was not smart enough to have finished grammar school and who had been in an asylum for the insane?

Once he was out of sight, she ran home all the way. She sat down at the grand and played Chopin. Mazurkas.

She played lively music with a bright beat. Music one could dance to. Music overflowing with happy feelings.

When Kitty arrived at the rendezvous an hour later, he was already waiting for her. She slowed her walk. She didn't want to appear too anxious. Really, he was much too handsome for her, measured by what she considered her own worth. His blue eyes were much darker than she had remembered them. They had a stern, serious look. He also seemed much taller than she remembered, standing there without his cap, his brownish hair all ruffled.

"How are you, Kitty?" He shook her hand in the hardy fashion of the day.

"Fine."

"Let's go to the *Stadtwald*," he said to her.

Kitty could only nod.

He reached for her hand and held on to it as they waited for the streetcar. To Kitty, holding hands with someone was a new and mysterious connection. It seemed to warm her cheeks and made her heart beat faster. Oh God, could it be true, really true, that all of life was so connected?

She felt a deep, incoherent shiver.

They climbed on the streetcar, heading for the *Stadtwald*, the main city park of Cologne. Getting together with someone, being with a boy, was all so new to her. It was almost a date.

When they arrived at the park, he still held her hand. "You're very quiet," he said to her.

"I am?"

"You are."

"Really?"

To her great surprise, his words did not make her feel uneasy. She felt terribly happy inside. She no longer felt the heavy weight of her isolation. Was it his hand holding hers? Was it his gentle voice speaking to her? Or was it his measured steps meeting hers?

All the time, as she walked along the path with him, she did not see anybody. She did not notice anything.

Suddenly, Robert stopped dead in his tracks and, turning to face her, he caught her eyes. "Why are you so scared, Kitty?"

"What?"

"Why are you so scared, I said?"

"Why do you say that?"

He shook his head slowly. "I've been watching you."

"You've been watching me?"

"Yes. I've been watching you. I've been watching you all along."

"You have?"

"Yes, I have." He looked down, embarrassed. "I've been watching you for weeks. The streetcar, remember? I watched you because you seemed so scared. It was so obvious. Not scared of me. Of course not. Whenever you were not aware of me, you looked so terribly scared."

He wouldn't take his eyes off her. She had to look away. It was all so embarrassing. "I did?"

"I watched you more and more because I wanted to know why you were so scared."

"You did?"

"Yes."

It should have embarrassed her that someone had made a study of her fearful ways. But it didn't. Somehow she felt at ease with Robert. For when she finally looked back into his blue eyes, she saw that they were gentle, that they were not demanding, correcting, or criticizing. Suddenly, she felt so free. "Why should you care if I look scared?"

"You're a very pretty girl." He changed the subject.

Kitty blushed. "Thank you."

"You're Jewish, aren't you?"

"Yes." Suddenly her voice choked.

"I don't ever want you to be scared of me."

She looked down. But out of the corner of her eye, she could still see him. "I'm not."

"I asked you to walk with me because I didn't want you to be scared of me."

"That's why?"

"Yes."

"You really mean it?"

"Yes."

Suddenly, right in the middle of the park, unaware of all the people around him, he folded his arms around Kitty, drew her gently against his chest and let her head rest against his shoulder. Though not yet a man, he held her like a man. Though not yet a lover, he held her like a lover. Seeing, feeling, understanding what could never be said in so many words: her ache, her fears, her isolation.

After a while, he let go of her.

The two of them wandered along the paths. They did not speak. Their silence was so very remarkable. There was a secret bond between them. To Kitty it seemed as if he were the sun and she the rain, joining to make a rainbow.

Suddenly, his arm reached about her and he turned her to face the pond. "Did you see that fish jump?"

"Yes."

"So recklessly?"

"Yes."

He shook his head. "He doesn't know."

"What?"

"He doesn't know anything about right or wrong."

She looked up at him. "No, he doesn't."

He turned her to him and gazed into her eyes. Yes, there was a knowing, an understanding, between them. With his body sheltering hers. With hers yielding to his. What a wonderful feeling it all was! If only he would know how much she had always wanted to be held like this.

They strolled along the paths for another hour. They fed the deer, they lay in the grass. Kitty picked flowers. But they talked only little.

"Thank you," she said to him when they had returned to their starting point. "Thank you so much."

It had been a lovely afternoon, an afternoon she'd never forget in all of her life.

It was only then that she noticed that his cheeks were coarse, pockmarked. As if he too were damaged, were less than perfect. In the end, she thought, nobody was perfect. Not even Robert.

"Will I see you tomorrow?" he asked.

Kitty nodded.

She watched him leave but the moment he was out of sight, she raced home, hardly able to wait to tell the world about her joy.

But there was no one to tell it to. There was no one who'd listen to her. There was no one who really cared.

Robert was not on the streetcar the next day. And not the day after that. Kitty kept on looking for him. For weeks she looked for him. Every afternoon. When she passed the stop where he would get on the streetcar, her heart pounded. But he was never there.

Surely, something had to have happened to him. Maybe he was afraid to see her again. Afraid to be seen with her because she was Jewish.

Yet the feeling of that afternoon in the *Stadtwald* lingered. Whenever she closed her eyes, she could still feel his arms around her. Then she would feel warm inside. A wonderful feeling. A feeling that she never wanted to lose.

Chapter 6

February 1938

A traveler returning to Cologne early in 1938, or to most German cities for that matter, could have been forgiven for observing that things had changed little since his last visit. For in all outward appearances the great cities of the Third Reich looked much as they always had. Less obvious to the visitor would have been a certain transformation in the mood of the German people. Even though most of them continued to extend to their visitors the mannered hospitality that had long been their hallmark, a new pride had grown within them, a certain hubris at once again living in a country that functioned better than most.

Deutsche Wertarbeit, the high quality of German workmanship, bred an air of superiority. Social compassion, as decreed by the state, found expression in the widely accepted Sunday *Eintopfgericht* (the one-pot meal to support the poor), and the Cologne-Hamburg Express, the first commercial attempt at high-speed rail travel, filled every German heart with pride. Of course, Hitler took credit for it all.

Everybody listened to the Führer's speeches, including most Jews, who analyzed them to gauge how great a danger they were in. If a speech contained no more than the usual hortatory invectives, it was dismissed as mere politics. If there were new threats, warnings of new decrees to come, the Jewish community became agitated, conjecturing endlessly about each new proposal and its possible implications.

In February 1938, Reggie had a terrifying experience. Two SS troopers showed up at her store and warned her, "Close your place or we'll close it for you!" She didn't ask who had sent them or by what authority they were making their threat. She simply closed up and went home, trying to figure out what to do next.

Everybody feared the SS. They were part of an elite corps, their job ostensibly to guard Nazi bigwigs. Their free lancing took them far afield from their official duties. They were both agents of the law and above the law, for they had no obligation to be consistent in the way they applied it.

Luckily, Ruth had been with her. Her calm put Reggie at ease. "Those SS troopers," Ruth said to her mother, "they act so tough and strong on the outside but on the inside, they are really scared, weak . . ."

"Scared, weak?"

"Yes, Mother, those men were scared. They were only acting on orders."

"You think so?"

"Yes, of course."

Reggie nodded. Yes, Ruth was smart. She understood. She understood a lot. Not afraid. Not afraid of men. Even those troopers. She was proud, self-assured, but respectful. She had all of the best qualities. She was a mirror image of herself. Ruth's birth had been like an immaculate renewal. Like a young nymph rising from a lake, Ruth had unfolded into a veritable likeness of her.

To Kitty the changes that were happening around her were difficult to comprehend. She wanted very much to understand the underlying meaning of it all. Why was she so different from all the others? Why was there so much anger directed against her solely because she was Jewish? After all, nobody ever asked a newborn if she wanted to be Jewish. Being Christian or Jewish,

German or Italian or British, for that matter, was no more than an accident of birth.

Kitty also wanted to admire the *Führer*, as most non-Jewish Germans did. She also wanted to drench herself in the fatherly love he avowed for the German people. She had often heard it said that the threat of international Communism had caused his rise, and that almost anything might be better than the spread of Bolshevism across Europe. Maybe he was right. If only Hitler didn't talk so much against the Jews.

In one of her daydreams she found herself transported to the great rally at Nuremberg. Smiling, carrying a large bouquet of flowers, she was waiting for the great leader in a long line of German girls her age. When he finally strode by, he stopped right in front of her. He looked straight into her eyes, his eyes gentle, not angry at all. He asked for her name, and when she told him that it was Kitty, he smiled at her like a father, patted her cheek, took the flowers from her and then walked on. She wanted to call after him, "I'm *Jewish!*" but he was already gone.

The reeducation of Kitty began one Saturday night in March 1938, just a month short of her fourteenth birthday. Though a mature girl physically, she was still a child emotionally.

She didn't really mind that her mother and sister left her alone Saturday nights. She was free to do whatever she wanted. No one was looking over her shoulder.

But when it got dark and the air grew heavy and oppressive, she wandered around the big house from floor to floor. She locked all doors and windows, and then rechecked them moments later. She picked up trifles, little things: a jewelry box in her mother's bedroom, a fancy necklace belonging to Ruth. She gaped at them, not really seeing them, then put them back again. She couldn't focus her mind or distract herself from the fear building inside of her. She closed the drawer but then, suddenly, she opened it again. What was that? It couldn't be! A party badge? The gold braided emblem of the Nazis, with the black swastika in the middle?

What was her sister doing with it? Was she a member? Oh, no, no Jews could be members.

When she finally sat down at the grand in the salon, she kept staring at the ceiling. Her sister! What was she doing with the Party emblem in her drawer? What did it mean? She just couldn't understand it.

After a while, she began playing. When she heard creaking noises, breaking glass, a distant howl, she stopped playing at once and sat there in terror as if anchored to the chair, waiting for a recurrence of the sounds. When there were no more sounds and everything remained quiet, she still remained tense, wondering what meaning she should attach to the sudden silence.

When the doorbell rang she was startled out of her wits. Who could that be? Nobody ever came calling on Saturday evening. The bell rang again much longer this time. She ran downstairs.

She opened the door. She couldn't believe her eyes. Two SS troopers in black uniforms. This was something worse than bad.

"Where's your sister?" asked the taller one.

She gaped at him.

"You've got a sister, haven't you?"

She nodded.

"I need to talk to her."

"Yes?"

"Don't you understand? I need to talk to your sister." His voice grew stern. "Ruth—isn't that her name?"

Kitty nodded again. Her sister? What about the Nazi emblem?

"Well?"

"She isn't here," Kitty responded in a small voice.

"She isn't here?"

"No."

"Why isn't she?"

"I don't know." Was it possible that Ruth had a date with the SS?

"Why not?" Suddenly, he pushed the door, forced it, and walked inside, his partner following him. "Why is she not here?"

Kitty shook her head. "I don't know."

"You don't know? Why don't you know?"

"I don't know."

"You don't know very much, do you?" Smiling at her sarcastically, he grasped her chin and raised it to make her look at him, an intimidation routinely used by the SS. "Who else is here with you?"

"I'm by myself."

"Really?" He turned to his partner. "She's by herself."

Oh, God, what had she done! "By herself!" she had said. One never said this to strangers. She knew better. Why had she ever said it? But they were the SS. How could she have done otherwise? They wandered around the house, looking into every room on each floor to see if she was really alone, to learn if she had told them the truth. Maybe this young girl who was so frightened was hiding some dark secret from them, some untruth punishable by arrest, or worse.

Upstairs in the salon, in the finest room of the house, they circled the room. "Not bad," said the one who had done all the talking so far, apparently the leader of the two. "These Jews know how to live well. What do you think, Hans?"

"Not bad, Kurt."

"What do you think, Hans, do you think she's telling the truth?"

They smiled at each other.

"She's a pretty one," said Kurt. He grasped her cheeks and spun her face around. "Pretty eyes, light skin." He stepped back. "Nice body. Doesn't look like a Jewgirl."

"Doesn't at all," Hans agreed.

Kurt reached his arm around her. He was a big fellow, a foot taller than Kitty. "Don't be afraid, little girl," he said to her. "We're not going to eat you. Really, you're very lucky. We're two of the nicest guys in the whole SS. Just ask your sister, Ruth." He smiled a dirty little smile. "Your sister who stood us up. Who was supposed to be here. Who you better remind not to cross us again." He spoke in a monotone, conveying his annoyance but not making much of it. "But, it's all right this time. You'll have to do. After all, it's all in the family. You, your sister, and the rest of them."

She didn't understand a thing. What was that about her sister? What had she done?

Kurt sat down on the couch. "Come here, little girl," he said, patting his knee.

Kitty froze. At first she stared at Kurt, and then she stared at the other trooper, the one called Hans. Whatever they wanted of her, she knew that she was in big trouble, that something bad was about to happen to her. Even in her confused state, she understood that much.

"*Komm doch her, hier, zu mir.*" It was a more gentle tone.

Kitty still did not move.

Suddenly, Hans pushed her toward Kurt. "*Geh' schon,*" he said. She lost her balance and tumbled toward Kurt.

Kurt grabbed her, his arms clinching her like a vise. He let himself fall backward. He kissed her. Then, using his knee, he forced her legs apart.

She struggled against him, trying desperately to get away. Instinctively she twisted her head away from him. Like an animal in a zoo, her gaze passed by him, blindly beyond. She did not want to see his black uniform, the smirk on his face, his lips that had called her "Jewgirl."

She thought of the fisherman sitting on the banks of the river Ahr in Bad Ems, tossing *"die kleine Forelle"* back into the stream. "*Warum?* (But why?)" she asked him.

"*Der muss noch wachsen* (Give it a chance to grow up)," he replied.

What do these men want with me? Am I not too little?

It was such an unequal struggle. "So you like to play," he said, flinging her to the floor. With his knee on her stomach, he ripped her dress with one giant tear. Then, clutching her chin with one hand, he used the other to tear away her bra and her panties.

Even though a scream seemed to rise within her, something also shut it off. Yes, screaming would make matters worse. Surely, it could not serve any useful purpose, for no neighbor was going to come bursting in to save her from the SS. She bit her lips and tightened her body. Whatever would happen to her, would happen, no matter what. It couldn't be helped.

"Let's see if you're as good as your sister," he said, forcing himself into her. Hans, sitting nearby, watched the proceedings. Kurt looked up at him. "These Jewgirls are hot stuff, don't you think, Hans?"

Kitty had shut her eyes. The massive weight, the piercing pain, the cutting jabs all made her feel lightheaded, even faint. Then she remembered: it would be over soon. Everything had an ending. That's what Papa always said. Eventually, everything ended, even the worst. Even her pain would end. Eventually they'd leave and, after a while, the pain would stop and she'd forget all about it.

When it was actually over and he finally got off her, she opened her eyes and stared straight ahead. She did not want to see him. Let him go away quietly, she said to herself.

Then it occurred to her that his friend probably would want to do the same to her. Of course! Why hadn't she thought of it? It hadn't ended. It wasn't over yet. But, at least she'd know what to expect.

"Well, Hans?" Kurt said, straightening out his uniform. "Your turn, my friend."

Hans did not answer him. She could feel his stare. After a while, looking out of the corner of her eye, she could see that he had risen and was walking out of the room.

"Let's go," he called back to Kurt.

Kurt followed Hans out to the hall. "What's the matter with you, buddy?" she heard him ask Hans. If there was an answer she did not hear it. She only heard the sound of their steps upon the stairs as they walked away. There wasn't another word between them. After a while, she heard the door close behind them and she stopped hearing their footsteps. Everything was quiet again. It felt as if they had never been there.

For a long while, Kitty didn't get up. She lay there in the middle of the salon, numb, thinking only that it was all over. She had survived. God hadn't let her die.

Little by little, her feelings came back. What had really happened? Nothing seemed clear any more. The only thing that was clear now was that she had been hurt, that she was still in terrible pain, and that she could feel a wetness between her thighs.

Bracing herself, she sat up. There was blood between her legs. Lots of blood had spilled on the Oriental! It had stained the Oriental!

Oh, my God, what will Mother say? Her good Oriental?

She pressed her torn panties between her legs and, with the blood still oozing, she struggled up to the bathroom. Upstairs she stuffed a towel between her legs, holding it secure with a fresh pair of panties. She stared at herself in the mirror and wiped the blood from the corner of her lips. She cleaned her thighs. Then she washed her face and brushed her hair.

When she returned to the salon, she rinsed the blood on the Oriental with a damp rag and then blotted it up the water. She ran back and forth to the bathroom upstairs to soak the bloody rag and wring it dry. Finally, she was satisfied. Her mother wouldn't notice. The Oriental had too many colors.

She dressed herself and set out for the Orphans' Home. She ran most of the way. She didn't want anyone to stop her and question her appearance by demanding to know what was wrong, what had happened to her.

She was fortunate. She met no one on the way.

When she reached the home, the housekeeper had her lie down in the medical room and called for the doctor. When he arrived, he sat next to her. All the time, while examining her, he also questioned her. Questions that doctors ask of children when they are brought in with skinned knees or sprained ankles. "How did you get hurt?" not, "What have you done wrong?" She found herself explaining things to him freely, as if she were explaining about falling out of a tree she had been climbing. About being home alone, about the SS coming to the door, about what Kurt had done to her on the good Oriental. He listened to her, not interrupting. He nodded often, but then when she had finished, he shook his head in disbelief. "What has this world come to?" he asked. "A child, only a child!"

He cleaned the caked blood from between her legs and applied a salve. Then he took a gauze pad and taped it tightly to her body.

After he had finished, while he was washing up, he offered to call her mother. Kitty wouldn't have it. She dared not give him the real reason—that her mother had forbidden her to ever go back again to the Orphans' Home.

The doctor's gentle way with her had relaxed Kitty somewhat, and when her mother and sister came home later that night, she blurted it out about the two SS troopers and how they had asked for Ruth.

Her sister gaped at her as if she, Kitty, had gone mad. "You really expect me to believe this," Ruth said, eyeing her mother as she spoke, "that they asked for me?"

But Kitty kept on insisting. "They did! I swear they did!"

Then her mother added, "Come on now, Kitty, do you really want me to believe that your sister has some arrangement with the SS?"

"Yes, they *did* ask! They asked for Ruth! For my sister! She was supposed to be at home, they said."

Her mother shook her head. "Your sister was with me all night. We visited friends." She turned to Ruth. "What about it? What about what Kitty is saying?"

"Come on, Mother! Why would I date the SS? Me, a Jew?" She stared at Kitty. "She's crazy!"

If Kitty had not seen the doctor at the Orphans' Home, she would have told her mother about the rape, the blood, shown her the bandages. But then, she thought, it wouldn't have made any difference. She wouldn't believe her anyway. This was the way it had always been.

She knew that Kurt had been with her sister. He had said so. It was hard to believe. Still, Ruth had always figured out ways to make people do things for her.

Kurt came again. He always came on Saturday nights when Ruth and her mother were gone and she was alone. It was as if he knew, as if Ruth had told him. She played his game. It was a game that was without rules, without contention, where she, Kitty, was always the wild joker.

Whenever the doorbell rang on Saturday nights, she froze in blocks of panic and inertia, reaching a state of strangling intuition. Kurt knew that she was alone in the house. Of course, she could always hide in the English butler. Squeeze into it and move between floors. Hope he wouldn't find her after he had broken down the door. But she trembled at the thought of it.

Sometimes Kurt brought her candy. He even talked nicely to her. "Kitty, my child, if you weren't a Jewgirl, I might quite like you."

There were other times when Kurt became angry with her for no apparent reason. Probably, she thought, for not knowing what he wanted of her. Hers was a hopeless situation. She was like an ant under a youngster's fingers. Appeals stood for nothing. She had no place to hide, where he would not follow, grab her, and scold her. Her life depended on his whims, on his moods, as did the amount of pain she would have to endure.

It was during these times, when she was repeatedly subjected to Kurt's sexual assaults and experienced an overwhelming sense of panic, that Kitty first discovered that her best defense was to stop thinking. It was like a conversion, like a passage to a new, less frightening response. There was less pain if she reacted instinctively, only with her body. For, if she didn't think, her body would eventually grow numb. When each episode was over and she found herself still alive, she could simply go on with her life and no longer think about what had happened.

Chapter 7

November 1938

On the 9 November 1938, *Kristallnacht* (the Night of the Broken Glass), hell broke loose for the Jews of Germany. The night was so named because the next morning the streets of Germany's cities were littered with pieces of glass that had been the storefronts of Jewish merchants. Hooligans had been encouraged to indulge their worst instincts, to strike out against Jews wherever they or their property could be found. The SS took it one step further. They joined in with the criminals to show them how it should be done. The police stood by and watched.

On that night when most of the Jewish temples were set afire, store windows smashed, and most adult Jewish men arrested, Kitty was alone. As the destruction started she was alone on the streetcar on her way home from work, and she was alone when she arrived home and listened to the mayhem far off in the streets. She had no idea where her mother was.

She bolted all doors and shut all the windows—not that this would do much good. She wouldn't dare refuse to answer the door for the SS. Eventually she sat down at the grand in the salon, staring blankly ahead, tuning into the sounds of the street outside. When she finally heard steps—and they were not the heavy boots of SS troopers—she began to relax.

It was her mother. She had brought Eric, one of her friends from the bowling league, along. A ruddy-looking man of slight build, no more than forty-five, wearing heavy, horn-rimmed glasses, displaying a hesitating, circumspect air. He was to hide in their home.

Ruth had also returned with them.

Kitty was no longer alone. Her family was together. Yet, in spite of that, one look into Eric's face made her panic deepen. He was even more frightened than she, if that were possible. For he was one of the few Jewish men of Cologne the SS had not yet found. There was little doubt that they eventually would find him. It was only a matter of time. Nobody escaped the SS.

Reggie took him into her bedroom. She had him climb onto the top shelf of the linen closet. Then she covered him with a sheet.

It was an altogether foolish gesture.

It wasn't long before the SS arrived on the street, their heavy boots resounding harshly on the pavement right outside the windows. One could hear them shouting out directions, hear them knocking on doors, even hear them asking questions. All along, they were getting closer. Would they pass? What vain hope!

When it finally came, it was a loud knock. "Open up!" The shout was unmistakable.

Reggie ran to the door.

"Open up at once!"

She opened the door.

The pair, black-uniformed SS, black boots and belts, their guns drawn, pushed their way inside. "Where is he?"

"There's no one here!"

"Come on! Don't cause yourself a lot of trouble! Where is your husband?"

"I'm a widow." Her voice choked. A nice try at sympathy.

"You're a widow?"

"Yes."

"Where's your boyfriend?"

"I have no boyfriend."

"Really?"

"No. You must believe me. I'm a poor widow who devotes herself to raising her two daughters."

They came up to the first floor and marched into the salon. They looked around and caught sight of Kitty, seated at the grand. "Come here little girl!" one of them shouted at her.

Kitty got up at once.

"Right over here." He pointed to a spot right in front of him. "Tell me, little girl, where's he hiding?"

Kitty bit her lips.

He grabbed her chin and made her look at him. She remembered Kurt and knew its clear message: "There's no use resisting!"

"Where?" was his one-word demand.

Kitty tilted her head toward the upstairs bedroom. It was so slight a tilt that only an expert eye would know its meaning.

He let go of her chin.

They found Eric in no time. Everyone could guess what Kitty had done. Ruth ran after them. She begged them to leave Eric alone. But they dragged him away, shoving him down the stairs between them. He didn't look back at Kitty. She wanted to tell him that she was terribly sorry.

Along with most of the Jewish men of Cologne, he was thrown into trucks and shipped off to Dachau or Buchenwald concentration camp.

After Kitty's "betrayal" of Eric, Reggie and Ruth avoided her even more than they had before. She had not had the courage to face up to the SS and lie. She, the one person who was such a good liar.

Of course, they never took into account her paralyzing fear at being summoned before an SS trooper. They had no knowledge of how she had already been broken by these experts at terror.

Most importantly, they took no cognizance of the fact that she was but a girl of fourteen, who, after her so-called "betrayal," needed her family more than ever before.

Kristallnacht marked the end of all self-delusion among the Jews of Germany. It was now clear to even the most German of German Jews that there was no longer any prospect for survival in Germany. All efforts were directed at getting out. It wasn't easy. A family couldn't just collect its belongings, say their goodbyes to neighbors, promise to keep in touch, give a last fond wave, and leave.

Where could one go? Who would take you? Most European countries would not allow Jews in, even temporarily. The rest of the world was virtually closed to them. Palestine, ruled as a British mandate, would allow but a few thousand a year. And the United States, its German immigration quota only twenty-seven thousand per year, wouldn't make any exception for the extraordinary situation developing in Germany. How ironic that the United States insisted on treating the German Jews as Germans, even though Germany had long since abandoned doing so.

This was only half the trouble. Once you had found a haven willing to accept you, the Nazis saw to it that you would leave with nothing with which to start your new life. There were taxes, levies, and assessments to be handed over to the German authorities. If after all this you salvaged a few marks, the legal exchange rate was such that you received only one-tenth of the actual value in a foreign currency. If you had a strong will to survive, and a great deal of courage, you got around the laws.

Ruth had made secret plans to leave for England. They involved a British tutor, Larry McDonald who, in addition to his job at the British consulate in Cologne, taught English to paying Jews. She was to receive a temporary visa through him upon her written promise to work as a maid.

A couple of days after *Kristallnacht*, when Larry McDonald came to deliver the documents, only Kitty was home. When she told him that she was Ruth's sister, he trusted her with the papers.

When Ruth came home later that day, Kitty handed her the documents and said, "You're leaving? You never told me! Don't you trust me?"

"Of course, I trust you. You're my sister, aren't you?"

"Why didn't you tell me?"

"It was a secret. It's all unofficial."

"Mr. McDonald trusted me."

"He shouldn't have."

Kitty walked away from Ruth, wondering what was going to happen to her.

She didn't have to wait long. That same afternoon there was a heavy knock on the door, followed by a hard, shattering scream. "Open up!" The SS had come back.

Ruth opened the door. She didn't ask them in. She talked with the troopers in low tones and Kitty, standing at the top of the stairs, unable to move, could not make out what was being said. She did sense from the tension in Ruth's voice that something was wrong. Their voices suddenly grew louder, more strident, and she thought that she heard her name. Yes, there it was again. She heard her name. Definitely! Distinctly! "Kitty." How, in heaven's name, could that be?

All at once, the SS troopers forced their way past Ruth and came right up the stairs. "You there, you come with us!" They grabbed her by her arms and dragged her along like a criminal. Ruth, catching one of Kitty's shoulders, tried to hold on to her sister, screaming, "She's not an orphan!" Speechless, Kitty gaped back at her sister who, still running after her, tried to hold on to her. "She's my sister, I swear!" Her voice nearly broke. "Why don't you leave her alone?"

They didn't pay any attention. They pushed Kitty ahead of them, shoving her so hard that she stumbled and fell to her knees. Without giving her a chance to get up, they grabbed her under her arms and, with her legs bouncing freely on the sidewalk, they dragged her limp body along.

With all this commotion, not one head turned. No one looked out. Windows stayed closed. The policeman, standing next to the curb, stared blindly past them. It was not that nobody cared, but rather that nobody dared to care.

Finally, lifting her, they tossed the limp girl into the back of the open truck. Like doomed prey, those already on the truck, watched the goings-on in silence.

When Kitty came to realize what had been happening to her, that she had been torn away from her family, she slid quietly into the far corner, moving away from everybody. She closed her eyes and covered her ears. She didn't want to see or hear anything. She didn't want to talk to anybody. For everyone had deserted her. Even God had let her down. He hadn't listened to her. There was no one who cared.

No longer could she cry. The tears were stuck inside of her, held back, like a dam restraining the flooding waters. Cut off, never to spill again! In this world where one did not cry. In this world where there was no place for children and their tears.

Yes, it was true. She was no longer a child!

She opened her eyes once more and her gaze locked on the shadowy legs right in front of her. Legs covered by crumpled, soiled pants. Legs in shades of grays and blacks. Legs fixed in place. Legs of old men. Of silent old men. Of feeble old men. Of helpless old men. Helpless just like her. Staring out into space. Saying nothing. Raising no objections. Thinking. Probably thinking about yesterday. About their families. Their little girls. Not wanting to know about each other. Know about her. All of them Jews! Standing there as if in a trance. Like nothing seemed to matter to them. All of them behaving like stampeding, gutless wildebeests, running away from the comrade cut down by the lion.

She closed her eyes once more. She thought about her mother and her sister. Of course, Ruth would tell her mother what had happened. Her mother would understand! She'd be looking for her. She'd get one of her influential friends to ask around. To find out what happened to her daughter. Explain to them how she had been taken away.

But suddenly, in spite of herself, her heart stopped and she broke into a cold sweat. What if her mother didn't believe that the SS had taken her away? Or, even worse, what if Ruth never told her? What if her mother believed that she had left on her own?

"Oh, my God, Mother what did I do wrong?"

The next morning when they arrived at Dachau it was still dark. The lights at the gate shone only weakly. It had been nine hours since she had been thrown onto the truck. She hadn't slept and her stomach was grumbling. The guard unhooked the tailgate, let it bang against the rear bumper, and screamed into the night, "*Raus!*" He pulled at sleeves and pushed bodies. "*Raus mit euch!*"

Kitty jumped off the truck. She looked around. There were other girls. She had not noticed them before. Suddenly, her heart opened up. She wasn't alone. She ran to where the other girls were. She recognized them. What luck! They were girls from the Orphans' Home. She counted them. There were only eight. She recognized Lore. Little Lore who was only twelve years old. Who was so timid and so scared. She took a place next to her, making sure her arm touched Lore's.

The men were marched to a nearby barrack. The girls were divided up, two for each barrack. Lore and Kitty were assigned together, Lore to the lower bunk, Kitty to the upper. It was plain luck that they would be together. Kitty was grateful for even this small favor.

Chapter 8

The Next Day

Nearby Dachau, a small town in the rural Bavarian countryside just ten miles north of Munich, lay one of the first concentration camps established by the Nazis. Later on, it would become known to the world as one of the more infamous extermination camps in the Nazi program to create an *Arische Reinrasse* (a pure breed of German Aryans). In 1938 it served mostly as an instrument of intimidation in their plan to force the emigration of Germany's Jews. Many of those interned were male heads of families who could arrange their freedom by providing written assurance that they and their families would leave Germany within sixty days of their release.

Of course, those who provided such assurances were betting they'd be able to find a country that would accept them and their families as immigrants, or at least offer them visitors' visas. They had better be successful at it, for once you were set free from Dachau there was no way of hiding from the authorities. It was virtually impossible to disappear into the general population, for everyone had to register with the police and produce papers upon the request of any petty functionary who demanded them. If someone who had obtained his release on the basis of a promise to leave Germany was still around after the stipulated date, he was returned to the camp, with his official records duly marked.

What about the young girls who had been shipped to Dachau?

The Jewish Orphans' Home of Cologne, which had held twenty-nine young boys and girls, had been cleaned out. There had been some expectation that the SS would be looking for the young males, and many of them had been spirited out of the Home. When they arrived and looked over the rest of the waifs, they selected eight girls for transport to the Dachau camp and shot the rest, including Rachel, Kitty's friend.

It was an easy bit of work. Each SS trooper made his own decision about which girls he would take and which he would shoot. Mausers drawn, they walked through the cowering children like sheep buyers looking over the offered stock. "I think this one will do," one of them might call out or, "This one's no good," and the youngster would either be loaded up for shipment to the camp, or BANG, shot on the spot. Altogether seven girls and three boys were killed that brisk, fall afternoon.

Lore was one of the children at the Home allowed to live a little longer. Kitty, who had never been a resident, was searched out later, probably because her name had been found or spoken at the Home. The SS were not inclined to allow anyone to believe a child might possibly be shielded from them by some trick.

On the first day in Dachau, all the girls were sent to the infirmary. A heavyset nurse in a starched, gleaming white uniform made them undress, checked them for lesions and sores, spread their jaws to look at their teeth, and rammed her fingers into their vaginal constriction to check for infections. After she had finished, she made them take showers. *"Ich will das ihr rein seit!* (I want you clean!) she screamed at them. Those who had not done a good job washing themselves, she scrubbed mercilessly.

All that night, Lore, numb with fear, swallowed her welling sobs, choking their flow like narrows restrain the flooding tide. Kitty held Lore in her arms, ignoring her own anguish, wiping beads of perspiration from her pallid forehead, trying to calm the little girl. "It's going to be all right," she said to her. "We'll make it through."

Even this tiny bit of hope, this consolation she offered Lore, was really a lie. She was not at all certain that they'd get through it. Yet her words were part of her repertoire for survival. If they helped her, they might help Lore, too.

This was all she could offer her friend—not that something dreadful would not happen to them, but only that they'd survive it. She was prepared to suffer, to withstand the onslaught upon her being, to endure the unspeakable. She'd offer up her compliance in a deal for survival. Even though she still had the ability to think and judge—the special qualities of being human—she no longer allowed herself to indulge those qualities. She had learned that already from Kurt, the SS trooper. Her best defense was to stop thinking. There was less pain if she reacted only with her body. If she didn't think, her body would eventually grow numb. She'd respond to each moment in a way that would help her survive. Like the callow deer in the forest, always at the mercy of fate, Kitty had learned to respond only instinctively.

Of course, it all had been such a big mistake. She wasn't an orphan. Whatever problems she had had at home, *she did have a mother*. A mother who was probably explaining things to some official right now.

But, all at once, a new insight overwhelmed her. What if her mother didn't wait for her? What if when she got back to Cologne—if she ever did get back—her mother and her sister had already left Germany?

At eight o'clock that night they came for Lore, tearing her out of her bunk like a chicken from its coop. As they dragged her away, the screaming girl looked back at Kitty, her eyes filled with unspeakable terror. Yes, Kitty thought, she was much too young to comprehend her fate, to understand what these adults might want with her. She was not primed for the worst, as Kitty was.

As the minutes passed, they seemed like hours. Before she knew it, she had drifted into one of her daydreams. Sitting at the grand in the salon, her eyes fastened on Papa, waiting for his nod. Her fingers stretched as far as she could stretch them. Ready to play his music.

"*Du, da, komm mit uns!*"

She didn't hear them.

"You, there, come along!" Suddenly, their flashlight blinded her. "Don't you hear us?"

She jumped from the bunk.

The two of them led her away, barefoot as she was, out the door, across the dark yard, stumbling over stones, on ruts and soft hollows. "Get going!" they growled. As much as she tried to hasten, they pushed her along faster, and she became afraid that she might be getting them angry by not moving fast enough.

They pushed her through the door of the barracks.

For a moment, the bright lights blinded her. She stumbled over a body. A soft, little body. A dead body? Her toes felt wet. Was it blood? She dared not look.

Finally, she was able to focus her eyes. The room was full of men, regular guards but also a few SS guards. They were all staring at her. She knew the stare. She knew what it meant.

"*Jawohl!*" One of them nodded, a touch of a smile on his face. One could read his thoughts: a virginal body, budding breasts, not the usual whore. A Jewgirl, but not too Jewish looking. A lamb to be savored, a tasty tidbit to satisfy the nastiest urges.

Standing there near the entrance, barefoot, in her slip, her hair disheveled, her eyes downcast, Kitty did not utter a sound. If this was her lot, so be it. She wanted to live. No matter what would happen. No matter what they would do to her. She had to make it back to her mother and sister. That's all that mattered.

Yet, she couldn't get that dead body out of her mind. No, of course, it couldn't be Lore. No, they wouldn't have. As long as she did what they told her to do, they wouldn't kill her. No! Never! They would want to use her again. As long as she didn't make too much of a fuss. Like screaming or crying or resisting them.

One of the guards came. *"Komm' mit mir!* (Come along!)" He shoved her into a room and pushed her down onto a cot. Instinctively she pulled her legs up to her chest and hid her face in her hands. As her body tightened, she felt the blows of a blackjack. *"Was ist denn los mit dir*? (What's the matter with you?)" someone screamed.

She didn't move. Like a lamb curled up before the slaughter, Kitty tried to shield her body from the merciless world.

He grabbed her by her hands, pulled her up so that her arms straightened right above her, twisted them, turning her body around, and dropped her on her back. Grasping both of her wrists with one hand, he jammed his knee into her crotch and with the other hand ripped the slip off her body, tearing both straps. Then, shoving his knee into her stomach, he removed her panties and her brassiere.

"Gut!" he said.

How practiced he was, she thought, just like Kurt.

She turned her head toward the wall. She closed her eyes. Not seeing spared her a small part of the pain. Besides, she did not want to convey resistance. That's what they hated most. It made no sense to resist. You never returned an angry look with an angry look. You never raised a hand to defend yourself. Certainly not in deed, but not even in your thoughts, for thoughts could be read on your face like an infection on your skin. If they read them on your face, they were punishable just like any other insubordinate act.

One after another they came that night. They came to "do it" to the Jewgirl. A conquest, which wasn't a conquest at all. Because she was a Jewgirl even if she did look Aryan. Yes, it was true, she didn't look Jewish. But it didn't really matter. Jews had it coming.

All the time, while she lay there crushed beneath those sweaty, foul-smelling hulks, she tried to think of Robert. She saw herself walking again in the *Stadtwald*, hand in hand with Robert, renewing his warm, shielding embrace near the pond. And like a secret, self-sustaining streamlet trickling deep in the hidden caverns of her mind, she heard the wild applause at the end of her Rachmaninoff concert in Cologne's great synagogue. Yes, it had been the greatest moment of her life. And through it all, as if trying to reach her from his cold grave, she heard Papa calling out to her, *Everything has an ending!*

Yes, there had to be an ending! There were so many of them. It was so far from an ending. All of them so big, so self-satisfied.

Little by little, the pain began to consume her. She was unable to distract herself any longer. For, whenever she thought that it was all over, another one came. She swallowed her screams. With her fists clenched, her eyes shut, and her neck wrenched, she just lay there, suffering the agonies of the assaults like a sinner flung mercilessly into the eternal firestorms of hell.

It was only many hours later, after she had been ravished over and over again, that they told her to get out. She tried to get up but she couldn't make it. The ache was unbearable.

Someone grabbed her arms, dragged her from the cot, pulled her out the door, across the freezing, rutty ground, and dumped her in front of her barracks, tossing the torn tatters that had been her clothing after her.

There she lay on the cold, bare ground, completely naked, covered only with her torn slip. A bloodied young girl, unattended and uncared for, shivering relentlessly. Quite an ordinary girl in her way. Pretty, yes. That's why she was still alive. So damned lucky for her. For a pretty Jewgirl had some slight edge over a homely one.

Everything was quiet now. Even in her delirium she recognized that it was all over. She had cooperated and she had survived. They had been satisfied, at least for now.

Two strong arms lifted her and carried her back to the barracks, easing her down on the bunk, covering her with a blanket. No one spoke. Everyone slept or pretended to sleep. She was thankful for that. She did not want to talk, she did not want to think. She wanted to sleep. She had to sleep.

It was six o'clock the next morning when they woke her. Her eyes were heavy. Her mouth was dry. Her body ached. Her stomach cramped with pain. She put on her torn undergarments. When she went to wash herself, there was a long line. There were only two wash basins for the whole barracks. There wasn't enough time. She dressed without washing.

Roll call was over quickly.

As she stood in line for breakfast, she felt dizzy. Her forehead sweated. Her legs felt wobbly. If she could only lie down. She wasn't hungry and wondered if they would take it as insubordinate if she didn't eat the bread they had given her. When someone asked why she was not eating, she gave him her bread. She drank something hot. It cleared her head.

She was sent out on a work detail with all the others. They marched to a nearby field. *"Zieh' das Unkraut 'raus!"* he commanded.

She weeded the hard soil with the others. Bending, tearing at the roots. On that cold November day she sweated profusely. Suddenly, she felt a burning pain in her stomach. The earth started to spin around her. Then, all at once, she collapsed.

The guard came over and kicked her in the stomach. *"Steh auf du Schwein!* (Get up you pig!)"

She couldn't get up.

He pulled her up by the neck but her body crumbled, blood oozing between her legs. He saw the blood on her shoes, on her skirt, on the ground. *"Verdammt! Was eine Schweinerei!* (Damn it, what a mess!)"

"Over here!" He called for two of the male prisoners. "Take her away!"

The men carried her to the infirmary. They sat her down on a chair.

Barely aware of where she was, Kitty instinctively held on to the chair. When she finally opened her eyes, she caught sight of the long, stub-pointed scissors, the gleaming, narrow knives, the chromed, plier-like tools neatly arranged on the cart next to her.

They Called Her Jewgirl

Oh, my God, she thought, what will happen to me now? What will they do to me next?

When the door finally opened, it was the same heavyset nurse, in that same starched, gleaming white uniform, who had examined her when she arrived at the camp. She wanted to get up and run. But she couldn't make it.

"Lie down over here."

She led Kitty to the examination table, helped her onto it, swung her dangling legs up and around, raised her skirt, and removed her panties, placing her feet into the stirrups. *"Was, im Himmel, haben die denn mit dir gemacht?* (What, for heaven's sake, have they done to you?)" Her tone was civil, even sympathetic.

She examined her, her fingers in her vagina. She shook her head. She puckered her lips. Then she looked up to the ceiling and thought for a moment, as if she wanted to make certain that there wouldn't be any trouble. After all, this was a Jewgirl. In the end, she thought, Hitler was right, insisting that they get rid of the Jews. They were Internationalists. They had worked for the other side in the last war. They had never believed in the new Germany, our free and united Germany.

What she now saw in front of her, what those men had done to this child, was this a vision of the new Germany?

Aber, die Schweine! (Those pigs!) They didn't care whom they had. Pigs, that's what they were. Sex! That's all they ever had on their minds. On their filthy, little minds. They were deaf to all the *Führer* was trying to teach them. Never thinking of the special responsibility of a German, of his dignity. A German, who had pride, who had culture. We're not a race of rapists, of sex maniacs! No better than all the others! No better than those degenerate Frenchmen. Those filthy, depraved Pollacks. Those raping niggers of Africa!

"I'll give you something for the pain," she said to Kitty.

The words were spoken more gently than any words Kitty had heard since her arrival in the camp. The nurse gave her a shot of morphine. Then she led her into another room and had her lie down.

Kitty's pain slowly disappeared. She actually fell asleep.

Later, when she opened her eyes again, the most intense pain was gone and the bleeding had stopped.

The nurse came back to the room. "You can leave now."

Kitty sat up and stared at her. She wanted to thank her, but the nurse looked away. She did not want her thanks. When Kitty got up to leave, she said, "*Danke!*" anyway.

The nurse gave an almost imperceptible nod.

Kitty lay down on her cot. She had received five stitches. She did not have to work the rest of the day. Soon she fell asleep and did not wake up until dark.

Chapter 9

Later That Month

The next two nights Kitty was left alone. She was lucky. She was too messy for them. They knew about the infirmary, the stitches and the crusted blood. She understood that. *Rein!* Clean! That's the way they wanted the girls. Everything was to be clean, super clean. That was part of the common identity her keepers treasured.

They also hated throwing up. They hated foul smells or sweaty breasts. That's what did Lore in. If a girl didn't appear neat and clean, all it took was one quick bang of the Mauser. Too messy, they said, throwing up when she should have been thankful to be alive. They didn't have to put up with those awful foul smells. On the third night they came back for Kitty. This time they were close to friendly, not at all like they had been before. They asked about her, as if they cared about her stitches, as if it mattered to them whether or not she was in pain. "*Komm mit uns!* (Come with us!)" they said, as if it were a request. It was not that they had suddenly found remorse in all they had done to her, but because there were now only four girls left. The rest, well, who cared? They hadn't been worth anything. Screaming, smelly bitches, who'd hate you even if you were a nice guy and tried not to hurt them. No matter how nice you were, they screamed their heads off.

Having decided that she wanted to survive, no matter the price, she even turned her head to her tormentors and forced a smile. They came for her every night. She even came to know some of them by name. She even talked to them. How painful it would be in later years to recall the civility that she had extended them. How much easier it would have been to recall a posture of defiance on her part, to say that there had been some line she had drawn that she would not be dragged across. But she didn't treat herself to this little deception. She remembered it as it was: her abject surrender and her cordial exchange of pleasantries with her tormentors. What difference did it make? As long as talking to them kept her safely alive. No, they wouldn't do away with her, this Jewgirl who wasn't like the rest. Not as long as she tried to cooperate, tried not to ruin a good time for them, did not cause them unnecessary bother.

Helping Kitty through this was a numbness that dominated her waking hours. Her body felt as if it had been swabbed with a topical anesthetic to make it less sensitive. She thought little and felt even less. She wouldn't allow herself to dwell on what was happening to her because it really had nothing to do with her. She was turning into an automaton. She reacted mechanically or as others willed it. The only thing that mattered to her was survival. To be able to live. To be free one day and go back to living that other life. If you didn't have that hope, you were already dead and they had won.

On the seventh night they came for her again. Her body was stronger now. She had survived this far, accepting her existence moment by moment, starting to build hope that she might indeed survive for a longer time. She was now better able to bear the pain because it had become part of her existence. She was like a blind person in a world of darkness, finding her way among the inevitable hurdles.

Clearly she was one of the lucky ones. She had pleased them. One could tell. For they no longer shoved her ahead of them. They no longer pulled her by her hair.

On this seventh night, when they came for her, they led her to a different barracks, a barracks filled with only SS guards, sitting around tables, drinking, laughing, showing little interest in her. She stood in a corner and waited. Nothing happened. By now she had developed a sixth sense about these things. She had a terrible foreboding. This was going to be something different. She didn't like the uncertainty at all.

Suddenly the door opened and a great hush descended upon the gathering. Two guards entered, a young boy between them. He was a slim boy, no more than fourteen or fifteen years old.

Momentarily the guards glanced at Kitty, but then they looked back at their charge. They grabbed him under his arms and ripped off his pants and all the rest of his clothing. The boy stood there totally naked, a virginal, vulnerable child, laid bare to the feral world around him.

All conversation had stopped.

The guards came over to Kitty, grabbed her by her arms and ripped off her slip. Before they could rip off her panties, she freed her arms, dropped her panties, and took off her brassiere.

Everyone stared at her. Then, in virtual unison, their heads turned to the boy.

"*Zeig' uns was du kannst, du arroganter Judenbengel!* (Show us what you can do, you arrogant Jewboy!)" One of the guards pushed the boy toward Kitty.

She stepped back, instinctively. She didn't quite understand. What did they want of her? Hadn't she always cooperated? Hadn't she always pleased them?

The young boy just stood there tight-lipped, staring at her with heavy but defiant eyes. At once Kitty recognized their fatal portent. His eyes told her that he was not yet reconciled to the savagery of the place, to the severity of their plight, for defiance had no place here.

His eyes searched her face, but then, suddenly, they dropped down to her body. Did she understand what they wanted of them? As if ashamed for his unspoken question, he looked away from her.

Oh yes, she understood! Yes, of course, she understood how they wanted to be pleased tonight.

Peering into his eyes, she stepped forward, looking for his "yes," his readiness. She was ready. There was no question about it. She'd do whatever they expected of her. It meant living. It meant surviving.

Then something happened that took her totally by surprise. The boy turned to them and spoke. *"Ich kann das nicht tuen!"*

She couldn't believe his words. *"I can't do it!"* he had said.

Why? But why couldn't he? Why in heaven's name couldn't he? What utter, utter foolishness! Oh God, would he ever pay for this! Pay for his defiance! No doubt about it! *She* had been ready! *She* had let him know! The only thing that mattered around here was to survive! Hadn't he learned that yet?

When the boy turned back to Kitty, his lips were determined, his chin jutting, and his dark eyes moist. The words were written all over his face: *"I'll never submit to them!"*

She lunged forward, wanting to go to him. To go to him in spite of his refusal. But, in the end, she didn't. In the end, she didn't move at all. If he wanted to defy them—which was a great folly, a very dangerous folly—that was his choice. It was his choice alone. It certainly wasn't hers. She guarded her body language carefully to make certain that it was understood that the boy had made his decision for himself only, not for her.

She watched as they severed his boyhood with a gleaming, machete-type blade. It was such a clean cut, like a sickle clipping the budding wheat. Not a sound came out of him. Not even a wince. Everyone was waiting for something to happen. But nothing happened.

In the end, they all applauded as they took him away.

Later that night they brought her a package, made of newspaper, blood oozing through the wrappings. "That's from your Jewboy." They placed it into her hands. "Your arrogant, dead Jewboy." They turned to leave. "You can have it as a souvenir."

It was on the twelfth day that Kitty was called to the *Commandant's* office. To her great surprise, Mr. McDonald, the English tutor, Ruth's friend, was there. They treated him with great respect. Kitty stayed with him for a while. He told her that he had made arrangements for her to go to England and work as a maid. Kitty couldn't believe the words. The part of her that believed in such things had long ago ceased to exist. He also told her that they would not allow him to take her along, but that he had left some money for her with the *Commandant* so that she could get home when they released her. She did not yet believe in the promised miracle. She knew only that when he left she would be left behind.

During the next three days Kitty waited, half wanting to believe, half-afraid to believe. She was ready to put Mr. McDonald out of her mind and spare herself further pain, but then, on the fourth day, early in the morning, she was called to the *Commandant's* office. They were releasing her. There was another girl by the name of Margot, an orphan, a girl about her age, with shallow, wandering eyes and a scab on her lower lip, who would be leaving with her.

When she asked for the money that Mr. McDonald had left for her, they laughed. "What money?" they said. It didn't really matter. After sixteen days in hell, the only important thing was that she was getting out.

Chapter 10

Late November 1938

Once through the gates of Dachau, Margot and Kitty would not trust themselves to look back. With a quick step and a much lighter heart, barely able to comprehend that the relentless, unpredictable terror of the camp had ended for them, they strode on, never stopping until, after several kilometers and many bends of the road, they were absolutely sure that they were out of sight of the camp. Only then did they appraise their plight. They had no money, they were cold, and they were more than three hundred miles from home.

They decided to see if they could find some way to earn the money they needed to get home. They did not dare go into the villages or cities for fear that the SS would hear of them and come after them again. They passed the harvested fields to their right and left. Whenever they caught a glimpse of a farmer, they trudged across and asked if he had any odd jobs they might do. They were invariably chased off, never with more than a word or two. They could well imagine the unattractive appearance they presented to the farmers, dirty as they were, with torn clothing. They suspected that the real reason they were given such short shrift was that the farmers guessed where they had come from and were afraid to get involved with anyone who might bring them and their own families under the scrutiny of the SS.

Their only good luck was that one farmer, while denying their request for work, did take pity on them. With a quick jerk of his head, he indicated that they might stay in his barn overnight. Later that evening he brought them bread and milk and told them to just leave the glasses and dishes in the barn when they left in the morning.

They left with first light, keeping the rising sun at their backs as they headed to the north and west, trying for the Rhine Valley. All through the long morning they tramped along the stone-faced highway, the rugged pavement tiring their feet. At about noon, a black Mercedes roadster passed them, pulling off the road about forty yards ahead of them. A hand came out of the passenger side and waved them on—an offer of a ride. They looked at each other as they walked slowly toward the car, trying to decide, unsure, but tired enough to be tempted, neither one of them confident enough to risk reassuring the other.

Margot was first to catch a glimpse of the SS uniforms. She grabbed Kitty by the sleeve and pulled her up short. Now Kitty saw them, too. Margot motioned to the far field off to their right, but Kitty was frozen to the spot. Though Margot tried to pull her along, Kitty couldn't move. Finally letting go, Margot hopped a short fence and ran off into the harvested field, calling back, "Come on, Kitty, hurry up." Kitty was fixed in place. When Margot slowed for a moment and turned back, she screamed frantically, "Kitty, for God's sake, don't you see who they are?"

Two shots rang out. Kitty saw Margot fall. For just a moment, she lunged toward her, wanting to run to her. Margot! But she choked off the scream with the palm of her hand.

"*Nun?*" One of the SS troopers called out to her. "Well?"

He wasn't really asking a question. There was no choice. She did not want to die. Not now.

"What a shame!" he said to her as he pulled her into the car and they drove off.

Sitting next to him, Kitty, rigid, terrified, tried to control the panic she thought she had left behind at the camp. What new horror was awaiting her?

When they arrived in a small Bavarian town, they stopped at an inn. "Take a bath," they told her. An old woman brought soap, towels, and clean clothing. After the bath she came with a tray of food. It was warm and smelled good, and Kitty ate heartily. She forced Margot's fate from her mind. Maybe Margot had survived the shots. Maybe they had missed and she had pretended to be hit, had played dead until the car pulled off.

But deep down she knew the truth. These people did not miss. Besides, Margot's body had jerked sharply before her legs buckled. She had been hit twice. Knowing the SS, both shots had found critical points in her body. There was no more left of Margot than a limp, lifeless corpse. It was she who was alive. And she wanted to continue to live, to go on, to get home to her mother and sister and leave with them for England.

She was not deceived by the bath, the new clothes, and the food the SS troopers had arranged for her. It was no longer anything new for her. They wanted to be paid back. She had learned to submit to whatever was demanded of her not because it was right, but only because it spared her additional terror, additional pain.

Early the next morning they boosted her onto the flat bed of a truck, telling her that the driver would take her home. Within less than an hour the truck pulled into another town. The driver told her she'd have to get out. This was the end of the line for him, at least for a while. She'd have to make her own way from now on. No, she couldn't wait for him, he told her brusquely. She could have reminded him that the SS troopers had promised that he would take her home, but she wanted no trouble with him. She did as she was told. Without a word, she climbed out of the truck and walked off.

For a long time, she wandered aimlessly around the town. She was freezing, but even in the cold she found herself sweaty and slightly dizzy, her walk heavy and her body feverish. As she was trying to figure out what to do next, she sighted a church in the distance, its lofty spire pointing like a long finger to the heavens. In her burning imagination, the finger was pointing at God as a witness to the evils below, to all the false words and easy excuses.

She headed for it. There had to be a respite somewhere, a place of quiet where she could finally find some peace.

She quickly reached the entrance. With all the strength left in her, she opened the heavy portal. Inside she waited at the entrance, momentarily blinded by the dark, wary of the quiet, taking in several long, deep gasps of air.

Yes, she was alone in the big church.

But this aloneness was of a new kind. For it was nothing at all like the death-sad aloneness of the camp, nothing at all like the dark nights that passed like long, sleepless eternities. Neither was it anything like the aloneness when, still in Cologne, sitting at the grand, she waited nightly for her mother and sister to return home. This was an entirely new aloneness, an aloneness that gave her a new feeling of peace.

She took a few hesitant steps along the center aisle. But the hollow, echoing resonance of her steps made her feel uneasy. At any moment, someone might scream, "Who goes there!" She sat down in the pew. That was much better. It eased her. She lifted her head and stared at the height of the apse. She observed the sun's bright rays, impregnated with the hues of stained glass, filter quietly into the church. Yes, this was different! This was quite unlike anything she had ever met up with. For here, sitting in the church, she could believe again. Yes, God was up there in the heavens! She could see Him! He was looking down on her! At this very moment! From way up in His heaven! A Christian God! Looking down at her sitting in his church! A God for everybody! A God for the poor, a God for the invalids! A God for all those away from home. A God for all those who were lost. A God who knew all about her pain.

With her eyes turned to the heavens, Kitty prayed to Him. "Please God, up there in the heavens, will you please help me!

Will you help me make it back to Cologne, even though I'm not a Christian?" She was in His church. She was asking Him for so little. "Please, *oh God*," she finally cried out, closing her eyes, "please, make my mother wait for me, so I can leave with her for England!"

She hadn't noticed the priest, not until he bent down to where she was sitting, placed his hand on her shoulder, and spoke in a most gentle voice. "What is it, my child?"

She turned her head and looked up at him. She met his eyes. She saw they were kind.

He gathered her face and held it gently. When he felt her tremble, he drew her closer to his yielding, robed paunch. "It's all right, my child, it's all right," he said to her.

For Kitty, being held by anyone was a strange, new feeling. When was the last time that anyone held her? When was the last time that anyone caressed her? Sheltered in the benign embrace of the priest, she felt again like a child in her father's arms. No longer could she hold back the tears. All at once Kitty started to sob wildly and, as he gathered her ever closer to him, she drowned herself in his robes. Like a miracle, her trembling passed and she became filled with a new warm and soothing feeling—a feeling of deliverance. Finally, she had reached port and had anchored safely.

Was this for real? Oh God, could it really be true that she was able to cry again?

She felt so safe. Even though she was still confused as to why she felt so safe. Even though she still remembered the terrors of the camp, her bondage. Even though she could still recall all the unannounced, sudden shoves and all the unexpected blows.

She wiped her face with the sleeve of her dress and looked up at the priest.

"Would you like to come to the rectory?" he asked.

Kitty could only nod.

The priest took her by the hand and, without saying another word, led her away.

Whenever the priest spoke to her, it was in a gentle voice. Whenever he looked at her, it was with a kind face. There was no more scowling, there were no more threats, no more smell of sweat, of caked blood, of splattered bodily fluids. Missing too were the sounds of others weeping or groaning. Instead, up in the rectory there were flowers everywhere. Easter lilies and African violets were in every room, filling the air with the most delicate aromas. Was she dreaming?

The housekeeper undressed her, washed her, and tucked her into a warm, clean bed. Alarmed by her state, the priest brought in a doctor. Yes, Kitty was indeed sick. She had pneumonia. The priest stayed with her at night and the housekeeper during the day, alternating as bedside nurses. Yet Kitty, even in her fever and delirium, still remained somewhat suspicious, wondering if in fact they suspected that she was Jewish. Did they know that harboring a Jew was a major crime? Even harboring a young girl like her? Especially a young girl who had been in a camp? Who might have escaped? But of course, they had to know, she finally reasoned. Who else would have walked into the empty church, in the middle of the day, so sick, so desolate, so alone? No, she wouldn't have to tell them.

As she began to recuperate, the priest talked about taking her to Switzerland. Kitty, trusting him more each day, explained that she had a mother and sister waiting for her, and that she wanted to get back home. Together she, her mother, and her sister would leave for England.

Yes, a child her age belonged with her mother, the priest agreed. However, when she was still not well enough to get out of bed after a week, he decided to take her to a nearby convent where she would be safer than at the rectory. In spite of everything, the Nazis respected the sanctity of the convents.

He moved her late one night. He came to visit her every day.

It took nearly three weeks before Kitty recovered and was well enough to travel. During that time, she had gained some weight and in the clothing they had found for her she looked a world better than she had when she came to them. She was ready to go home. It was arranged that one of the nuns would accompany her to Cologne.

The trip was uneventful, but when they arrived at Kitty's home, no one was there. All the evidence indicated that her mother was gone just for the day, as she so often had been when Kitty was last home. Kitty insisted that it would be all right to leave her. "My mother will be back soon," she assured the nun.

She agreed. The nun took Kitty's face, held it tightly against her bosom, and looked up to the heavens. *"Gott im Himmel wird dir helfen."* Yes, God in heaven would help her. He would help this little Jewish girl.

Biting her lips, she stroked Kitty's cheek and shook her head. Then, all at once, she turned and left.

Alone once more, Kitty sat down on the steps and thought how lucky she was to be home again.

When her mother arrived toward evening and found Kitty waiting for her, she seemed barely surprised. "So, you're finally back," she said rather calmly. It didn't seem to matter much to her mother whether she'd come back or not.

Kitty had been away from home for over five weeks. She had been ready to tell her mother about everything that had happened to her. She ached to unburden herself. But the shame of all she had undergone, of all she had done—that was how Kitty thought of it—made her hesitate. Her shame was too difficult to explain, too complicated for her mother to understand.

Still, she had to say it. "All the time I was gone I kept hoping that when I got back, I'd be able to talk to you," she sighed.

"Really?" Reggie pursed her lips, nodding. "Well, let me tell you something. I don't want to hear about it. I've got my own troubles. All the time you were gone, did you ever care what was happening to me, your own mother?" she continued. "I should have left and just let you worry about yourself." With that she cut off the conversation and left Kitty wondering why she had come back home.

Yes, it was hopeless to talk to her mother. It had always been. Play it safe, she thought, as she had with the SS, as she had in camp, as she would now with her mother. After all, she wanted to get to England, and her mother offered her the best chance of doing so.

Eric, having been released from camp, had already left for England with Ruth. Mr. McDonald was also gone. He had left her papers at the British consulate. Many others had left, and those who hadn't left were trying desperately to find a country that would accept them. It was well into the eleventh hour for the Jews of Germany.

Kitty knew this, not just from all the talk but now, more compellingly, from her own experience. In the end, all she wanted was to survive. To do so, she had to escape Germany.

Of course, had Reggie inquired about Kitty's absence, she might have found out about the cruelties her daughter had suffered. But that wasn't her style. That had never been her style. For Reggie had a sense about life—like many of her countrymen, both Jews and gentiles alike—that to suffer adversity strengthens character. That to be able to deal with the worst calamities was a prerequisite for survival.

Never mind feelings! Never mind weakness! The world was there for the strong!

If there were ever one thing that Kitty could admire in her mother, it was her determination, her unfettered guts. In spite of her great disappointment in not being able to talk to her, Kitty had confidence, at this important moment in her life, that no matter what it took, Reggie would see to it that they made it out of Germany.

Chapter 11

July 1939

Kitty and her mother left Cologne Airport on the morning of 21 July 1939. Each was allowed to carry one hundred *Reichsmarks*, about twenty-five dollars. A white-smocked matron stripped and searched them for valuables, particularly diamonds, pawing their hair and fingering all of their orifices. The inspection came up empty, and they were cleared. Their passports were duly stamped, and they were allowed to board the plane.

Not until they had crossed the English Channel and saw British soil did they breathe easier. Reggie turned to Kitty and smiled. "We made it!" she said. "We made it out of hell!"

Kitty smiled back at her mother with a bland stare. What did she know about hell?

Reggie patted the back of Kitty's hand. "You did well," she said.

Suspicious of any compliment from her mother, she asked, "I did?"

"Yes, you did," Reggie nodded. "Give me your purse."

She handed it over.

Reggie emptied Kitty's purse, tore out the lining and there, at the bottom, between the seams of the butted leather, a slight bulge could be felt, though not seen. "Feel it," she said to her. "Go feel it!" she insisted when Kitty made no move.

When Kitty felt the knotted seam, her heart skipped a beat. Her mother repeated. "You feel it?"

She nodded.

"Five and a half carats!"

"Yes?"

"I fooled them, didn't I?"

Kitty nodded again.

"The sons of bitches!"

A shudder ran down Kitty's spine. The thought that her mother had sewn a diamond into her purse and risked the wrath of the SS to get it out of Germany was too much for her to contemplate. She might have been thrown back into Dachau. No diamond in the world was worth that risk.

London was in its last days of peace. It would be a little more than a month before Great Britain would declare war on Germany, following Germany's invasion of Poland. Even though most Britons were aware of Hitler's persecution of the Jews, they tended not to welcome foreigners other than tourists or those on a short visit. The Jews arriving in London daily, with no place else to go, seemed to be settling in for a long stay. One would be wise to speak German only in a whisper.

Kitty and Reggie moved in with Eric. He had rented a two-room apartment, a big letdown from their generous accommodations in Cologne, but they were glad to make do. Their bigger problem was that they were refugees in a strange land, speaking English poorly and, indeed, speaking among themselves in the language of Britain's enemy.

While the subdued resentment of the English people posed daily stresses and inconveniences, their real concern was that the English Channel might afford little protection if Hitler chose to invade the British Isles, the next part of his master scheme for the Third Reich. If he did come to Britain, one of his first acts would surely be to round up his escaped Jews. The only hope of the

German expatriate community—Jews and anti-Nazi Christians alike—was that the rest of the world would recognize the enormous danger Hitler posed and band together to repel him with a united front before it was too late. This strident pleading for a strong stand against Hitler, which seemed certain to increase the prospects of another great war, further alienated the German expatriates from the general British population, most of whom still hoped for peace.

On their third day in London, Ruth arrived to greet them. Reggie had not seen Ruth for more than six months, and mother and daughter hugged passionately, a greeting Kitty had not been given when she returned from her own odyssey.

"I told them that my mother had just arrived in London," Ruth related joyously. Then she added petulantly, "Really, Cambridge is a hick town. Nothing's happening there." As if it were entirely natural to do so, without a word to Kitty or Eric, Reggie and Ruth disappeared into the next room, closing the door tightly behind them. They had a lot to talk about, talk that was none of Kitty's business.

Eric smiled knowingly at Kitty and shrugged his shoulders. She looked away from him; whatever she felt at this moment, it was *her* secret. Whatever her pain, it was her pain. Besides, who was Eric, anyhow? Her mother's boyfriend. They were not even married, just sleeping in the same bed. Her father's bed. Well, not really her father's bed, but in his space were he alive. It sometimes seemed to her that Eric was trying to learn more about her so that he would some day be able to replace her father. It was an eventuality she would never allow to come about.

The human spirit is at times wondrously resilient, and soon the horrors of the camp seemed to fade in Kitty's memory. Of course, such memories do not really disappear but simply bury themselves so we will not be reminded of them during every waking hour, so we can go on living in the present and planning for the future. After one week in London, Kitty did start thinking ahead, and she suggested to her mother that she would like to move out. Maybe it could be arranged to have her stay with

They Called Her Jewgirl

Ruth's sponsors who, with the help of Larry McDonald, had brought her to Cambridge. She didn't mind being a maid, she assured her mother. After all, what other job could she find for herself?

"You do whatever you want," her mother said.

So with daily encouragement from Kitty, and no impediment raised by Reggie, Ruth arranged it. Kitty was looking for some small measure of independence from her mother in the arrangement. As things turned out, she obtained a great deal more.

When Kitty stepped from the railroad car, she put down her suitcase and took a long, deep breath. So this was Cambridge! How peaceful it was! There was no sense of urgency here. There was no hint of the imminence of war. The fresh summer greens of the chestnut trees sparkled in the gleaming sunshine. Couples were strolling leisurely along the sidewalks, arm in arm, their conversations fading into the wide, open spaces. Long ago she had stopped believing that a world like this still existed.

Standing there alone on the platform, she closed her eyes. She let the new calm fill her insides. It was a wonderful moment to cherish.

In the stillness of the moment, she hadn't noticed the tall, elderly man approaching her. "Kitty Korten?"

She opened her eyes and turned around. "Yes?"

"I'm Henry Woods."

This was her first meeting with Professor Woods of King's College, Ruth's sponsor, a lean man with a slightly bent walk and kind, grayish eyes. He took Kitty's hand and led her along to the exit. He stopped in front of two women. "This is Mrs. Woods, my wife, and this is my daughter, Jessica. We've all been looking forward to meeting you."

For a second, Kitty frowned and dropped her head, like she usually did, in total disbelief. *This wasn't for real. They had said they'd been looking forward to meeting her, their new maid? They were actually welcoming her!*

Suddenly, she realized that this was all very different. She wasn't confronting her mother! She raised her head, met their eyes, smiled, and spoke in the best English she could muster. "My name is Kitty."

They smiled at her.

Altogether, they walked from the station, Kitty between them, Henry Woods patting the back of her head, guiding her along, gently, even caressingly. As Kitty looked coyly up at him, she gave him a smile. Vague memories of that other loving force in her life, her own father, stirred in her. No longer did she feel that old, pressing sense of urgency.

"It's all right, my child," he said, nodding, looking back at her. "We know it hasn't been easy."

It was a wonder that Kitty could ever again trust another human being. But in the need for loving contact, hope springs eternal, and over the next months Kitty would be eased into a special trust of the Woods.

It all turned out so well. Living with the Woods in Cambridge brought Kitty her first extended happiness in a long, long while. How little human warmth and love had been needed to bring it about. She was part of a family.

She loved them and they loved her. She was going to school again and made friends. She knew it could not last, but it would be an hiatus of sorts. A normalcy, if there were such a thing. Mrs. Woods, her mother, Mr. Woods, her father, and Jessica, her older sister.

Kitty began the process of easing more and more of her painful past out of the inventory of her reflections. Her dreams were of the present. Though Germany had been in a state of war with England since September, Kitty felt safe.

On Sunday mornings, in King's Chapel on the university's campus, she prayed with her new family. The old church, so rich, so beautiful with its tall spires, its Gothic arches, its carved, worn pews, seemed so enduring, so unfailing. The rich tones of the choir, the solemn old hymns, the chanting congregants so secure in their beliefs. As she was praying to a Christian God again, she closed her eyes: "Please God, whoever you are, let me be part of them! I don't want to be Jewish any longer!"

When the service ended, she walked with her new family, Mrs. Woods holding her hand, squeezing it as if she wanted to confirm that Kitty was part of them. On the lawn outside the chapel, in the bright sunlight, the minister greeted his parishioners. "Thank you for coming," he said to Mr. and Mrs. Woods, shaking their hands. Kitty suffered a moment of panic. Jessica was next, and then . . . would he extend his hand to the maid, the Jewish maid?

When it came to her turn, Mrs. Woods, her arm around Kitty's shoulder, said, "This is our Kitty," and the minister smiled at Kitty and shook her hand.

Kitty had her chores to do, but it was never a long day for her, and the evenings were an opportunity for a quiet time, not holed up alone in her room, but surrounded by generous and loving people. In those days there was no central heat in most English homes, and as winter came, they spent the evenings gathered closely together in front of the living room fireplace. Mrs. Woods knitted while Professor Woods pored over his academic tomes. Sometime he would stop reading and ask Kitty about how she was doing in school.

At other times Kitty played the piano. Or Mrs. Woods would join her on the cello. When she was alone, Kitty would play for hours, nocturnes, songs without words or impromtus, mostly melancholy music, musing upon the fleeting images of all that was now lost to her, never to be regained. There were times, many times, when Kitty would just stare into the fire, letting the heat blush her cheeks. She would let her mind stray off into nothingness, dreaming one more of her many dreams. The most beautiful of all was the daydream, in which she was not afraid, in which nobody threatened her.

About eleven months after her arrival in Cambridge, her mother called to let her know that she had obtained their American visas. Their stopover in England had ended. Kitty was to leave for London at once.

The parting was short. She kissed and hugged each member of the Woods family. She held back her tears. In her mind she was already back with her own family. She had to be strong.

The boat left from Southampton before dawn. German bombs had leveled most of the city, and there was a blackout. The boat was dark. But when she arrived at her cabin, she found a dozen red roses there. "Kitty, much luck," the card said. It was signed, "The Woods family."

Chapter 12

July 1940

Like a gardener tending a budding flower, the United States caused Kitty, now sixteen years old, to blossom into a strikingly attractive young woman. Her pale, whitish cheeks put one in mind of a white Easter lily, while her cocoa brown eyes resembled its dark, toasted stamen. Her childhood curls had given way to a crowning blossom, an upswept, bouffant coiffure so popular in those days.

Still, her uncertainties and her disquiet were much apparent. Whenever she tried to make up her mind about anything at all, her brow wrinkled deeply and her lips edged rather awkwardly to one side. Confusing reality with illusion, uncertain as to which way to turn, which way to jump, she seemed like a lamb lost in the wilderness, trying to find its way in the chaos of its young life.

Yet along with all of these outward signs of confusion, a new, more pragmatic balance of character had ripened within her, for she often broke into a surprisingly irreverent lightness of being, into bubbling chatter, behaving as if she were without a care in the world, confusing the rhythm of life with authenticity. Still at other times, when she fell into deep musings, she took on a far-off look, and when asked about her apparent melancholy, she professed a sober regard for life's inevitable hardships. These opposing themes mirrored what she had been taught in music, where counterpoint—the combination of independent, contrasting themes—imbues it with a well-rounded cast, great strength, and, yes, even beauty.

Kitty had a great deal in common with the young men and women among the German-Jewish refugee community in her new hometown, Chicago. Though none of the others had been in a concentration camp (by now, she herself had only the vaguest conscious recollection of that horror), they had similar childhood memories and shared the special experience of having had their young identities undergo an abrupt disruption. Eager to embrace their new culture, they tended to emulate American manners, dress wildly American, respond with less respect to those in authority, and speak frequently out of turn—all contrary to their austere German beginnings—which incited the dismay and exasperation of their elders. The culture shock that had disrupted so many immigrant American families earlier in the century now afflicted the German-Jewish émigré community.

Among the elder European refugees, however, uprooted as they were from their homes, there was resistance to the corruption of treasured old values. Finding themselves among strangers speaking a different tongue and behaving in unfamiliar ways, they clung to what they had always believed in as a way of preserving their memories, their affinities, their very identities. One of the old values to be treasured was that physical intimacy was reserved for marriage. Reggie's shameful image as the "Merry Widow of Cologne," living with Eric without the blessing of marriage, evoked much pressure from the refugee community, until the "sinners" were finally forced into marriage. After the wedding, Eric tried to take on the role of head of the family. He was hardly a match for Reggie. It seemed to Kitty that he much too easily succumbed to the whims of his new wife. But, after the wedding, Kitty found him more attentive to her than he had ever been before.

Even though Kitty still lived with her mother, her sister Ruth, and Eric, she quickly became independent. She found part-time work in a music store and two years later, when she was eighteen, after graduation from high school, she was hired for a permanent position. In the evening and on weekends, she gave piano lessons. No longer could others dictate who she was or what she would be. She was her own person, financially independent, in control of her own destiny.

About the same time, in the summer of 1942, two years after her arrival from England, Kitty fell in love with a young refugee, Henry Morgenthal, also an émigré from Cologne. She knew little about Henry except that their parents knew each other. Barely two years older than Kitty, they were drawn to each other like honey gatherers drawn to the buds of flowers. They had so much in common. Hadn't they both escaped from Cologne? Weren't they both refugees from the same evil monster?

Kitty soon found out that all émigré families in America were not alike, just as they had not been alike in Cologne. Henry's father had been one of the men in the Jewish Bowling League of Cologne, and Reggie's reputation as a flirt was well known to him. Reggie's illicit cohabitation with Eric had so badly tainted the family that Kitty, a child of that family, was equally disgraced. For wouldn't she bring the problems of her family to her relationship with his son?

The Morgenthals' icy reception confirmed to Kitty what she had understood from her childhood: that, even though shrouded, her past was far from buried.

When Hermann threw open the door and she saw his broad grin, his twinkling eyes, it felt like she had come home again. "Reggie, my dear," he said to her, "how wonderful to see you again!" They embraced and kissed. Then he took her elbow and led her into the living room. "How are you doing, Reggie, my dear?"

Reggie gave him a wry smile. "Wonderful, Hermann!" She had always been impressed by Hermann Morgenthal, so much a man of the world. Hermann was suave, even elegant in an Old World fashion. Though of average height with thick, black eyebrows, graying sideburns, and a dominating nose, this was a man who knew how much respect he was owed.

"I'm so glad to see you again." Lee, Henry's mother, greeted Reggie and Eric with an overwrought smile. A small, unpretentious woman who, though stout, had a pretty face, acting overly proper in her Old Country way.

They all sat down.

Hermann held up the musty bottle. "*Niersteiner Auslese* '39!" He set up the glasses. "May I?"

Reggie nodded, smiling. How wonderful it was to have a taste of the old times, to know that not everything had been lost. That there still was someone who remembered the good times they had had in Cologne, at the *Kegelklub*.

For a few moments, after Hermann had poured the wine and they all had said their *Prosit* they gazed at each other with vacant eyes. For, in truth, in spite of the hearty greeting Reggie had received from Hermann, they acted like strangers, unable to break loose from the rigid proprieties that had always governed their conversations, which were so much a part of their German upbringing. Even though their circumstances had changed, even though they had outgrown the élan of their earlier lives, they all still wore the stocking-capped faces of their past.

Finally Reggie burst out. "You've got a wonderful son, Hermann."

Hermann nodded. "Yes, of course."

"An officer in the army."

He nodded again.

She wasn't ready to go on, even though she had wanted to. There was something strange going on here. She could sense it. There was a lurking hesitancy in Hermann's voice that made her feel uncomfortable.

Suddenly Hermann's face grew stern, even strained. "I asked you over for a reason."

Reggie nodded. "I understand."

"I hope that what I'm going to say will stay within these four walls?"

Reggie nodded again. "Of course, Hermann."

Hermann got up from the chair, stared at the ceiling, and slowly shook his head. "I don't think the marriage is a good idea."

Reggie raised her eyebrows. "Why, Hermann?"

He kept on shaking his head. Then, suddenly, he turned and stared at Reggie. "You should know why."

"No, I don't, Hermann." She squirmed in her seat, not certain what he meant by that remark.

"Really?"

"No, I don't." She grew irritated at his insistence.

Hermann waited, giving her time. "Henry will be overseas..."

Reggie nodded. She didn't like this cat and mouse game. What the hell was he leading up to?

"To fight in the war..."

"Yes?"

"Tell me, who would take care of Kitty if anything happened to him?"

What an absurd question, Reggie thought. Who'd ever think about that sort of thing? "What do you mean, Hermann?" she said.

"Let's say something happens to him. He gets killed. Of course, I pray to God he won't. But, what I mean is, after all, it's war. He might not come back. There might be a baby. Who will take care of the mother and her child?"

Eric, who had been silent up to now, spoke up. "I can only say that I would be glad to take on that responsibility."

Hermann reached for a cigar, bit it, wet the tip, and lit up, blowing the smoke away from everyone. Then he sat down again. "So you think that you will take care of her? Take care of Kitty and her baby?"

"Yes. Of course."

"Really?"

Eric blushed.

Reggie knew what Hermann was really saying: that Eric was a divorced man. That he had lived with her in an illicit arrangement. That her daughters had been exposed to unseemly cohabitation. "Not right," that's what Hermann would say. "You people just don't qualify."

Eric's expression grew suddenly stern. "She'd be very welcome."

Hermann took a long puff on his cigar. He pursed his lips. He wasn't going to play around any longer. "They can wait!"

Reggie shook her head. These were two young people. In America. Hermann didn't understand. "What if they won't?"

"I'll insist."

"You'll insist?"

"You can count on that!"

"But why? Why, Hermann?"

"He won't get one penny from me. *Not one red cent!*"

Finally the matter was in the open. The gathering in of the clouds, the somber drizzle, had finally turned into a drenching downpour. That's what he had meant. That's what he had meant all along.

Reggie leaned forward, giving Hermann a sidelong glance, frowning. "Hermann, please, these are two young people...You can't really mean that?"

"If Henry goes against me, *that will be it*. He knows, when I say something," he paused and then slowly and with determination spoke again, emphasizing each word, "when I say something like that, he knows that I mean it."

If there were ever a moment in her life when Reggie felt diminished, when she felt put upon, it was right at this moment. This man had given her the eye just minutes ago, had embraced her like a long, lost love when she had arrived. Yet this same man, whom she remembered as the biggest flirt in the whole bowling league, had the audacity to forbid the marriage of her daughter to his son. Because her daughter wasn't good enough. He forbade it by threatening to disinherit his son.

Yes, of course, this was really all about a rich man's money! Everything with Hermann was about money and the power it gave him! God, at one time she had actually admired this man, successful as he was! But now? How easily she could read his mind. His son was marrying the poor widow Korten's daughter! Of course, in his eyes, her family was not classy enough. *Eine Schauspielerin! Ein Flüppchen!* (Yes, an actress! A floozy!) But always good enough to let him pinch her butt.

Reggie sat up, erect. "They won't need your money!"

Hermann only shrugged. "That will be up to them."

Lee, Hermann's wife, spoke up. "I want my son to be happy. He won't be happy with your daughter. I know he won't. He doesn't understand. They come from different homes."

Reggie's face hardened. "I see."

Lee added, "I'm so sorry."

"Sorry?" Reggie shook her head, gazing at this woman, Hermann's wife. "You're sorry, is that what you said?" Reggie's sharp retort surprised everyone. "We're not good enough for you? Is that what you're saying to me? Kitty's home is not good enough for your great son, for your precious little boy?" She took a deep breath. "Let me tell you something. They're going to get married whether you like it or not." She got up from the chair. "Come on, Eric!"

Eric got up. They left without saying goodbye.

Even though she felt slighted by Hermann's reference to how he was going to control his son by denying him money, Reggie sensed a sudden pride at being in America. She could speak out without recrimination. There was no class distinction in America. No one was better than she was. This was no longer Germany.

Two weeks before Henry left for overseas duty with the army, Kitty and he were married. In the midst of all the cultural upheavals of a world at war, family advice to follow time-honored European class distinctions sounded absurdly out of touch with what seemed to be the new realities—it sounded even quaint, almost archaic. To be fair, it must be said that no advice from any quarter could have derailed Kitty and Henry's plans to get married. They were too much in love. If there were problems in her family, so be it. He was marrying Kitty, not her mother, not her sister, not her family.

Chapter 13

April 1945

With Henry overseas, the Morgenthals accepted what was, after all, the inevitable. Little by little, their earlier opposition to their son's marriage grew into measured approval. All things considered, he could have done worse, they said to themselves. They came to realize that class distinctions, like those played out in Europe, stood for little in America. Their hold on their son's future was no more than a mirage, a false vision that had been left over from earlier days.

Kitty was grateful for their change of heart. After all, she was who she was—whatever her family represented hadn't been her doing—and she was thankful that finally her parents-in-law had made a distinction between her and her mother's reputation. Even Reggie rejoiced. Kitty's acceptance by the Morgenthals, who once belonged to the elite of Cologne's Jewish community, brought Reggie much satisfaction, all the more because Ruth had "abandoned" her and had moved to California.

Kitty spent most of her weekends with her parents-in-law. They took her to operas, to ballets, bought her new dresses, jewelry, and other trinkets. She couldn't help but overflow with gratitude for all of their generosity.

More than anything, Kitty found a new wholeness in her relationship to her father-in-law. In her starry-eyed notion of its meaning, her father-in-law replaced that lost idol of her life, her own father. Even though he looked much like Henry, he reminded her of these two most important men in her life.

But eventually, all this attention from her parents-in-law felt more like an attempt to control her life. For it seemed to Kitty that in their eyes, she still was the daughter of that "loose woman," even though they never remarked about the "Merry Widow of Cologne." Before long she came to realize that what had initially seemed to be approval of her marriage to their son was really an attempt to remake her, to try to erase the blot on her family by exposing her to the finer things of life, to try to fashion her into a new, well-bred and sophisticated young woman.

In the end, what they really wanted was to supervise all of her weekend activities. When she finally balked at having them be a part of her every weekend agenda, they accused her of committing a perfidy of one kind or another. They accused her of engaging in secret activities of some sort. This, of course, was a total distortion of the truth. They simply didn't trust her loyalty to their son. In their accusatory zeal, they even threatened to write to him overseas about their suspicions.

In hindsight, everything about these weekend visits had been wrong right from the start. In the end, her father-in-law wasn't at all what she had imagined him to be. Something new and entirely different developed in their relationship.

She first noticed it when he kissed her so ardently. A kiss that took her so much by surprise that, intuitively, she pushed him away. When he smiled back at her with that demeaning sneer of his—which, for some unknown reason, seemed so familiar to her—he intimated that, to him, her rejection was only a dare. For, the next time, expecting the same rejection, he grabbed her more determinedly, locked her firmly within his strong arms, and forced his lusty instincts upon her.

It all happened so unexpectedly. It happened on a Monday morning in April 1944, when Hermann drove Kitty to work—Kitty having spent another weekend with her parents-in-law. To her great surprise, instead of heading south, he drove north on U.S. 41, leaving Chicago.

"Where are we going?" she asked. "Aren't you taking me to work?"

Hermann remained stone-faced.

She asked him once more. "Where are we going?"

He turned to her, his face impassive. "We're going on a trip."

"What do you mean, we're going on a trip?"

"Yes, we are," he nodded.

"What do you mean? I can't just take off from work."

"I called your boss and told her that you were sick."

"You did what?" He had called her boss and lied. He had treated her as if she were a child. She didn't want to go on any trip with him. "You take me home at once!" Her voice was strong, firm.

Hermann just kept staring straight ahead.

"I want you to take me home at once!" She was wild. When he didn't answer, she repeated. "I said to you, *Take me home at once!*"

He paid no attention to her.

"Don't you hear me?"

Hermann just stared straight ahead.

Kitty gazed at his impassive face. The stern look, the firm lips. What was wrong with this man? Was he crazy? "What do you think you're doing?" she screamed at him. "I don't want to go on any damned trip with you. I need to go to work."

There was only the slightest hint of a smirk on his face.

"No kidding?"

Something was definitely wrong here. Something was very wrong. For some reason, she held herself very rigid. "Stop the car . . . now . . . at once!"

Hermann paid no attention.

He was up to no good. "Stop the car at once!" she screamed at him.

He still did not respond.

"Stop! Right now! Right this minute!" She screeched, leaning forward, trying to distract him.

He just kept on driving, staring straight ahead.

This was just too much. She boxed his arm. She pulled at his coat.

All at once, without any warning, Hermann's closed fist landed across her face. He turned, his eyes furious. "What the hell is the matter with you?"

The blow had been so powerful, so brutal, that Kitty was thrown into deep panic. Grim visions reverberated in her head. It all seemed so familiar. The merciless intimidation, the cruel coercion, the icy scorn! Yes, of course, it was an abduction! That's what it was! Right here in America!

Instinctively she grabbed for the door handle. "Let me out!" she screamed at him.

Hermann just looked straight ahead and kept on driving.

She opened the door a slit. The graveled shoulders swished by. They were going fast. Fifty miles an hour. Maybe even faster. *Margot! Run, Margot, run!* Oh God in heaven! She must get away from him! Get away from it all!

Suddenly, Kitty thrust the door wide open and, bracing herself against the running board, flung herself away from the car. She flew right past the shoulder and landed in the tall grass of the ditch. Rolling over and over, she slowly came to a rest.

For a long moment, she lay there in the tall grass, totally stunned. Then, aware of no pain and sensing that there was nothing broken (or was this again the numbness of the camp?), she thanked God for having let her survive her frightful leap.

Hermann brought his car to a halt. She watched him back up to where she was lying in the ditch. She couldn't think. Her mind was a total blank. She seemed paralyzed as he rushed over to her, grabbed her waist, and held her up as if he were a parent and she an ill child.

When a truck stopped right behind Hermann's car, the man called out. "Is everything all right?"

"My daughter is sick," Hermann called back to him. "Stomach cramps or something. I'm taking her to a doctor."

The man looked at him quizzically.

For a moment Kitty wanted to scream, "*This man's kidnapping me!*" but not a sound came out of her.

Before anyone could say anything more, Hermann had lifted her into his arms and carried her back to the car.

She couldn't believe what was happening. What was the matter with her anyhow? Why hadn't she called out to this man? Why hadn't the man questioned Hermann?

But, of course, she knew. He wouldn't have believed her anyhow. No one had ever believed her. "I've been abducted by this man!" she could have called out to him. I've been abducted by this older man, who's acting so concerned, who looks so respectable? I've been abducted by this older man who seems to care so much for me, his daughter, sick with stomach cramps, needing to be taken to a doctor?

They drove on for another two hours, way past Milwaukee, Hermann watching her out of the corner of his eye. She did not speak to him or demand her freedom. There was no point in trying. It was hopeless. It was hopeless to fight him. She could feel it in her bones. He'd do whatever he had to. It really didn't matter where they were, here in America or back in Germany. It didn't make any difference. There was no use trying to get away from him.

Finally, when they came to Sheboygan, he parked the car in a large square.

"We're going to eat," he said to her.

As she plodded along next to him, he suddenly reached his arm around her and looked at her quizzically. "Why are you so afraid of me? You know, I could be your father?"

Her father? That's what she had thought once. But he was nothing like her father. He did not even resemble her father. Who did he think he was, anyhow? Taking her away against her will? What was that? Is that what fathers did?

No! That's what men did!

Yes, he was just like all the rest of them!

For a moment she thought again of breaking away from him and calling out for help. "I've been abducted," she'd explain. "I've been abducted by this man." She'd point to her father-in-law. "That well-dressed older man over there!"

She thought better of it. Who'd believe her? He'd explain. He had a way of explaining everything. He was such a smooth talker. They'd only gaze at her as though she were crazy.

Yes, it was an indefinable, abject fear that held her down, kept her from acting. It was as if she'd been doused with noxious gases.

Still, in spite of her fears, she blurted out, "Please, let me go home!"

He looked back at her without acknowledging her. He just squeezed her shoulders and smiled.

She felt limp and impotent. It upset her that she would feel that way here in America. After all, this was not Germany. This was a free country, a country where you were free to do as you liked. A country in which you were not to be coerced, not to be abducted.

But something deep inside of her was making her the way she was. It kept her from acting. As if she were drifting on a shoreless ocean, unable to control her fate, forced to submit to her appointed destiny.

"Come along," he said to her as they entered the restaurant. "You're really very lucky."

There it was again—that smirk on his face. You're really very lucky! she repeated to herself, trying to find the key to an old, forgotten refrain, to a cadence that would complete a connection to other coercions that carried the same smirk.

They sat down. "I simply don't understand why you wouldn't want to be with me."

She looked away from him. But from the corner of her eye, she saw him dig into his pocket and pull out a little box. He grabbed her hand, turned it up, and placed the box in it. "Here," he said to her, "a little something for you."

She dropped the box. "I don't want it." What was he trying to do? Buy her? "Whatever it is, I don't want it," she repeated. Then, suddenly, she got up and walked away from the table.

He came running after her and caught her by the wrist. He took her hand and put the box back into her palm. "Take it," he said to her.

Kitty tried to twist free from him, but he held on to her wrist. "Open it!"

People were staring at her as though she were on stage. She felt so foolish, standing there in the middle of the restaurant with her father-in-law. Her head was spinning. "Why?" she said to him, pursing her lips. "I told you already I don't want it!" But she was choking on her words. As she looked about, she could see heads turning away. She opened the box. It was a diamond ring. A diamond ring in a garnet setting. Expensive! Also very crazy!

He led her back to the table. "Take it," he insisted.

She looked at him. "Why would you give me a diamond ring?"

"Because you're my daughter-in-law."

"Because I'm your daughter-in-law?"

"While my son is overseas, it is my job to take care of you, isn't it?" He chuckled out loud. "Take it," he said. "You're being ridiculous." He shook his head. "Didn't your mother teach you anything? When you're given a present, you just take it and say thank you."

He took her hand and put the ring on her finger.

Kitty bit her lips and looked away. Yes, she knew! What he was doing was wrong. It was terribly wrong. She would never be able to claim that she didn't know that it was wrong. She shook her head. Why was she so much at his mercy?

He ordered cocktails. "Drink," he said to her. "It's good for you. It will settle you down. You will feel much better."

She looked up. She looked into his face, an impenetrable face, a poker face. For a moment she thought that he wore black boots. Then she looked past him. She did not want to look at him any longer.

"Drink up," he insisted. "I want you to drink!"

She drank. She drank because he commanded her to drink. It was as if she had been conditioned to follow his orders. She drank because she didn't want to think any more. She didn't want to think about anything. About anything that was happening. Right now, all she was capable of was to await the next moment, react to it, get past it. She shook her head. It was so damned familiar.

She drank more than she should have. What else could she have done? Make a scene? Make a scene in the restaurant? She drank too much. She wasn't used to drinking. When they finally left the restaurant, she couldn't walk straight. She hadn't noticed the curb and fell. He picked her up.

Across from the restaurant, on the other side of the square, he checked into a hotel. She followed him. Upstairs, in the room, he carried her to bed. He took off her dress. He unhooked her brassiere, removed her panties. Then he undressed and lay down next to her.

She felt him touch her nipples. She bit her lips. When he tried to kiss her, she turned her head away from him and pulled her legs up to her chest. He palmed her thighs. She clenched her fists. Then he forced her legs apart. She tried to push him away. He was too strong.

She turned her head away from him. Her mind searched. It searched all the time. It searched deeply into the past. It searched and searched. Had she ever escaped? She couldn't remember.

That evening, in a hotel in Sheboygan, her father-in-law raped her. Yes, that's what it was. He acted as if she belonged to him, as if she were part of a bargain. It was as if he had a right to her, having given her a diamond ring. A ring she really hadn't wanted. A dinner she hadn't asked for. A trip she had been forced into. As if having sex with her, the daughter of the "Merry

Widow of Cologne," was but an undisputed consequence of the circumstances of her life.

He even became angry with her. He said that she kept herself too stiff. That's when he hit her. He hit her across the face because she didn't know how to be a proper victim for him. He said that she didn't even know how to have sex right.

After it was all over and he finally turned away from her, she quickly dressed and, without speaking another word, ran out of the room. Outside, in front of the hotel, she asked for directions to the railroad station.

Yes, she had been assaulted! Right here in America! God, she could scream out loud! She had let it happen! Why?

Clutching her handbag under her arm, biting her lips, she hastened to the railroad station. She did not see anything or anybody. Her steps were wobbly. At times she tottered, as if in turbulent waters, tossing past heavy swells and deep whirlpools.

When she arrived at the station, there were no trains until late that evening. She sat down on a bench. That's all she could do. She never lifted her head. She didn't want to look at the world. She didn't like it. An abandoned child, she was now a grown woman still unable to deal with life.

All the time she kept watching the door, waiting for him to come after her. If he came, she'd run out the side door. But he never came. He never looked for her. She knew that if he had wanted to find her, he would have looked in the railroad station. But he didn't.

Yes, of course she knew. He was finished with her for now.

Chapter 14

February 1946

Kitty's mother-in-law never found out about her husband's abduction. She continued to invite Kitty to visit with them on weekends, unaware of the changed relationship between Hermann and Kitty. She never suspected that whenever Hermann found himself alone with Kitty, he would humiliate her with sexual innuendoes, paw her shamelessly and, when the opportunity presented itself, force her into a sexual tryst.

One could say that Kitty was the ideal victim. Like a well-timed swoop of a falcon, he descended on her, without failure, without mercy. Kitty, a helpless prey, primed by the sexual assaults of the SS and by the gang rapes of Dachau, became enchained like a slave to her master.

Of course, she could have talked to her mother, tell her what Hermann was doing to her. But she didn't. She knew her mother would only blame *her*. She could already hear her words. "What do you mean Hermann attacked you?" she'd say to her. "An old man like him?" She'd frown. "You couldn't defend yourself against an old man like him?" her mother would shake her head in disbelief. "I don't understand it. I don't know what's the matter with you, anyhow."

In the end all she told her mother was that she did not want to visit her in-laws on weekends. "I have no time for myself," Kitty said to her. "They always insist that I come and see them. It's the same story every weekend."

"Tell them you're with friends."

Kitty tried her best to stay away. "I'm busy," she said to her mother-in-law. "I'm going on a trip with friends."

"Friends?" her mother-in-law questioned. "What friends?"

Kitty lied. "Friends from work."

"Friends from work?" she asked. "They're married?"

"Some of them are."

"I see!" The skeptical tone in her voice seemed full of reproach.

Embarrassed, Kitty added, "But they're nice."

There was total silence on the other end.

"They're really very nice people," she repeated.

"Well," her mother-in-law replied, "we will definitely expect you next week."

It was like an order, so characteristically Teutonic in nature, maintaining that a married woman has no business "running around."

All that changed after that November day in 1945.

It all happened on one of those weekend visits to her parents-in-law. Kitty didn't feel well. She had stomach cramps, and she wouldn't eat. She also felt dizzy, like throwing up.

She wanted to go home. They wouldn't have it. They insisted that she visit *their* doctor. "We are very concerned about you," Hermann said to her. "After all, you're like our own daughter."

Kitty protested. She protested vehemently. She even begged them. Hermann acted as if she had insulted him. Her mother-in-law agreed. She had no choice. They insisted. As always.

Of course, Kitty could have simply left. She could have told her in-laws that her well-being was her concern, her concern only. That whatever was wrong with her was something that she alone would deal with and that it was up to her family, her mother and Eric, to take care of her.

Kitty said no such thing. Having been coerced so many times before, a pervasive pattern of yielding to "orders" had arisen in her, something that defied all reason. For even though she was now in America, far removed from the Nazis, her in-laws constantly reinforced the resigned responses that had been forced upon her so much earlier in her life.

Dr. Martin's office was on the second floor of a converted apartment building. They made her sit between them, not giving her much space. They watched her all the time. They sat there waiting in silence, not speaking a word.

Dr. Martin finally appeared at the door to the waiting room. He was an old man with a high, furrowed forehead, a leathery scalp like the skin of a worn softball, and narrow, fragile facial bones shielded by a pallid, cadaverous layer of skin. He was a skeleton of a man, ambling along like a zombie. "Ve vill see you now!"

He handed Kitty a gown and told her to get undressed. He made her lie down on the examining table. He listened to her breathing, pressed all over her stomach and then, lifting her legs into the stirrups, forced his gloved fingers inside of her. "Relax," he told her, "it von't hurt."

The examination took a long time.

When he finally finished, he told Kitty to get dressed. He left the room. She could hear him talking to them. He was telling them about her, telling them about things that were private. Personal, intimate things.

When he returned, his face was stern. "You must go to se hospital at once," he told her. "I'm making all se arrangements right now." He placed his hand on her shoulder. "You must take my vord for it. Your parents-in-law vill take you."

"But . . . ?"

He gave her a smile, but his smile was false.

When she returned to the waiting room, she asked them, "What's going on here? Things were happening that she did not understand.

But all she got was silence. She thought that they stared at her in a rather odd way, as though she should know. Know what? Her mother-in-law seemed angry, barely able to contain herself, ready to turn her anger into fits of rage.

They took her to the Alliance Hospital on Irving Park Road. They went around the back, avoiding the lobby, up the service elevator, Kitty between them, they guarding her. Upstairs, on the fifth floor, they marched her to the waiting room and made her sit between them.

After a while, a nurse came for her. She led Kitty into another room. She read the sign above the door: *Operating Room!*

"What's going on here?" she asked the nurse. "What are you doing to me?"

The nurse turned to her, surprised. "You mean, you don't know?" she asked.

"No, I don't know," Kitty answered. "No one told me."

The nurse shook her head. "You're pregnant, of course." She stared at Kitty, astonished at her ignorance. "We're getting you ready for an abortion."

She was flabbergasted. "What?" she cried out. "An abortion? You're getting me ready for an abortion?"

The nurse nodded.

She couldn't believe it. An abortion? It couldn't be! This was absolutely crazy!

All at once Kitty got up, tore herself free from the nurse, and fled the room. An abortion, she had said! Were they crazy? She had to get away from them all! Shaking her head wildly, Kitty ran down the hospital corridor, screaming, "No, I won't! No! No! I won't!"

When she saw the stairway, she dashed toward it and hurried down to the first floor. She had to get away from them! Get out of this place!

But the exit door wouldn't open. No matter how hard she tried. She shook the door. She pulled at it. It wouldn't open. She pounded the door. She kicked against it. It still didn't open.

Her mind was flooding with things. She was out of breath. She started to sweat. What could she do now? She had to get away, get away from them all.

She decided to run back into the hallway. She hurried along the first floor corridor, toward the lobby. But then, suddenly, she stopped dead in her tracks. Where was the lobby anyhow?

But it was too late. They were waiting for her. A nurse grabbed her. She tore herself free. But exhausted as she was, another nurse easily caught her again. She couldn't fight them off any longer. There were too many of them.

Upstairs, the operating room nurse, Dr. Martin, and her parents-in-law were waiting for her. The nurse led her away. "Get undressed," she ordered, handing her a hospital gown.

Kitty stood in the corner and took off her clothing. She did as she was ordered.

It was at this moment—a moment in her life that she would never forget—the moment right after she got undressed, standing in the anteroom stark naked, the nurse keeping an eye on her, making sure that she did what she was told, that she realized that she would always be a victim. For the rest of her life. Even here in America. That she would always be like a hostage, subjected to the whims of her captors. That she'd never have any say about anything that really mattered to her. For, right now, right at this moment, they were going to take something from inside her body, a new life that belonged to her and not to anyone else. Something that was only for her to decide to keep or not to keep.

She covered her face to hide the seeping feelings. But the tears broke out anyhow. They came from way deep inside of her like an opened sluice. Tears that intimated the hidden, binding shackles that kept her from doing what was her right to do.

She turned away from the nurse, ashamed to let her see the tears, the tears that were about things she would never understand.

Of course everyone—her mother-in-law, Dr. Martin, the nurses—thought that she had had an affair while her husband was overseas fighting for his country, sacrificing himself so she could be free.

Except, of course, Hermann. He knew. He knew the truth. He had lied to everybody. It had been an easy lie. Dr. Martin, in the shadow of Hermann's power and money, had brought her to this godforsaken private hospital, where an abortion would be blanketed by total silence. Everything fell into place. It was so obvious—her mother-in-law's anger, their insistence on the abortion.

There was no more escaping. The nurses held her down so she could not move. It was all so familiar. Being held down. Her powerlessness. The pain. The surrender. Everything hidden behind closed curtains. A prison where she was at the mercy of her captors.

When it was all over, everyone quickly disappeared. Kitty dressed herself. She decided not to think about it any longer. Whatever had happened, happened. There was no use crying over it. Thank God, she was still alive. She had survived, and she had to go on with her life.

She knew the words. An echo from deep inside of her. An echo from a time far away.

Chapter 15

July 1946

Going north on Lake Shore Drive in Chicago, just past the Edgewater Beach Hotel, they turned west into Bryn Mawr Avenue and took a sharp turn south into Kenmore Avenue. Henry and Kitty had arrived at the Ardmore Apartments, their new home. A furnished apartment with well-worn, prewar furniture.

Henry had returned from the war more than a year after it had ended. No longer the young refugee who had escaped Hitler's fangs, but a U.S. Army officer, toughened by war's circumstances, hardened by the realities of surviving on the battlefield.

Kitty could see the change in his face. His slack mouth had firmed and his chestnut eyes no longer flinched as they once did. A young man of average height, with a strong nose and a full, black head of hair, he was not a handsome man. But he seemed full of confidence, having participated in a successful war, an experience that seemed to give his squarish face a ripened balance.

"It's not at all bad, is it?" she asked him after she opened the door, smiling at him, awaiting his approval. She had found the apartment all by herself—apartments were still in short supply right after the war—plunking down a five-hundred-dollar bonus to the rental agent, which was really—she had to admit it—a bribe.

"No, not bad," he said, "not bad at all," inspecting the kitchen that was no bigger than a large closet.

The apartment had a Murphy bed, one of those beds that when not in use stored upright behind French doors in the living room, the only full-sized room in the apartment. Kitty rushed to demonstrate it for him. "Isn't that clever?"

"Very clever."

Henry stepped to the window and opened it. He stared into another apartment right across a narrow airshaft no more than four feet wide. Kitty watched as he closed the shades. Privacy was not the apartment's best feature, especially in July, with everyone's windows open. But, in spite of the small size of the apartment, in spite of the neighborhood's congestion, Kitty was happy. To her it signified the beginning of a new phase in her life, even if it had only offered her living space in a barren cave.

"I'm going to make dinner," she announced.

For nearly half an hour Kitty busied herself in the kitchen. She peeled potatoes, sliced them, cut up onions, and put them all together in a pan that she brought to a wild sizzle. She mixed different greens for the salad. Then, removing the wrappings from the steaks, she dangled the raw cuts in front of Henry. "Porterhouse," she said, giving him her best smile.

"Great!"

When they had finished the meal, Henry wiped his mouth. "Wonderful," he said to her, "a great meal." He got up from the table and, pulling down the Murphy bed, stretched out on it. "Come here, honey!"

The moment she had feared so much had come! The moment when he would ask her to come to him. When he would want to make love to her. Like the unraveling filaments of a bad dream, a thousand threatening images shot across her mind's screen.

Petrified, she stared at him. "I've got to clean up," she muttered.

"That can wait."

"Please!" She bit her lip.

But deep down she knew. She knew that for Henry, having waited all these hours, these days, these years, this was the moment to make love to her, make love to his wife. He had every right to want her. Now! Right now! He had every right to expect that she'd also want him.

When she finished cleaning up the dishes, she smiled at him warily. "Give me a minute," she said as she disappeared into the bathroom.

Tight-lipped, her throat constricting and her mind whirring, she tried to lock the panic inside. But her insides felt like a steam engine that, having reached critical pressure, waited for the releasing thrust. It would be easy for him to tell that she was not very amorous, that she was not "dying" to welcome him back home.

She lit a cigarette, inhaled deeply, and stared at the smoke as it scattered into nowhere. "I've got to!" she said to herself. Then she took a long, deep breath, trying to steel herself against the fluttering frenzy inside. "I must! He's waiting! He's my husband!"

She undressed, put on cotton pajamas, applied some lipstick, a little rouge. She did not want to appear too seductive, too sexy. It was so easy to lose one's control, to lose control over one's emotions.

She held on to the door, waited, trying to calm herself. Finally, she found the courage to face her returned husband and stepped out from the bathroom.

But to Henry, eyeing Kitty as she emerged from the bathroom, it was all a great disappointment. She wore no sleek, lacy gown, no fragrant perfume, no welcome smile. She was nothing at all like the Kitty he had left behind. Nothing at all like the Kitty he had dreamed about when, wallowing in the starless trenches of Normandy, he diverted himself with seductive images of the wife he had left behind.

Was this how he was going to be rewarded for all those years he had to be away from her?

What he saw now, the way she appeared to him (something that would forever remain deeply furrowed in his mind) was but a dutiful gesture, exacted solely by his male place in the scheme of things. Nothing more!

But then, when Kitty bent down to put out her cigarette—she had picked up smoking while he was gone—when he caught a glimpse of her young, delicate breasts, their crimson nipples riding freely within the loose confines of her pajama top, at that very moment, as at the rise of a curtain, he forgot everything about his disappointment. For even though it was no more than a stolen glance, he found a new focus for his lustful imaginings.

Of course Kitty had completely missed the moment, the moment she had bent down and bared her breasts. Like a rose oblivious to those who behold its beauty, she had not fathomed the extent to which she had stirred Henry. For she casually walked away from him, pulled the drapes shut, turned off all the lights, and came to bed.

For a long time she lay quietly next to Henry, enveloped by the total darkness, not moving, wishing she were not where she was, unable to speak to him, to speak to him about the lurking disquiet inside of her, about her growing panic. Her mind was a total blank. No, not really a blank. It was charging forward, going somewhere, filling her with qualms and terrors. Running amok. But in the end, still going nowhere. How would she ever be able to make him understand? She didn't even understand it all herself.

She sighed deeply.

Still, after a while, it seemed to her that he had sensed her unease. For, when he turned her to him and drew her face to his chest, he held on to her so caringly, not at all the way she had feared. He held on to her as if she were his daughter and he her father. That made her relax somewhat. For his caress seemed to spring from some kind of benign love.

After a while, as if responding to the chaste nature of his embrace, she forgot why she had been so scared. When his fingers grazed her cheek, passed over the ear lobes to cup the back of her head, she let him kiss her lips gently, tenderly. Maybe, she thought, if she didn't think about it, everything would yet turn out all right. But the more she tried not to think about it, the more something else, something beyond herself, seemed to be gaining control over her. In spite of his caring devotion, her lips remained taut, unyielding, and when he finally turned her head to him and peered into her eyes, she had to look past him. And when his lips brushed along her ear, alongside her cheek, her head drew backward, away from him. It was just the smallest fraction of a millimeter, but she knew that it had to appear as a clear movement, like the involuntary blink of an eye whose lash had been touched. All along she remained passive, stiffening ever so slightly when she felt his hand touching her breast, unbuttoning her pajama top, grazing her nipples.

Then, all at once, as if stung by a scorpion, she twisted away from him.

It was at this moment, the moment he touched her nipple, that it had felt as if a strange hand had tried to burst into a private space that held her innermost, most intimate secrets.

God in heaven, what would she do now?

In her rational self, in her thinking self, she wanted so badly to give Henry the assurances he wanted. Her shrinking away must have seemed like a rejection, a rejection that might plant seeds of doubt for years to come!

She gave a deep sigh.

But it seemed that a rabid lust had taken control of Henry, probably heightened by her impassiveness, by her reluctance. Whatever she had been thinking, it was all too late now. He lifted her hips and, tugging at her pajama bottoms, quickly slipped them off.

All along, she felt herself straining against him. She turned her head and closed her eyes. She tried to twist away. But, as she tried to get away from him, he held her down, pried her thighs apart and, pressing them down to the bed, brought his fiery body down on hers, forcing her into total submission. Frantically, Kitty turned to the side and threw him off, pulling up her legs, curling like a child. But he quickly rolled her on her back and thrust himself into her once more.

Kitty clenched her fists. Yes, it was happening all over again. She lay stiffly under him, no longer resisting but altogether unyielding and unresponsive, not wanting him, not holding on to him, not sharing his passion.

Yes, there was no doubt. She had failed him.

After the lovemaking had ended and Henry lay spent at her side, the trembling started. At first it was barely noticeable. The panic showed mostly in her face—the frightened stare, the deepening frown, the slight twisting of her mouth. Soon it was followed by a tightening of her body, a rigidity that attempted to hold back the next phase, which, before long, caused a rhythmic, jerky shaking of the whole body. Each of these sequential signs signaled the next, deeper envelopment, like a dark cloud shadowing the landscape before the first drop of rain. She vainly tried to bring each stage under control. But, before long, she was completely trapped by uncontrollable bodily rhythms that jolted her upper body, growing ever more pronounced, taking hold of her as consistently as a piston's stroke follows the explosion inside the cylinder. Finally she yielded, no longer able to hold the turmoil within her.

With all of her resistance broken, the shaking became ever more frantic, claiming her complete will, growing into a rhythmic forward thrusting of her shoulders, a contortion so violent that her head bounced freely front to back, intermittently lolling side to side. So savage was the thrashing that it seemed as if she were being tortured on a rack. It was not quite an epileptic seizure—certain elements, the foaming at the mouth, for one, were missing—but a fit of equal severity.

Henry, aghast, watched it all. He stood by helplessly, astounded at the violence of the attack.

Eventually (it might have been no more than fifteen minutes), the shaking stopped. With her back arching frenziedly, her face twisting grotesquely, Kitty let out a final screech and collapsed into a rigid coma, which caused her to lose all awareness. She lay there, totally exhausted, in a deep stupor, her breathing, though shallow, now peaceful.

After a while she regained consciousness.

Of course, Henry hoped that the demon he had brought forth had been recaged. "What happened?" he said to her. "I feel responsible."

As her body started to relax, she mumbled. "It's nothing. It will go away." She avoided his eyes.

Still, baffled by the violence of the attack, he considered the remark a total misreading of what had just occurred. "We need to talk about what just happened. This is not the way things work," he said.

Kitty's face darkened. "I don't want to talk about it."

He spoke once more. "We've got to find out what this is all about."

"It's nothing."

"Whatever it is, we've got to try to straighten it out!"

"Straighten what out?" Kitty said angrily.

"Our sex life, of course."

"Is that all you can think of? Is that all that I mean to you? Someone to use for sex?" She seemed beside herself, unwilling to deal with his oblique criticism. "Why don't you go and find yourself somebody if that's all you want me for."

He was flabbergasted. "That's not at all what I meant and you know it," he replied. "All this time I've been waiting to be with you. Waiting to love you. Can't you understand that?"

Kitty turned away from him. For some reason, his words seemed to have calmed her. Yet her calm lasted for only a short while. Soon new words of his would throw her into yet another rage.

The moment Kitty realized that he was discussing her condition with his father, she tore the phone from his hand, and started to hit him, which, to his mind, was totally out of proportion to the provocation. It seemed like such a frantic act. Kitty gasped heavily and, with her face contorting, she screamed at him, "You damn bastard! Don't you understand anything?" Her eyes seemed to pop out of her head. "Don't you think I have feelings? Why in hell did you have to call him?" She waited, gasping heavily. "I'm not an animal! I have feelings!" Kitty, hearing her own screams, was shocked at the harshness of her voice. Her words had burst out of her as inevitably as a ball of fire bursts from a Roman candle. She turned away from Henry, sensing the source of it all. "You're just like him!" She ran into the bathroom, slamming the door shut.

Within minutes, she returned fully dressed. Grabbing her keys, she ran out of the apartment. She had to get away from him!

Outside, she had no idea of where to go or what to do. She meandered along Bryn Mawr Avenue over to Broadway, her gait wobbly, uncertain. She didn't see anyone; she didn't recognize anything. At the corner of Broadway and Bryn Mawr she paused and waited. She waited for something, somebody.

She was all mixed up, disjointed, not remembering anything or anybody. Why was she where she was? What was she doing here? Maybe she'd turn back. But no, she had to get away, she needed to go on.

She wandered south, along the darker parts of Broadway, where there were no more stores. On and on she wandered, seeking something that would distract her from her rage. Calm her. Something unimportant. Something pleasant. Something away from everybody.

Five more blocks, still she walked on. Six. Finally, at Argyle Street, she entered a restaurant. She sat down at the counter and ordered coffee.

She needed time to think. She needed time to think about something. Something important. Something that was bothering her. Something that was on her mind. She drank the coffee slowly. But no matter how much she tried, she couldn't figure out what it was.

When she paid the bill and left the restaurant, he was there. "Go away! Get away from me, Henry!" She recoiled as though he were her enemy. Then she hurried along Argyle away from him. She never looked back. Yet, all along, she knew that he was following her.

Going east, meeting Kenmore Avenue, she slowed. At the corner, she came to a complete halt, trying to decide which way to go—north and back to the apartment, or east toward the lake. She sighed. For some reason, she couldn't make up her mind.

When he came up to her and took her elbow, he only said, "Let's go home, Kitty!"

She shook off his hand. She was too mixed up. She didn't want him.

His arm reached around her. "Please, Kitty, let's go home." Gently, firmly, he tried to direct her north, to lead her back to the apartment.

She resisted him. But his arm didn't let go. She was being restrained by his strong, overpowering arms. Arms that felt like a straitjacket. Like straitjacket from her yesterdays, causing an unexplained panic in her. All at once, she tore herself free, momentarily staggering from the sudden spin. When she found her balance again, she spurted away in the direction of the lake.

As she raced toward the lake, she felt an unbearable terror driving her on, a terror that she could not explain. She ran across Sheridan Road, not hearing the screeching brakes, not knowing where she was or where she was going, never slowing or stopping. Above all else, she knew that she had to "get away."

Finally, she found herself standing at the far end of the Edgewater Beach Hotel's promenade overlooking the lake, staring down at the rolling surf, trying to figure things out

God, how mixed up she was! How unhappy she was!

She forced back the tears. Crying always made her feel weak. She must find out what was happening to her, what it was that was causing her to feel the way she did.

When his hand grasped for hers, it felt no longer like a forcing grip. It felt like a gentle, caring hold. It did not frighten her. It reminded her. It reminded her of something. Something that had happened somewhere? Somewhere, at another time? God, where did it happen? Where was it again?

Yes, of course, she knew, she remembered: Cambridge. Henry Woods taking her hand and leading her along, glancing back at her as they walked away from the station, smiling at her.

She gave an almost imperceptible nod. A silent nod. She let him lead her away. She didn't speak another word. The silence bred its own balm. Slowly she sunk into a frizzled, tired numbness and the turmoil, the anger in her, gradually diffused.

Upstairs, she sat down at the kitchen table. Henry warmed up coffee, still not saying anything. But then he reached across the table and took her hand into his. "We need to get some help," he said to her.

She didn't answer him.

"We need to get help," he repeated.

Kitty stared ahead vacantly. She really couldn't talk.

"I would like you to see a psychiatrist."

She shook her head. "I can't go on like this."

"I know."

"I'm at the end." She spoke quietly, shaking her head slowly. "I'm no good for this world."

"You'll get better."

"I can't go on any longer."

"You need to see a psychiatrist," he repeated. "We must get help."

"I'm so sorry."

"Why?"

Kitty lifted her head and fixed her gaze on Henry. "For causing you so much trouble."

"You couldn't help it. We'll talk to a psychiatrist."

"You know that I love you, don't you?"
"Of course, I do," he said.
"That I'm grateful that you care for me?"
"I am your husband, am I not?"

Still, a dense and perplexing fog hung over her. Her love for him was entangled in an unfathomable web of contradictions. When she finally asked it, she nearly choked on her question. "Tell me, what is wrong with me?"

Henry got up slowly, walked over to where she was and, bending down to her, he took her face into his hands and held it close to him. "That's what we're going to find out," he said, forcing an assuring smile that concealed his own confusion.

For several days they didn't talk about the incident of that night. Kitty recognizing her self-defined failing, tried her best to make him forget. She prepared special dishes that she knew he liked, told him that she loved him, touched his cheek, even kissed him. She tried to ease the strain between them in her own special way. Henry, noting her valiant struggle to ease things, didn't make the appointment with the psychiatrist. After all, seeing a psychiatrist meant that you were "crazy." At least, that's what it meant in those days.

On the fourth night, after they had eaten dinner, finally, over coffee, he suddenly looked up at Kitty. "We really can't go on like this," he said to her, shaking his head.

"Like what?"
"Like this. This strain, this tension."
She looked away from him.
"I mean, something's troubling you. I can tell."
She took a deep breath.
"I can feel it every time I touch you."
She raised her eyebrows.
"You shy away. You shy away from me."
"I do?"
"Yes, you do."
"I'm so sorry."

"What's more, I feel that you resent me."
"You do?"
"Yes, I do."
"What do you want me to say?"
"Only that you know. That you're aware of it. That it bothers you."
"I know."
"Then, tell me why?"
"I don't know."
"Do you have any idea?"
"No. Do you?"
"Of course not. Otherwise I wouldn't have asked."
"I can't tell you either."
He spoke in a tentative voice. "Would you like to see someone?"
"See whom?"
"Somebody to talk to about yourself?"
"You mean a psychiatrist?"
"Possibly."
"Do you really think so?"
"I wouldn't ask otherwise."
Kitty looked down and shook her head. "I can't do it."
"Why?"
"I don't know why." She shook her head more vigorously. "I can't do it!"
"One visit?"
She looked up again. "One visit?"
"One visit."
"Are you sure?"
"That's all we'll plan."
"All right then. If that's all you want. One visit."
She glanced downward as he reached for her hand. The moment had come. She could tell. Her heart was beating faster. He wanted to know. He wanted to know what she didn't know, what she couldn't remember. She knew there was something, something that made her act the way she did. If only she could

remember. She also wanted to know. But she was so afraid. So afraid to know. It would be bad. So very bad.

The psychiatrist met with Kitty for over an hour. He examined her reflexes and at the hospital drew spinal fluid to rule out neurological causes.

When Kitty and Henry returned later that week for the results, he explained that there was nothing physically wrong with her, that there were no physical reasons not to have normal sex or to expect that sex would be painful or uncomfortable. Her convulsions, he said, were a manifestation of great anxiety and obviously indicated emotional problems. "It is quite possible that you will be fine for long periods of time," he told Kitty. "Still, the general view that a psychic disease will cure itself or can be ameliorated by an extraordinary effort of will is erroneous. This is not a fixed illness, which restricts itself to only a few attacks, but it persists as a rule over long periods in life."

He recommended analysis.

"I'm all right," she said to Henry later on. "There is really nothing wrong with me."

"Really?"

"I might need an analysis."

"Yes, an analysis."

"That's what he said."

She was so relieved. After all, these were only emotional problems. They couldn't be very serious. An analysis? Of course, she needed an analysis. But thank God, she said to herself, she was all right.

For Henry the question arose as to whether the expectation of a neurotic phenomenon was enough reason to go into a long-term cure. After all, the cure, as psychiatry prescribed it, was without guarantee of success. In addition, the illness was seldom considered a legitimate suffering and it carried that label as a social fact.

But more than anything, there was an unspoken agreement between Henry and Kitty that at this point in their lives, the high cost of an analysis was way beyond their means.

Chapter 16

December 1951

Kitty never saw the psychiatrist again.

For more than five years, between July 1946 and December 1951, Kitty lived the life of a typical young married woman of those postwar years, establishing a home and starting a family. She bore two sons, joyful events in any circumstances, but particularly joyful for her in that they gave her troubled life a new focus. She also renewed her interest in music and enrolled in the Chicago Musical College, while Henry began working toward his advanced degree in clinical psychology.

With Kitty's music taking up those scant minutes a day that caring for her children did not absorb—she usually played in the evening when the children were asleep—little time was left for reflection on her disturbing past. In this busy setting, she was able to close off most of her fears and anxieties. It would be difficult to imagine Kitty finding this level of normalcy had she not come to feel so needed.

Yet Kitty's problems did not simply disappear. Even setting aside for the moment the question of whether or not her childhood would ever be buried so deeply that it would not compromise her ability to lead a productive life, all physical manifestations of her problems were not entirely gone. Her tremors and their ensuing spasms occurred episodically without apparent provocation. She did not stop her wanderings at night and her sexual frigidity persisted, though less often followed by tremors, probably as a result of Henry's greater patience. Henry and Kitty went on together, doing their best to make a good and stable home for themselves and their children. Had you asked them to comment on their life during these years, it is likely that they would describe their marriage as a good one.

The truth is that both Henry and Kitty lived their lives putting off all that could be put off, knowing all along that the truth might be a sticky, bloody, even fatal revelation.

But the quiet routine of Kitty's existence was shattered when her mother-in-law died in December 1951.

Kitty tipped her head toward the bedroom. "Go see your mother." They had arrived quickly after the doctor's call. Hermann, Henry's father, was out of town.

Henry sat down instead. "No, thanks."

"For the last time?"

"You heard me," he said.

"She's your *mother*!"

"I know that," he said.

There were certain things in life you had to do. The death of one's parent was an end. An end to being a child. Especially the death of a mother. She shook her head in disbelief. "I'll go see her."

When she came back from the bedroom she said, "I closed her eyes."

For the next two days, Kitty and Henry stayed over. Kitty made meals for the two of them, her husband and Hermann, his father. As a matter of fact, she took over the household.

What unknown forces had driven her to assume the dead woman's role?

On the third night, right after the funeral, after she had retired to the guestroom, Kitty's tremors started.

Holding her hand, Henry sat next to her, waiting, knowing that there was nothing he could do. He could only wait for the eventual, physical exhaustion that would sap the tremors of their energy. Instead, the tremors went on and on and grew in violence, ending in a convulsive seizure, with Kitty eventually losing control of all of her bodily functions.

When the rhythms slowed momentarily, she whispered to Henry. "Please, take me home! I can't stay here any longer!"

Henry and Hermann, their arms cross-locked, carried Kitty out to the car. Holding tightly onto their necks, she controlled the spasms as best she could until she was safely in her seat. Then she turned to Henry and stared at him as if she had just escaped a nightmare. "I'm so glad to be away from him!"

Henry could only shake his head. What was causing these seizures? What was the link to the terror he'd seen in her eyes?

It made him think of that German prisoner in Avranches, in Normandy, screaming his head off, all through the night. Germans bombing their own to help them escape. *"Nicht mehr!"* he'd scream. "No more!" Gone crazy! Shaking down to the bones. Just like Kitty. Couldn't quiet him. Driving everyone bonkers. Not letting anyone sleep whenever those German planes came over at night. Until that one night when the screaming stopped. The quiet so puzzling. So damned puzzling. Not a sound. Not even the burst of a gun. Just complete quiet. Except for the drone of the plane's engine overhead.

His body was found later, thrown behind the hedges. His mouth ajar, blood still oozing.

"Gone crazy!" they had said.

Life had been so simple then, so easy to digest. It was life or death, nothing between.

Kitty was scared of something real. Something that was real to her. Not a plane. Of course not. For this was a different, a more complicated world! Also a more compassionate world! But what was it?

He took her hand into his. He looked into that tortured face of hers. A face muzzled by abject terror. As if she had been tossed into the fires of hell, the flames enveloping her, slurping at her flesh, consuming her.

Henry gave a big sigh. God Almighty, everything was so difficult! So difficult to figure out! He closed his eyes, shook his head. Subconscious! Unconscious! Suppressed traumas! Projections! Conversions! All the tools of the Freudian trade! Deep, hidden valleys filled with lost, shadowy fears! Utter confusion! Revealing false answers! Benign failures! Irrational reality! And, in the end, so often, only quiet, penetrating desperation!

What was it all about?

A deep chill came over him. Yes, life was a lottery! Totally at random! Starting off full of promise. Hoping, trusting. Then, fate turning the key. Inconspicuously, turning it one way or another. Opening the gates or locking them. Admitting the fortunate. Letting them enter into those glorious, gilded halls of mindless self-satisfaction. Banishing the luckless, imprisoning them in the helter-skelter world of misjudgments and miscalculations.

Well, that wasn't quite true. More often than not, it was the weak who were caught in the web of irreversible fate. Like Kitty. Never willing to fight for that piece of good fortune that should have been her due!

Maybe he was being sentimental. One needed to be realistic. Assess the possibilities, the probabilities, all the angles. Try to find causes, reasons. Explore everything. Open her up and reach inside of her. Find out how actions caused reactions, how everything was interconnected. One life, two lives, three lives. Her life, his life. Mind, body. Madness, saneness.

Yes, there had to be a link. There had to be some sort of a link.

Kitty did not sleep that night, nor did she sleep the next day. She awaited each new jolt. With the spasms escalating, reaching a new, savage stage, they continued without respite for hours at a time, no longer episodic but almost incessant.

By late afternoon, Henry called the psychiatrist, the one who had recommended analysis. He moved Kitty to a hospital. There, with constant, heavy sedation, he kept her sleeping for nearly a week. Gradually her body came to relax and, after the spasms had abated for more than twenty-four hours, the consulting doctors talked about her release. As Henry awaited the final word, he watched her studiously, looking for those deep shadows that came over her before each attack: the holding back, the tightening of the neck muscles, that fixed look of terror.

"I think I'll be all right," she said as they walked along the dark, cavernous hospital corridor. She had said it for Henry's sake. She still felt uncertain. Her heart was beating fast. She was trying her best. All she could do was hope, hope that she'd make the transition back into the real world without a hitch.
"Of course you will be," he said.
As they left the hospital, she bit her lips, trying not to think of things. But the words came out of her anyhow. "Why does everything seem so familiar?"
"I don't know."
Suddenly, she turned and looked back. She saw it in big letters: ALLIANCE HOSPITAL.
By the time she reached the car, the tremors had started again. Henry rushed back into the hospital. When he reached the psychiatrist, he explained to him what had occurred.
"Get her out of Chicago at once," he said to Henry. "Have her visit a friend or relative, but get her away at once."
At the airport, later that evening, Kitty waited for the flight that would take her to her sister Ruth in California. She had quieted. The spasms had stopped.

As they turned off Sunset Boulevard, Ruth swerved into Beverly Glen Road, finally slowing down as she wheeled into a side street and drove up a gated, red-bricked driveway.
Kitty was starry-eyed. "What a beautiful place you have."
Ruth smiled vaguely and parked the Fleetwood in the garage. Kitty followed her sister into the house.

The entrance hall seemed as large as a ballroom, with an open staircase winding up to the second floor. Just like in the movies, Kitty thought. "My suitcase," she reminded Ruth, "I left it in the car."

Ruth smiled. "Later."

The maid greeted them. "We'll be on the terrace." Ruth hesitated for a moment. "Some coffee. Bring some cake."

They both walked out to the terrace. Kitty waited at the edge of the steps that descended to the garden. Something was wrong here. She could tell. "What a lovely place," she said anyhow. Her stomach had tightened.

After a while she sat down with Ruth. For an instant they looked at each other. Then Ruth avoided her eyes.

"I need to talk to you, Kitty," she said.

"Go ahead."

Whatever was it that Ruth wanted to talk to her about? It could have waited. She had arrived but minutes before.

Ruth sighed, then pressed her lips together. "I don't know how to say it."

"What is it, Ruth?" She tried to catch her eyes.

"It's just that you're my sister."

"So I am."

Ruth took a deep breath. "I have a six-year-old daughter."

"Of course, Cindy."

"She's never seen . . . how should I say . . ."

Of course! Kitty understood at once. She nodded. "A crazy woman?"

"No. That's not it. What I mean . . . like Ma said when I talked to her, you get those fits! I mean . . . Cindy's only a child . . ."

"I understand." Was she angry? Was she disappointed?

"I reserved a room at the Ambassador."

"I'll find my own room." She was no child.

"It's already paid for."

"I can pay for my own room. Thanks, anyway. This wasn't necessary. There's no reason why you should have to put up with me."

Ruth gazed at her sister. "I'm so sorry."

"Why should you be? I had no right to impose on you."

Kitty did not leave right away. She had made a mistake. She had to wait, try to get a hold of herself.

After a while, after she had had some coffee, after some meaningless inquiries about each other's husbands, Kitty finally rose. "Will you please call a taxi?"

"I can drive you wherever you want."

It was easy to tell that Ruth was relieved. She wasn't wanted here. Ruth, as always, had readied her game plan. "Thanks, Ruth, but I'd rather be alone."

For all the days following the death of Henry's mother, and then through the week of Kitty's hospital stay, Bobby and Danny had been left in the care of Reggie and Eric. They would now stay on for the duration of Kitty's trip to California.

"What do you hear from Kitty?" Eric asked when Henry came for a visit. "Is she feeling any better?"

"Much better," he said. "She's having a great time in California." He didn't reveal his concern about Kitty not staying with her sister.

Reggie brought in the boys. She held on to Danny while Bobby jumped into his father's arms. Then, without so much as a greeting, she declared. "All I can say to you, Henry, is that you just cannot go on like this."

Henry, surprised by her grim words, let go of Bobby. He had really come to see his kids, not to be admonished by his mother-in-law. "What do you mean by that?"

"What I simply mean is, that you cannot let Kitty go on ruining your life."

Eric elbowed Reggie, nodding toward Bobby. Neither Reggie nor Henry paid any attention to him. He quietly took Bobby and Danny out of the room.

"No one's ruining my life. The way you talk, one might think that you believe she's concocted her sickness."

"Well, with your smarts, I'm surprised that you take it all at face value. All I can tell you is that it wouldn't be the first time she's pretended to be sick."

"What do you mean?" Henry asked, riled by her insinuation. "What do you mean, *pretended*?"

"All I can say," she said, extending a theatrical pause, her patronizing smile clearly disdainful, "you shouldn't believe everything she tells you. I've been around her for too long. I know Kitty better than you or anyone. I hate to say this to you, but your wife acts out a lot of fantasies. She always has. Yes, I know it, she's my own daughter. But I must warn you that she's an accomplished liar. I've known it all of her life." Looking downward, thrusting her chin forward, shaking her head slowly, she intimated deep torment. "I wonder what terrible things she's told you about me."

"That's enough now!" Eric had returned. "I don't want to hear any more of this." He seemed angry, but his was too civilized, too feeble an anger, useless for dealing with Reggie.

"Mind your own damned business!" She stared at him. "This is about my daughter! This is my business!" She turned back to Henry. "I think, as her mother, I owe it to you to tell you the truth."

Henry had long known of the antagonism between mother and daughter, but there was a level of resentment here that he had not expected. "All right then," he said, his lips pursed, nodding weakly, "you might as well let me hear what you call the truth. You might as well tell me why you feel she's playing a game with me."

Reggie's stern, grim-faced gaze caught his eyes. "I feel so sorry for you, my boy. You're such a naive young man. True, I'll admit that when I was your age, I was even more naive than you. I also trusted everyone. I trusted Kitty's father when everybody warned me that he was a pitiful good-for-nothing."

"What was it that you wanted to tell me about Kitty?" Henry said, showing his impatience.

"When I was a young girl, way back when . . ." she raised her eyebrows, "what I lived through . . ." she nodded slowly, "during those awful days in Berlin . . . was worse than anything with the Nazis."

"What do you mean?"

She closed her eyes and shook her head. "I was right there," she bit her lips, "when they killed her!"

"What, in heaven's name, are you talking about?"

"What am I talking about, you ask?" She waited. "But, of course, you wouldn't know." She nodded slowly. "Of course, you weren't there, were you? That's right, you weren't even born yet."

"Really?" Henry raised his eyebrows with the insult. "So, tell me, what has Berlin got to do with Kitty?"

Reggie didn't seem ready to return to this time and place; she was still back in that other time. "Those raping bastards! Those brutal beasts!"

"What?"

She nodded slowly. Finally she spoke. "They killed her!"

"Who?"

"Rosa, of course!" Reggie wiped her tears. Then she looked away, into the distance.

Eric interrupted. "Revolutionaries. That's what they were. That's who she hung around with. In 1919. After the war. The men of the *Freikorps* killed this friend of hers. Rosa Luxemburg. That's what she's so obsessed about. I know all of her stories. I've heard them a million times. All her excuses. But, mind you, they are not really excuses. They are explanations for all that bitterness in her."

Reggie stared at Eric, her face steely. "Bitterness, is that what you're saying? I was bitter because we had nothing to eat, because we had nothing to live for?" She waited but Eric remained silent. "So, what did you do, Mr. Righteous? Lie low? Turn tail? Crawl into some hole?" Her stare didn't leave him. "You goddamn chickenshit! You call yourself a man?"

Eric bit his lip.

Yes, Henry understood: Berlin of the rowdy twenties after World War I. That's where she had grown up.

Reggie looked into the distance. *"For once you must try not to shirk the facts; mankind is kept alive by bestial acts."* Reggie stared at Henry, a grim expression on her face, nodding. "You know the line?"

"Yes. I know."

"Brecht!" she added. "Yes, Berlin! It was the worst of times..."

Henry nodded, his mouth open. Still astonished at the outburst.

"We're all children of our times. You understand?"

"Yes, of course."

Reggie waited. Her face was still grim. She seemed to be collecting herself. Finally she went on. "All my life I wanted to make certain that what I had to go through wouldn't happen to my girls. Do you understand that? Do you understand what I'm saying? All I ever wanted for my girls was for them to be strong. Not to fall prey to those bastards, those men! But to be a good parent and raise your children right you need a partner, a partner who's on the same wavelength as you."

"I'm waiting." If this all was about Kitty, it took her a long time to make her point.

Reggie shook her head. "Her father did it! He's the one who ruined her! Ruined her forever!"

Henry felt her stare. She seemed to be watching his expression.

"I'm telling you! That's why Kitty is the way she is today. He never understood a damned thing about raising a girl. Never understood that a girl must grow up strong. Just like a man! Must learn how to deal with this world, learn to withstand the onslaught."

Reggie looked away from him. She looked down, closing her eyes, shaking her head.

"They're all *bastards*! All of them! That's what they all are: *bastards*! Those men! Those sex-craved men! Those raping maniacs!"

Henry stared at Reggie. His stare was stark, unrelenting. "You mean every man? All of them? Every one of us?" He was angry. So that's what Reggie was all about. "You cannot blame your whole damned life on those days in Berlin! On those men! Is that when you formed your opinion about men, all men?"

"Opinion? What do you mean by *opinion*? I'm talking the truth! I *know* what they're like!"

Henry had long suspected that there was more to Reggie than her one-note toughness had revealed. Now today, she had started out promising to tell him about Kitty and ended up sharing details of her own life, her own beliefs. "But that was then," he said, "all this happened a long time ago. What has that got to do with Kitty?"

"Her father ruined her. Kitty should have been strong. Like me. Like her sister."

"We're not all made of the same stuff," Henry protested.

"But we all have to deal with the same world." She gazed out into the distance as if totally possessed by her insight.

Henry shook his head. Whatever he'd say to her wouldn't make any difference. This was a determined woman. But he had to say it anyhow. "I'm sorry you feel this way. Yes, it might be the same world, but we all see that world with our own eyes. That's why we don't all deal with it the same way. Maybe it would be better if we all saw it the same way. We were not all in Berlin. Kitty has certainly seen her own horrors. This is not a contest to find out who has seen the worst horrors."

"This is my own daughter we're talking about, Henry. These boys are my grandchildren! I beg you—may God forgive me—listen to me: *you must put her away*!" Reggie shook her head as if she was pained for having delivered the hard truth. "Believe me, I know what I'm talking about. Put her away before it's too late! You can do it, I know you can. You're smart. You know about psychology and all that business. Put her away!"

Henry tried to keep his composure in the face of all of his anger. She was getting to the guts of things. "Tell me, please, why do you want me to put her away?"

Reggie gazed out into the distance, frowning. "He spoiled her."

"Her father?"

"Yes." She nodded again. "She was his favorite. He was obsessed with his *Goldkindchen* (his golden child). That's what he always called her. That's why she turned out so much like him."

"And what does that all have to do with her sickness right now? With her tremors, with the shakes?"

"It's all put on. Believe me! When she's sick, she gets her way. Her father did all this to me. When her father was still alive, he pampered her. He catered to her. He catered to her every whim. He let her get away with everything. That's the way it always was with him." She removed a hanky from her sleeve and wiped her tears. "It was like an addiction with him. It cost me a fortune in doctor bills, in nurses, in worries."

"Well, I don't know what happened in Germany with you and Kitty, but Kitty *is* sick right now, and when she gets those shakes, I know that she can't help it. I know that she tries to stop them. I do not doubt it for a minute. I have no reason to doubt it. I have never caught her in any lie either, on any matter, not ever. I know she would never deceive me intentionally. It wouldn't be like her."

To his great surprise, he wasn't really angry at Reggie. Maybe, he thought later on, it was because he was grateful that at last he had heard firsthand how much his wife was despised by her mother. It would help him deal with Kitty.

"I feel so sorry for you," Reggie said to him.

"Don't!"

She shook her head. Obviously, she was dissatisfied that her son-in-law had not bought it all. She just sat there, still deep in her thoughts of the past. Finally, she rose from the couch. "I feel so sorry for you, my boy." For a moment, she just stood there, facing Henry, undecided. Then, finally, she spoke her last words,

"All I can say is, *you'll find out*. Sooner or later, *you'll find out*." She turned and left the room.

Henry sat quietly for a long minute. Mother and daughter. Of such different cloth. Viewing the commonality of their experiences so differently. Each seeing fragments, very different fragments. Understanding so little of each other. Understanding so little of the life they had lived together.

Chapter 17

January 1954

When Kitty walked across the tarmac, her bearing was relaxed, her step easy. Her gleaming white suit offset her deep tan. The California sun, the soothing sands, the rolling waves, the lightness of the outdoors, were all still with her. There was nothing to remind Henry of her breakdown, nothing to indicate the hidden stresses that had so badly torn her apart just weeks ago. It was as if she had shed all the constricting impulses that had contributed to those terrible tensions within her.

When Kitty saw him, she ran to him, threw her arms around his neck, and kissed him. "I'm so glad to be back," she said. "I've missed you so much."

"I missed you too." Henry was surprised at her ease and her ready affection.

"How are the boys?"

"They're fine. And California, how was California?"

"L.A. is beautiful. The palms, the beautiful homes, the beach, the sun. It's another country, almost another world. I loved it."

"Your sister? How is she?"

"She's fine. I didn't spend much time with her. It was better that way."

A few weeks after her return from California, Kitty's health gradually deteriorated. She was back in her old surroundings. Most ominously, she succumbed to convulsive fits at almost any time, any place: while lunching with her friends at Berghoff's, while toasting newlyweds at the Empire Room of the Palmer House, while browsing at Marshall Field's where she tore down a rack of clothing during her spell. These spells came over her without warning. They were like an abrupt metamorphosis, turning her into an emotional hemophiliac who, with a sudden dearth of platelets, was no longer able to close off the deep wounds inside.

Yet there were also months of remission, interrupting her deterioration, and during these periods Kitty could still function reasonably well. This, of course, created a temptation to deny the inevitability of the dark storm these seizure-like episodes portended.

Kitty's experience with those who had promised to help her look into her past had not been good either. Exploring causes by examining their effects promised no relief, no understanding, certainly no resolution.

"Sex! That's what they always talked about! How sex should be pleasant!" she complained.

Like that psychologist, the one Henry had befriended at the university, the one who each time she'd visit him couldn't remember what they had last talked about. Of course, what they had last talked about was sex. How she should learn to breathe deeply and relax. As if that effort would make it fun. After months of weekly visits, she still felt the same.

Who else was there? Oh, yes! Of course, the analyst! Yes, she had finally consented to see the analyst. She couldn't stand his mellow voice. Speak up, Dr. Lessner! I can't hear you! He was always asking her, "Kitty, tell me, what is on your mind?"

"Nothing," she would answer him, "nothing at all." Then he would shake his head. "You must relax, my dear," he'd say to her. "You must let your thoughts flow freely, let go, tell me all about them." But, of course, she couldn't let go. If she could have let go, she might not have been the way she was, might not have needed him. How could he fail to understand that? And the money he charged. There were many better uses she could put all that money to, uses that would benefit her whole family.

All those doctors, with their high-sounding words for things, with their degrees covering the walls of their offices like wallpaper! All they did was make her feel incompetent to do anything to help herself!

Kitty could not adapt her greatest strength, her will to survive, to the process of healing her tattered psyche. All she could do was to accept her fate as it confronted her daily and pray that each new day would be less painful than the day before.

Even Henry had given up. The dire foreboding of a catastrophic ending, of a total shipwreck, had purged all hope in him. He could not control the uncontrollable. All that was left to him was the agonizing anticipation of the impending calamity.

Henry sat next to the stage. With the dim, bluish lights bathing her loins, the girl's nude body arched backward, straining against her angled knees, while her dark, erect nipples undulated above a delicate, virginal face and her outstretched arms gyrated fluently to the heavy beat of the tropical rhythm. As if her hands were not her own, she caressed her thighs with delicate strokes, feigning deep ecstasy. Yet she also employed a coy hesitation with each bending and twisting, pretending an innocence, an elusive modesty so paradoxical, yet still so very convincing.

When the music stopped, Henry applauded. The girl gathered her clothing and left the stage. The lights went on and the room felt cold and sharp again.

After a while, she returned from the dressing room, clad in a silky black dress that clung to her soft, exquisite body like a delicate shadow. At once, she caught Henry's eye and smiled at him. Without waiting for him to acknowledge her smile, she came and sat down next to him.

"I'm Cherie!" She placed her hand on his thigh.

Henry stared at her, surprised, but ensnared by her brazenness. How young she was! Seventeen? Eighteen? So pretty! Turned-up nose, moist, dark lips, delicate cheeks, a fine neck. An innocent face.

"What's your name?"

"Henry." He looked around the room. Eyes turned away.

"You going to buy me a drink?" She squeezed his thigh.

He had been caught off guard. "A drink?"

"Yes, a drink." The bartender came over and faced him.

"No, I don't think so."

With her satiny palm caressing his cheek, she leaned toward him, baring two yielding young breasts, her playful, brown eyes looking up at him. "Please, just one?"

Goddamn, she's doing it to me! The tricks of the trade, as obvious as the hawker's bark. Suddenly, he felt guilty. What the hell was he doing here anyhow? There was Kitty, her problems, her anxieties. That's where he belonged.

Belonged? Really?

Who had ordained where he belonged? God? Nature? Or was it some vaguely designed reduction to order? Shit, there was no order. Only social constrictions. Rules imposed by uninformed experts, by trite dogma or willful authorities. How could he ever find the right distance between himself and the immediacy of his urges? If God hadn't meant it so, why had he bestowed this powerful passion in him? "Well, all right, then," he replied, "but just one."

She nodded to the bartender. He poured out a pinkish drink and set it down next to her.

She took a sip. "You come here often?"

He shook his head. He wished her hand were still on his thigh or holding his cheek. Such a tender touch. Was it all fake? "What made you a stripper?" he asked.

"Dancer," she corrected.

"Yes, dancer," he repeated. "What made you a dancer? A very good dancer, by the way."

"Well, thanks." She took a big sip, nearly emptying the glass. Nothing delicate here, he thought. All business. Nothing real. Damn, he had fallen for her seductive bait. Why hadn't her stripping been enough for him? "Tell me, what got you into stripping, I mean dancing?" he repeated.

She looked puzzled. "Why do you want to know?"

"Just wondering."

Crazy how his curiosity always overtook him. He was obsessed by curiosity. All of his life! Even way back in Cologne. As a young lad. Riding the streetcar. Trying to figure out why people were the way they were. What they did. Why they were so glum.

For heaven's sake, let off already! he said to himself. Savor the moment! Find its pleasure! Enjoy it! Don't muddle things up!

"Got to make a living. That's all." She looked up at him. "Doesn't everyone?"

"Of course." What concern was her life to him anyway? "You're really very good."

"Thanks." She finished her drink. "Doesn't do me much good."

"What do you mean?"

"Girls like me are a dime a dozen."

"Another drink for the lady?" the bartender had come back, interrupting.

She squeezed his thigh. The same trap. It upset him. "No, thanks."

She turned to the bartender. "Give me a minute." Then she turned to Henry. "They make us hustle. All the time." She gave a deep sigh. "Most of the guys just want to talk. That's all they want to do."

Suddenly, his curiosity got the better of him. She had understood. About men. Their needs. Their need to connect. To talk. That's all they really wanted to do, she had said. Most of the time it wasn't sex. It was their fear of loneliness! Of feeling lost!

She was right! Yes, she was damn right! She had a soul, she had a heart. Even if she herself hadn't connected. Even if she had failed. Look at this fresh-faced young kid, he said to himself, choosing this dead-end life. Whatever made her do such a self-destructive thing?

"Okay, I'll buy you another drink."

"Never mind." She broke into a crafty smile. "Let 'em wait."

Suddenly, totally unexpectedly, their eyes met without taking measure of each other and a conniving smile passed between them, which was a little bit like a conspiracy.

"You from here?"

"Of course not." She raised her eyebrows. "Who's from here? Everyone's from somewhere else. Escaping from somewhere, running away from something." She closed her eyes. "Never mind. Forget it."

He nodded. "I see."

"Topeka."

He nodded once more.

"Topeka, Kansas."

"I see." He hesitated. "Been back?" He wasn't sure why he'd asked.

"Of course not. Would I go back? You know the first question my mother would ask?"

"No."

"What have you been doing?"

Suddenly, he felt sorry for her. She was just a young kid who had taken the wrong track, who hadn't yet learned that making a life required more than a pretty body with sex appeal. "You can always work in an office."

"Me? Work in an office? Christ! What would that do? That would be the end of me. I couldn't do that." She shut her eyes. "Besides, who would take care of my kid?"

"You've got a child?"

"Little girl. Two years old. Real cute."

"And you work here?"

"What else can I do? I quit school." She shrugged. "Works out fine. When my boyfriend gets home, I leave. He takes care of the kid."

"Marriage?"

"Who knows."

The bartender had come back. He stared at her. "Get moving, kid," he graveled.

"Fuck off!"

She turned to Henry and whispered into his ear. "That bastard!" She placed her hand on his and said, "Thanks, pal."

He raised his eyebrows. "What for?"

"Never mind."

When she got up, she looked about herself as if she were lost. He felt sorry for her. Just a young girl on display. Like a bird in a cage. Took a wrong turn. Missed a step or two here or there. A few bad choices. Overwhelmed by life. Trying to get out of the rut she had carved for herself. Frustrated by her limitations. Probably failing.

"See ya' round," she said as she walked away from him, her eyes grazing the ground as she slowly disappeared.

That night he understood better than ever what it meant to be constrained by a chain of circumstances.

Lying on his back, he cradled the girl in his arms while her head rested on his bare chest and strands of her hair fanned across his body. He was her lover. Man with woman, father with child, life with death. All irrevocably linked. So fatefully preordained. Like a connection to the cosmos. Cruelly finite.

It couldn't be real. It was all a dream.

In his mind's eye he could still see her moist vision. Was it Kitty's? No. It wasn't Kitty's. It was someone else. Some other girl's eyes. But who?

He remembered the movie, Joan Crawford (what was the name of the movie again?), her eyes shiny, full of tenderness, full of feeling. Oh God, why couldn't it ever be?

Soggy, tender sentiments! So hard to come by! So dangerous! So fraught with perversions! Vulnerable feelings open to abuse! So easily taken for fatal weakness! Yes, of course, it was true: only the strong survive. Only the strong go on living without feelings.

What really are the sexual feelings once the juices are spent? What really lingers of the melody once the music stops? Moments pass so quickly. You want, you have, you leave. Suddenly, there is no more. The oddity of a lost ending. Two lovers, their embrace, their disjunction.

He wanted to hold on to her, keep on cuddling her in his arms. Suddenly, he shrank away from the illusion. Yes, it was only a momentary respite from life! A respite from the real thing! From the cruelty of the universe!

Henry opened his eyes. Little by little the world came back to him. It couldn't be helped. It had been but a moment. A rare, throwaway moment.

Chapter 18

April 1954

When April rains darken the spring skies, our optimism seems to turn into pessimism. Some would call this the stuff of folk tales. They insist that moods are not controlled by the weather, but by events in our lives.

The trouble started on that afternoon in April. 1954. Henry and Kitty were driving north on U.S. Highway 67 from Davenport to Clinton, Iowa. The highway, old and narrow, lacking shoulders, badly in need of repair, paralleled the Mississippi River as it wound along a swampy, uninhabited corridor. Lush green vegetation hid the waterlogged underbrush that lined the highway away from the paved surface.

Henry's ultimate despair had been building like inevitable fate, like a silent slide on an icy road that would end in the bowels of a ditch. He knew that, in light of Kitty's gradual deterioration, her unexplained outbursts of rage, her convulsive spasms, her so-called "fits," something needed to be done. A "change of milieu," taking her out of her everyday surroundings, like after her collapse following his mother's death, when she had flown out to California to visit her sister, might be helpful.

But he knew too well that this was no more than a stopgap solution.

All of his appointments—Henry had opened an office as a marriage and family counselor—had been canceled for a week. The boys were well taken care of by the housekeeper. Even though he considered the trip no more than an escape, he welcomed the respite from his tumultuous life with Kitty. In his presence, she would not drown herself with Seconals, she would not be smoking in bed or driving a car in the twilight of awareness. If the fits came, he was prepared to deal with them—that is, mentally prepared.

But, as a matter of fact, he was not!

Right out of the blue, Kitty broke into their peaceful, uneventful silence. *"Let me out of the car!"* Her voice was shrill, determined.

A chill came over Henry. This was absurd! Totally without reason! Why in hell would she want to get out now? Yes, her craziness was starting up again.

Trying to keep his cool, he disregarded the remark and kept his eyes focused on the winding road.

She turned toward him, her eyes icy, scowling. *"I said that I want you to let me out!"*

For a moment, he glanced at her and met her eyes. "Why? What's the matter?"

"Don't you hear me?" she snarled at him. "I want to get out!" Her voice was drenched with full-throated rage. "I want to get out right now!"

Out of the corner of his eye he could see her reaching for the door. "I can't let you out here. It's all swamp," he explained, slowing the car.

She held on to the handle but didn't open the door. For a moment, it seemed to him as if she were jogging her head to clear it, as if she were trying to stop herself from doing what she was doing. But apparently she could no longer hold things back. It was too late. With her face twisting grotesquely, she suddenly lunged at Henry and, grabbing his head, she turned it away from the road. "You . . . goddamn you . . . you listen to me!" she screamed at him. "Where in hell do you think you're taking me?"

He shoved her right back into her seat. "Damn you! Can't you see that I'm driving on a narrow highway? Are you trying to kill us both?" This was absolutely crazy! Why in the world did she want to get out now?

But Kitty wouldn't stop. "I said I want you to let me out!" Her shrill, staccato voice nearly drained her speech.

He shook his head. What in hell had gotten into her?

"Right now!" she screamed, growling, pursing her lips. "You, you let me out right now!"

For Chrissake, woman, what is the matter with you? Can't you see there is no room to stop, no shoulder to pull onto, no place to walk along the road? "We'll be in Clinton soon," he said, quietly but firmly. "You can get out there. I promise!"

"Stop the car!" She opened the door a slit.

"I can't. There's no place to stop. It's all swamp. Just wait till we get to Clinton. I promise, I'll stop."

It seemed that she finally sensed that he was not just humoring her, that he intended to keep his word, and she let go of the door handle. "How far is it to Clinton?"

"About ten miles."

"All right, then." She turned her back toward him. "You better let me out then."

What a marvel! She had listened to him! He could breathe easier. At least he'd have a chance to think about it all for a while, to figure out what was going on with her. What to do next. In a way, he was kind of surprised that she had given in so easily. But then her mood swings had always come suddenly. One moment she would be fully at ease with the world, the next she would behave as if she were possessed by some ungodly power.

For the time being, he said no more.

When they reached the outskirts of Clinton, he pulled over to the sidewalk, stopped the car, and turned off the ignition. He must keep his word or she'd never trust him again.

"You sure you want to get out?" He hoped the question would be better received now that he had stopped, when she could see he was prepared to live up to his word.

If she received his question better, she did not let on. For she didn't answer him. She didn't even look at him. She got out of the car and slammed the door behind her.

As she lingered on the sidewalk, trying to orient herself, Kitty felt a great sense of relief that, finally, she was away from him. She was alone. Yet now that she was away from him, now that she was free, she couldn't remember what had set her off or what she was free from. She was so mixed up.

At last, clutching her handbag under her arm, biting her lips, she started off toward the city. Her legs felt not quite like her own, which caused her to walk wobbly, unbalanced. What did she want to do anyhow? Where did she want to go? God, she couldn't remember. She couldn't remember anything. Yes, of course, she needed to get away. Just get away. From him. She had to go on. She had to go on in order to save herself. It really didn't matter where she ended up.

With her eyes fastened upon the sidewalk, she walked on, not looking at anything or anybody. Why had she done what she had? What was it about Henry? What was it within her that had told her she must get away from him? If only her head would clear up. She felt like she was cascading down a river, totally out of control, using up the last bit of strength that was left in her.

During all this time, Henry just sat there, watching Kitty lose herself in the distance, thinking about how crazy it all was. There really hadn't been any argument, any fight. Right out of the blue, she had asked to get out of the car, to get away from him. Crazy, that's what it was! Totally crazy! But then, when one thought about it—this was not the first time the question had come to him—was she really trying to get away from *him*? Or, if not from him, from whom?

Finally, when he had almost lost sight of her, he started the car and followed. She might have quieted. She might have changed her mind. When he saw her, he drove past her and stopped just beyond the next intersection. He left the car and waited for her. When she saw him, she quickly crossed to the other side of the road. He returned to the car, pulled ahead of her once more, and parked again. This time, when he waited for her, she was less than twenty feet away from him. He watched her hesitate. Then, too late to cross over to the other side, she resumed her pace as if she hadn't seen him.

He grasped her arm.

"Leave me alone," she screamed at him, tearing herself free.

He grabbed her arm once more. "Why don't you cut out this foolishness?"

"Just leave me alone," she repeated. But her voice was thin, without determination.

"What are you going to do?" His tone was quiet, considerate. "I'll leave you alone, but just tell me what you're going to do."

"None of your business." Once more she twisted herself free.

He caught up with her again. "All I want to know is what you intend to do, and I'll leave you alone."

Kitty's eyes turned to him, suddenly fierce, defiant. "If you don't leave me alone, I'll scream!"

He could sense her desperation. The prospect of her screaming did not appeal to him. Already people were staring at them. "Maybe I can help you find whatever you're looking for. After all, I know the town."

"Where's the railroad station?" Her question had come out of the blue. She looked away from him as if embarrassed to have asked so prosaic a question.

"That's easy," he said, somewhat relieved. "Two blocks ahead. You can see it from here." He pointed toward it.

But she had already walked on. He wasn't certain she had heard him. He returned to the car and waited. Trains were infrequent these days, certainly from Clinton. If she wanted to go back to Chicago, she might have a long wait.

After a long while Henry drove on to the station and again waited in the car. He waited another long thirty minutes. Let her quiet down, he thought.

When he finally walked inside, the waiting room was empty. It had been bypassed by time. There were no train schedules posted on message boards, no flashing lights, no movement of baggage, no signs of passengers arriving for their departure times, no knots of relatives to see them off. High above, the arched ceiling, blackened by rancid steam from huge radiators, spoke of total neglect. In the center of the room, an old woman, holding on to her grandchild, sat alone on one of the high-backed, wood-slatted benches left behind from the station's better days. The lack of traffic suggested that no trains would be leaving for Chicago any time soon, if at all.

He spotted Kitty, the back of her head peeking above the high bench in the far corner. She was waiting for the train that wasn't coming.

He sat down next to her and stared at her stoic face. He took her hand, placed it upon his knee, and squeezed it ever so lightly. She gave no response. Her thoughts seemed far away. With his forefinger he wiped a lonely tear from her cheek. Then he cleaned off the smudged mascara with his handkerchief.

Kitty's agitation was linked to something he had done in some way or another. He couldn't tell what. Something he had done had frightened her, angered her, panicked her. Something that *he* perhaps had not been aware of. Nevertheless, it had been something he had done, or maybe had said or suggested.

Finally, he rose and, holding her hand, he said to her, "Let me take you home, Kitty."

As he lifted her to her feet, he reached his arm around her and, holding up her slumping frame, he led her out of the station. All the way to the car, he did not speak a word to her. He opened the door and eased her onto the seat. She never lifted her head. There was nothing left in her. She seemed totally drained.

He drove across the Mississippi along U.S. 30, back toward Chicago. He'd get her home. She was better off at home than in a strange city.

Just west of Morrison, Illinois, less than fifteen miles outside of Clinton, the sky turned suddenly black. Henry slowed down and turned on the headlights. All at once, a torrential downpour pelted the car and all the windows fogged up instantly. He wiped the inside of the windshield with his hands. "Damn it," he declared, "the rain's really coming down." He glanced at Kitty, slumped deep in her seat, oblivious to what was going on. "It's going to be tough driving home in this kind of weather!"

Kitty's gaze remained fixed on the steamed-up window.

As he drove on, trying to find his way through the storm and the blinding darkness, her silence began to annoy him. He tried to reason himself out of his gnawing irritation. But his anger wouldn't let go. It kept on simmering within him. Yes, of course, everything was always loaded on his shoulders. The whole damned, fucking world. All the time! Always! There was no end to it.

He gave a deep sigh.

Be reasonable! Try to understand! She can't help being the way she is! he said to himself.

But all the reasoning, all the understanding in the world couldn't suppress those strong feelings within him. Like an aching tooth, he kept on going back to the soreness, wanting to touch it, probe it, challenge it. "Are you ever going to talk to me?" he finally asked, staring at her.

Controlling his irritation, he waited for her answer.

After a while, he continued. "Well, I guess not." He nodded. "All right, then. I'll shut up."

Out of the corner of his eyes he watched her body straighten. She took a deep breath and turned to him, her lips pursed. "Let me out!"

The same old craziness.

"Let me out! At once!" she repeated. Her voice was surprisingly strong.

She opened the door. He could hear the tires splash across broad puddles. He grabbed her arm and held on to it.

"Let me out!" she screamed, trying to free herself from his hold.

Henry tightened his grip. "No! You can't get out now!"

Twisting away from him, she freed her arm. Taking his eyes off the road momentarily, he found her arm again. He held on to it with all his might. Kitty let go of the door and, pulling at his hair, tried to free herself from his grip. She yanked his head so violently that he couldn't help but jam his arm across her neck, pinning her to her seat. Then, pulling off the road, he brought the car to an abrupt halt.

"You goddamn stupid bitch!" he screamed at her. "Do you want to get us both killed?" Empty words but, of course, he had no others.

"You let me out!" She twisted herself free of him.

It didn't matter any longer. He didn't resist her. He had had enough. He really didn't care any more. Let her do whatever she wanted. This time she had gone too far.

Kitty slammed the door shut. The hard rain pelted her face, nearly blinding her. She wiped the pasted hair from her eyes. She tried to remember why she had to get out of the car. Yes, of course, it was to get away from him. That's what it was!

But why did she need to get away from him? And now, now that she was away from him, what did she want to do? Where was she anyhow? Where did she want to go?

Finally she turned and slowly, carefully, plodded her way along the squashy shoulders. Yes, she needed to get away from the car and from him. With the rain pelting her, she did not see much. The soft mud stuck to her shoes like wet cement. After a while, she crossed over to the pavement. It was easier to walk on the highway.

On and on she walked. The rain washed her cheeks. Her coat had soaked through to her dress. Every so often she slowed to wipe her chin. But always she walked on. Not knowing where she was or where she was going. Oblivious to the world around her.

Finally, she saw the gray, dim outline of a boulder and reached for it. She wiped it with the sleeve of her coat and, lifting herself, she sat down. She needed time to think. Figure out what to do next. Find some answers.

If only she could start her life over again. She'd do something different. She'd be someone different. But there . . . oh, my God . . . there it was again . . . that face . . . that same face . . . that face that was driving her on and on . . . driving her absolutely crazy.

Suddenly, giant tears rushed down her cheeks. She covered her mouth. Oh God, why won't it ever end? Why did the torture have to go on and on! Why did she always have to see that same ghastly, shapeless face?

But her silent screams were lost in the blackness of the night. She was alone. All alone. As she had always been. Alone in this world where no one ever heard her cries. Where no one ever listened to her unending despair. Her despair about all those things that were churning around in her head. Her despair about all those things she tried so hard to remember but couldn't.

In the meantime, Henry, slumped in his seat, exhausted from all that had occurred during the past few hours, could only shake his head at what he had witnessed. He had to ask the question: What had happened this time to trigger her madness?

But as time passed, he couldn't help but worry about Kitty roaming about in the cold, drenching storm. He buttoned his jacket and turned up the collar. Outside, the hard rain soaked his hair, pasted his pants. As he trudged along the soft, sticky shoulders, across deep puddles and sudden hollows, his eyes quickly adjusted to the darkness. He walked and walked, on and on, looking for Kitty. Where could she be? How far could she have made it in this foul night?

When he finally saw her, perched on top of the boulder, sitting there motionless, her hair stuck to her face, her open coat falling to the sides, he gave a sigh of relief.

But the moment she saw him, her eyes burst wide open and, jumping off her perch, she ran away from him. She ran in such great panic that when she slipped and fell to her knees, she jumped up instantly and continued running away from him. Splashing through large, black puddles, she escaped into the night.

He chased after her. "Come on, Kitty, please!" he called out after her.

But she didn't seem to hear him. She ran on and on. When he finally caught up with her and touched her—not wanting to spook her by grabbing at her—she swerved into the highway, slipped on the wet cement and, with her arms outstretched, fell face forward across the lane.

There were no cars. He grabbed her outstretched arms and turned her on her back. He needed to hurry. Kneeling on the concrete, he slid his left arm under her shoulders, his right arm under her legs, and lifted her to his chest. Slowly, carefully, holding her close to him, he trudged back along the shoulders and found his way to the car. He put her down on the seat, started the engine and turned on the heater. He brought the suitcase from the trunk, took out a shirt, and wiped her face. He dried her hair and cleared the soaked curls from her eyes. Then he removed her coat and took off her shoes. He raised her arms and lifted the dress over her head. He took off her undergarments and dried the rest of her body.

After he had dressed her in dry clothing, he wiped his own face. He needed to get her home. He would change later. With the heater going full blast, he would be dry soon enough.

Kitty had buried her face in her hands. She didn't want him to hear her sobs. She had remembered everything that had just happened. She didn't understand it. Why had she been so desperate to get away from him? Finally, she spoke. "I'm so sorry," she said. "Will you ever forgive me?"

Henry reached out to her and stroked her hair. He seemed thankful that it was all over, that the madness was done with. That she was herself again. "Of course, I forgive you."

"I don't know what came over me," she said. "I can't think straight any more." She shook her head. "I'm so afraid to think."

He pulled her close to him, letting her head fall to his chest. "Let's forget it," he said. "Let's forget about it right now."

She closed her eyes. "I can't! How can I forget it?" She shook her head. "There's something. I know there's something. There's something about you."

"About me?"

"I don't know. But there's something." She opened her eyes wide and gazed at Henry. "Your face! Yes, it's your face!"

"I look like him, don't I?" He didn't want to say the word. It might drive her into another rage. But he knew that she meant his father.

Kitty gaped at him, her eyes dazed, her heart pounding like crazy, but she said nothing. She said nothing at all.

Chapter 19

October 1954

He had come in the back door on an early Monday morning. Kitty was still sitting at the breakfast table. Henry had gone to work. The kids were off at school.

She looked up. "What are you doing here?"

He smiled at her with that familiar, mocking smile of his. "Why, of course, I came to visit you."

She knew better. Her father-in-law never did anything without some damned good reason. "To visit me? At this hour?" She hadn't been alone with him since Henry had returned from the war.

He took off his hat and coat and sat down across from her. "Yes, I came to visit you. Why is that so unusual?"

Her face dropped. She knew the words. His "innocent" questions. She remembered his ruses, his lies. His fake charm. "I really don't want to see you."

"Why?" He frowned. "Your own father-in-law? Why wouldn't you want to see me?"

She pursed her lips. This was not going to end well. What did he want from her anyway? "Why don't you just leave."

"Leave? You're asking me to leave? That's not very hospitable of you. And all along I thought you'd be happy to see me. After all, we haven't seen each other for such a long time."

"That's right. For a long time." She recognized the empty, devious grin he always put on while his cunning words were picking her brain.

"Aren't you happy to see me?"

"No." She needed to get away from him. "I want you to leave!" To her surprise, her voice was firm, insistent.

"So, if I won't?"

She reached for the phone.

He jumped up and tore it away from her. "Not so fast, my dear!" He shoved her back to her chair. "You're not getting rid of me that easy."

"What do you want?"

"What do I want? What do I want from you?" Suddenly his face turned grim. *"What do I want?"*

She waited.

"Your husband, my son, called me the other day, asking a lot of questions. Questions about you and me. About the war years. Something about a car. You always imagining me, instead of him, sitting next to you."

She bit her lips. God Almighty, what could she do now?

"He said that's what you had told him. That you became upset whenever you sat next to him because he looked so much like me. That you went crazy in the car and nearly jumped out."

She remained silent.

"He asked me what I had done to you while he was gone during the war." He kept on staring at her, waiting for an answer.

She didn't say anything.

"What did you tell him?"

She looked down, biting her lips. "Nothing."

"Nothing?" His voice was unrelenting. "You told him nothing? You want me to believe that you told him nothing?"

"Nothing."

"Let me tell you something." His face remained inscrutable. "If you had told him nothing, he wouldn't have called. Isn't that right?"

"I told him nothing."

"You told him nothing? How in hell did he know why you jumped from the car?"

"He doesn't know."

"What do you mean, he doesn't know? He told me that he was certain that it was me who you wanted to get away from."

"He's only guessing."

He leaned back. He seemed to be thinking this over. Then he bent forward again, grasping each end of the table. "I want you to be clear about one thing!"

"And what is that?" Suddenly she had regained her courage. She wouldn't let him threaten her. This wasn't the past, when she was alone, without any support. There was Henry, there were the kids, her friends, her neighbors.

He grabbed her hands. *"Not one word!"*

She jumped up and ran to the front of the house. But as she tried to open the door, he caught up with her. He grabbed her wrist and dragged her back to the kitchen. "What in hell do you think you're doing?" He plunked her down on the chair. "Don't think for one moment that you can get away from me." He sat down again. "I haven't finished yet."

She buried her face in the palms of her hands. She didn't want to see him.

"Let me make myself perfectly clear: one more word to Henry and you've had it." He tore her hands away from her face. "Look at me when I speak to you!" He grabbed her chin and, raising it, forced her to look at him.

She shuddered.

"If you tell him any more, even one damned word—about you know what—you've had it. I think you know me well enough. I'm not playing around. I'll come back and I'll shut you up for good. What happened between you and me, never happened. Is that clear?"

She nodded.

"If I get one more call from Henry, if I find out one more thing that you've told him, that will be the end of you. You can count on it."

She bit her lip.

He grabbed her wrist and held it in a vise-like grip. "I'll get you! I promise! One more word!"

She nodded.

Then, as he stood up, he seized her neck with one hand and with the other grabbed her hair, pulling her head back, forcing her to look at him once more. "I'll break your pretty little neck! You understand that?"

She nodded once more.

When he had left, she sat back in her chair. She could not remember anything. Her mind was a blank. Nothing about those war years was clear any longer. But then, to tell the truth, she was really afraid to think about it. It would be bad, so very bad.

He came back many times. He'd sit in the kitchen and talk to her, making certain that she was still unnerved by his presence, watching her quake when he made any threatening move, all of it intended to keep her from talking coherently about anything that he had been involved in.

Except that one morning in the spring of 1956 when he came, rapacious as a savage bull, barely able to control his rage. "What in hell did you tell him?"

She tried to get away from him, but he grabbed her hair and pulled her to him until their faces were no more than three inches apart. "What did I tell you?" He yanked at her hair. "Didn't I warn you? Didn't I tell you what would happen if you talked to him?"

She nodded.

"You talked to him anyhow. Accused me. Told him about being pregnant."

She shook her head. She hadn't told him.

"Who do you think I am?"

She shook her head again. What was he talking about?

"Do you really think you can fool around with me?"

"No."

He let go of the hair and pushed her backward. "Who do you think you are anyhow?"

She stumbled. Oh, my God! The baby! She hadn't thought about the baby! "Please!" Kitty held her belly full with her six-month pregnancy. Couldn't he tell that she was pregnant?

He pushed her ahead of him. "You crazy, stupid bitch!"

When she lost her balance right at the basement steps, it was already too late. She slid down the stairs, all the time holding on to her stomach, hitting the back of her head as she landed at the bottom on the cement floor.

She bit her lips but no matter how much she tried, she couldn't get up. She felt her stomach. Thank God, the baby was still kicking.

That was the day Bobby saw him leave. School had been dismissed early. "Don't you tell anyone you saw me," his grandfather bellowed at him. The frightened eight-year-old rushed down the stairs and helped his mother up. Little did Bobby know then about the impact of this chance meeting with his grandfather.

It was way past midnight on that same night that Kitty, dressed only in her nightgown, sat at the Knabe Grand, her arms dangling to her sides. The steely glare of the street lights, flickering from behind the trees like an old movie reel, swathed her with an eerie luster, giving her face a shadowy cast. The stoical way in which she sat there concealed the inner struggle she was waging. Like a strained rumbling beneath the earth, presaging a fissure's rupture, she tried desperately to contain the dizzying turmoil within her.

Her life was a total mess!

Shaking her head, she sighed deeply. What was she going to do?

Then, suddenly, she recognized the connection: her heartless, merciless father-in-law, a refugee from Nazi Germany, had been schooled in the same cold-blooded methods from which he had fled. What merciless fate had thrown her into the madness of his life?

Suddenly, without any warning, she pounced the keys with all the passion she could muster, immersing herself in her music, bringing forth those familiar sounds that always felt so lucid and comforting. No more thinking! No more remembering! God, how she loved Chopin! How she loved his preludes, particularly the twentieth, with its big minor chords, with the solemn, rhythmic beat of the largo. With all those pessimistic phrasings. Speaking so loudly of his desperation. Yes, Chopin's. Even Chopin.

How his music could soothe her! Like a sedative! Like an anesthetic! For, as she played on, her playing made her feel light, giddy. She felt as if she were drifting in a balloon, way beyond the clouds, apart from the world below, freed of everything that was troubling her.

She played on and on, no longer aware of where she was or of the hour. Finally, with the last notes of the prelude fading gracefully, the sorrowful chords still lingering in her head, her fingers came to rest on the keys. How long would her playing hold back the terror? How long would it be before her music would no longer offer her a safe escape? It was like a game of hide and seek. The delicious thrill of hiding within the rapture of her music was always followed by the naked panic of being discovered, of being found out, of giving up her silence.

For a long time, she sat there silently, her fingers still on the keys, her face cast in a death mask, her hollowed cheeks ashen, her slumping mouth cowering with new fear. She hadn't noticed Henry coming into the room until he was right next to her. He had come to question her, as always. Instead of leaving her alone, alone to permit her to calm herself. Alone to permit her to gather her own strength, to let her deal with what she needed to deal with. Alone to permit her to shepherd those ominous thoughts through her consciousness and out of her mind.

Instead, since the Iowa trip, he constantly pressed her, cajoled her with his questioning.

"Why don't you come to bed?" he said to her.

"Why don't you leave me alone?" A little too sharp, she knew at once. After all, it wasn't his fault.

"It's three o'clock in the morning. Why are you playing?"

She shook her head. "Do you have to ask?"

"I can't help it. You woke me."

"Sorry! I'll be quiet. Go back to bed. Get some sleep."

He gazed at her. "What's wrong? What's the matter with you, anyhow? Can't you sleep?"

She bit her lips, trying to hold back her mounting anger. Why couldn't he leave her alone? There he was, prying again. "Can't you see? If I were asleep, would I be here?"

"I'm only trying to help."

"I don't need your help. Why can't you leave me alone?"

"Why are you always so angry with me?"

She buried her face in her hands. "For God's sake, I'm not angry with you!" But, of course, it wasn't the truth. At least not the whole truth. She was angry. She was angry because he was always prying. Trying to dig up the buried past, instead of leaving it alone. She didn't want to know.

Henry, I can't deal with you any longer!

But Henry wouldn't let go. "What is it about me that always makes you so angry? There must be some behavior of mine, maybe some mannerism I'm not aware of, that sets you off."

"Please, not now. Please!" God, how he could irritate her.

"Why not? I can't sleep anyhow."

"I don't know what it is. As soon as I figure it out, I promise you'll be the first to know."

"I don't understand anything any more," he said quietly.

"Why don't you just leave me alone? You *do* understand that's what I want, don't you? Can't you get that into your head?" But she knew him well enough to know that even insults would not drive him off, that he wouldn't leave her alone. Or couldn't. He needed to fix everything, to have everything in order, to be in control at all times.

"Because we can't go on like this."

She did not answer him. Still sitting motionless at the grand, she just stared ahead. Maybe she'd play some more, something quieter. He'd leave eventually. When she lowered her head to find a starting place on the keyboard, her neck muscles tightened into a spasm and her breathing suddenly quickened.

He seemed to have noticed her flinch from the pain. "If we don't know why all this is happening, maybe we should try to find out."

"Why don't you just put me away?" She heard the harshness in her voice, and she looked at him to see how he had received her words. Their eyes met and she felt his pain. He couldn't help the way he was, as she couldn't help the way she was. "This isn't fair to you," she went on with less bitterness. "It isn't fair to the kids. It isn't fair to my unborn child. I realize that." She looked up at him but before he could utter any of his flip assurances, she continued, "I know I belong in an institution. I can't deal with my life any longer. I don't know any more what's going on inside of me. Maybe I'm really going crazy!"

"No, you're not going crazy. And nobody's going to put you in an institution. You need someone to talk to. Someone who can help you understand what's going on inside of you." He reached for her. "Why don't you come to bed?"

Holding on to her elbow, he helped her up. She seemed worn down by his persistence and went along with him.

"Get some rest."

He helped her to bed, but he did not lie down with her. Instead, he sat on the far end of the bed, facing her. "Tell me, whom do I remind you of?" he asked her.

She turned away from him.

"My father? Do you see *him* when you look at me? I *do* look a lot like him, don't I?"

"Why can't you ever leave me alone!" Her mind was spinning. She was losing control. It was always those damned questions. She buried her face in her hands.

"All right, if I must, I must," he said finally.

But, of course, he wouldn't leave her alone. She knew that he was only waiting for another chance to begin probing again. He was always watching her reactions, overruling any reluctance to question her.

"I can't think of anybody other than my father whom I could possibly remind you of."

She could see herself again sitting next to him in the car. Yes, she did not want to look at him.

"It's my father, isn't it? I remind you of my father."

"No!" she screamed at him. "Will you stop it already?" But she knew it was too late. He wouldn't stop.

"My father! Yes! Of course, it's my father!"

"Why can't you ever leave me alone?" she screamed, still fighting the connection he seemed so intent to force on her. "You always want to pry things open. It's like an addiction with you. I don't want to think about certain things. Can't you understand that?"

He didn't listen to her. "Was it when I was overseas, when my parents made you spend those long weekends with them?"

"Stop it! Stop it already!" She screamed through clinched teeth, nearly choking on her heavy breathing. Rolling her head from side to side, she clawed it as though it were ready to burst open, trying to cap the erupting volcano inside. He was pulling the ground right from under her. She was plummeting down a bottomless shaft.

But to Henry everything was clear now. He was connecting effect to cause, understanding the underlying reasons, touching off the recall-triggering mechanism. "Why are you so afraid to think about my father?"

"I don't want to hear any more!" With her eyes popping out of her head, Kitty's face twisted into a monstrous grimace. "Leave me alone!" she screamed. "I don't want to hear any more!"

Henry knew he was on the right track. There was no stopping him now. "Could it be that he tried to make love to you?" Finally, his suspicions were out in the open. Finally.

"Stop it! I tell you, stop it!"

Suddenly Kitty jumped out of bed and ran into the bathroom, locking the door behind her.

He ran after her and pounded on the bathroom door. "Open up!" he yelled. She did not answer him. He heard her open the cabinet and turn on the faucet. He knew at once: Seconals. "Open up!" He pounded on the door. "Open up right now!"

There was only silence.

"Come on, Kitty," he said in a calmer voice. "Stop this foolishness. It's painful for me, too. But we can't run from it forever."

But Kitty's mind was clear now. He had afforded her no respite, allowed her no escape. She needed to take charge of her own life. Be in control again. Make her own decisions without others telling her what to do. Without him making new demands on her. Neither he nor anyone else.

"Kitty, open the door. This is ridiculous. No one's trying to hurt you."

She didn't answer him. There was no point in it. He'd only continue questioning her about things she didn't want to talk about. About things she didn't want to think about. Certain things needed to remain unspoken. Personal things. Painful things. Things that she would never talk about. Never in her life.

She leaned against the sink and stared into the mirror. Was that really her? Her face so out of joint, her hair so unkempt? Oh God, she didn't look like herself! She looked like a stranger! She hardly knew who that was, that person she was looking at in the mirror. God, if it were only possible to start all over again! To be born anew! To be born in some other place! Into a different world! Knowing what she knew now. Making no more mistakes. Well, maybe some. Yes, of course, everyone made some mistakes. It couldn't be helped. But no more mistakes like the ones she had made. Big, frightful mistakes.

All the time Henry waited. On and on he waited. Give her time, he thought, time to settle down. But then, the moment came when something within him told him he had waited long enough. Taking two steps backward, he plunged forward, shoulder foremost, throwing the full weight of his body against the door. The door didn't give. He backed up again, a bit farther back this time and, plunging forward once more, hurled himself against the door even harder. Still the door held. Again and again he threw himself against it until, finally, the frame loosened and the door gave way. But only inches. Kitty's limp body, partly visible behind the door, was blocking it. Pushing hard, he forced her body back inch by inch, far enough to allow him to squeeze through.

There she was, still clutching the empty bottle of Seconals. He took it from her. There were no pills left in it. Four had spilled on the floor. Four out of a dozen. Yes, she had taken eight, pregnant that she was. With his arm reaching under her full belly, he lifted her and made her kneel in front of the toilet bowl. Then, holding her chin in his left palm, his right hand grasping her cheeks, he forced his index finger deep into her throat. She gagged, tried to pull away from him. He forced his finger ever deeper, as far as it would go, until, arching forward, she vomited. One after another, she spit them out, all eight of them. The pills floated in the bowl, a beautiful sight, all of them soft but still intact.

He carried her back to bed, Kitty shivering throughout her body. He covered her with a blanket. When the shivering didn't stop, he spread a second blanket over her and tucked both blankets under her shoulders. He sat down next to her and, holding her hand, he gently stroked her forehead. Little by little, Kitty quieted and the shivering ebbed.

A child, he thought, that's what she really was, a child. A child who had lost all hope. A child who had been terrorized by a cruel tyrant. Frightened to death. Unable to cope any longer. Unable to deal with her world any longer.

When Kitty finally opened her eyes and looked up at Henry, she sighed. "I've done it again." She shook her head. "What's the matter with me, anyhow?"

"You were scared," he said. "I understand."

"No, you don't."

To Henry's amazement, she seemed much calmer than when he had found her playing her Chopin earlier that night. "Everything is all right now," he reassured her. "You're fine and that's all that matters." He did not want to cause any more pain. He wanted to leave her be.

"No, that's not true. I'm not fine at all." She shook her head emphatically.

"Everything's going to be all right."

"No, it won't be."

Henry sighed.

"The next time," she clamped her lips, holding back her feelings, "when I won't be pregnant, you won't stop me."

She was driving a stake into his stomach. Whatever was it that kept her from talking? All he could do was shake his head.

"There'll be a day—and it won't be too far off—when you'll wish you had never bothered with me."

Chapter 20

September 1957

It all happened on a Monday morning. It was a year after Kitty's third child had been born, a girl.

His early appointments canceled, Henry decided to go home. To his great surprise, his father's DeSoto was parked in front of the house. What was he doing at his home? Uninvited. Unannounced. Expecting, of course, that his son would be away at midmorning.

Henry unlocked the front door and quietly slipped inside. An eerie silence greeted him! Not a soul was moving about! He tiptoed through the hall and sneaked past the living room as if back in Normandy, combing the nooks and crannies of a deserted cottage, soaking up the razor-edged vigilance of danger, searching out the enemy, ready to confront him at a moment's notice.

When he came upon the bedroom he was totally unprepared for what met his eyes. There was Kitty, naked, lifeless, sprawled across the bed, her face ashen white, her bottomless eyes staring vacantly at the ceiling.

Grabbing her wrist, he felt her pulse. It beat only faintly. She was still alive.

Suddenly, remembering the DeSoto, he raced back outside. His father was gone. Damn it! Too late! He got away with whatever he'd been doing! His father had heard him! He'd run out the back door!

Henry rushed back to the bedroom and covered Kitty with a blanket. Tucked it in. Then he sat down next to her and placed his palm on her forehead. Her skin felt chilled, clammy. What in heaven's name had he done to her?

"Say something!" he pleaded.

She didn't stir.

"Come on! Speak to me, please!"

She gave no response.

He grasped her hand. Her hand was cold, inert. He raised her arm. The arm felt heavy, leaden. He lifted her leg. The leg was rigid. It would not bend. Her body felt paralyzed. Frozen solid.

"It's me, Kitty!" he pleaded.

For a fleeting moment he saw the flicker of an eye, as if a shadow had shot across her face. He waited. He waited endless seconds, hoping that something more would happen. Some other response. Another sign. But nothing else happened. She just lay there, oblivious to him.

"He's gone! You needn't fear!" he reassured her.

Little by little, he became convinced that she was in a state of conversion hysteria caused by deep anxiety. Her perceived fears had been too great and had been converted into physical form, into what might be called a possum-like defense. Into "playing dead." Into becoming invulnerable to predators.

Suddenly, he noticed a slight parting of her lips and a barely perceptible nod toward her legs. He understood. He began massaging her calves. Soon he worked on her thighs, relaxing the fierce spasms that had caused the rigidity. After a while, he bent her legs. He massaged her arms. Then he carefully bent her arms. He massaged her neck, gently turning her head from side to side, loosening the stiffness. Little by little, he managed to relax all of the inflexible muscles.

She wet her lips. Her eyes turned to him. "He was here," she whispered. She clenched her lips, choking off the deluge like a dam holds back the flooding waters.

"My father!" he said.

She nodded.

"What in hell did he do to you?" He shook his head.

She took a deep breath and sighed.

"I tried to catch him."

Suddenly, she pursed her lips and shook her head. "I can't go on any more!"

"He ran out the back door as I came in the front. I'm certain."

"He's going to kill me!"

"What was he doing here?"

"Please, you must put me away. *Please!*"

"What did he do to you?"

"I belong in an institution. With all the others." She gave a deep sigh. "I'm telling you, he's going to kill me!"

"Nobody's going to kill you."

She shook her head. "I have to get away. Away from it all. That's the only place I'll be safe."

"What did he want from you?"

"Please!"

"I saw his car. Why was he here? I don't understand."

"Why can't you leave me alone?"

"I will. The moment you tell me why he was here."

"I don't want to talk about it." She turned her head away.

"If, after all that's happened, you still believe you can protect yourself by not talking about it, I can only say . . ."

She started to sob. "That's all you ever want to do is talk. I don't want to talk any more. Just leave me alone!"

"Okay! If that's what you want, I'll leave you alone!"

He was angry even though he knew he shouldn't be. After all, it was Kitty who suffered. But one can't solve problems by denying them. He knew that. She had to know that, too.

Nothing more was said between them. Kitty kept on staring at the ceiling, afraid to talk, rock the boat, cause any problems. She just lay there, silently. But after a while, she did speak. "It's all my fault." She shook her head and, turning to Henry, she fastened her eyes on him. "God, you look so much like him."

Yet at the very moment she'd said it, it struck her that his eyes did not hold the same look of scorn, and that his lips did not bear that familiar, demeaning smirk.

"I know I look like him," he nodded.

"No, you really don't." She shook her head. "I don't know why I said it."

"I understand."

"I'm so sorry." She looked at the ceiling, biting her lips. "I've let you down. You have every right to know." Suddenly, she could feel her heart beating faster. What was she doing? Had she lost all of her senses?

"Maybe."

"You have a right to know why your father was here," she continued. Was this really *her* talking? Had she lost all control over what she was saying? "It's just . . . oh, my God . . . I'm so damned scared."

He grasped her hand. "I understand."

She turned away from him. Yes, of course, it was about his father. His own father! How could she ever tell him? "I really can't talk! You must believe me!"

"Why? What are you so afraid of?"

Suddenly, she looked up at him, still uncertain. Then, all at once, seeing that his eyes were kind, not at all threatening, the words just spilled out of her. *"Because he'll kill me!"*

Henry gave only a slight nod, a skeptical nod.

She shook her head. It was just as she had expected. He didn't believe her. *"You must believe me!"* she protested. *"He said so! Please, you must listen to me! He said so, many times!"*

Henry shut his eyes and let his head sag.

Oh God, what was she telling him? He didn't believe her. *"Do you hear what I'm saying? He's tried to kill me! Do you understand that?"* Suddenly her head was seething again with that old, dizzying feeling that came with not being believed. It was like a frail quiver, a quiver as delicate as the intricate weavings of fine filigree, which always filled her with that fragile, tangled lightheadedness.

Oh God, what had she done?

With her mouth twisting, she held back the scream that was edging to the surface. In the end, panting heavily, exhausted from her frightful panic, she let go and emitted a deep, painful sigh. *"I'm so scared!"*

"I know you are."

"I can't go on anymore. You must let me go."

"I won't."

"Please, you must! I beg you, you must! It won't end!"

"It *will* end. I'll see to that."

"No, it won't. There's nothing you can do. There is nothing anyone can do. It will *never* end!"

"It *will!*" He clenched his teeth. "You can count on that!"

"I can't talk anymore. I'm too afraid to talk. To talk about anything. He'll kill me!"

"Is that what he said?"

"Yes! Yes! That's what he said: he'd kill me! He'd kill me if I told you anything, anything at all about what happened, about what he had done."

"During the war?"

"Yes!"

"When I was gone? Overseas?"

"Yes!"

"Is that when it all happened?"

"Yes!"

"I'll get him for this!"

"Oh no, you won't!"

"I will!"

"He'll come back! I know he will. I can't stand it any longer!"

"He won't!"

"Oh no, he will."

He looked at her. He looked right into her eyes. "You must talk. You must talk to me. You must tell me everything. If you don't, I won't be able to do anything. I won't be able to help you."

"But I'm so afraid!"

"If you don't talk, we won't have a chance. His threats will go on and on. I need to know what happened today and all the other times he threatened you." His voice was soft and low. "I need to know what happened during the war."

She closed her eyes and sighed. A deep shudder filled her chest. Yes, there was his face again! Always coming back! That towering rage on his face! His deadly threats. Forever! Oh God, how long was this going to go on? Would the tyranny ever end? No! It would go on and on. It was going to destroy her. She would always see him, right there, right in front of her, in her dark, private vision, threatening her, possessing her.

She shook her head. Something had to happen. Yes, deep down, deep in her heart, she wanted to be free of him. Be released from her prison. Be able to open those weighty, embattled gates of her isolation.

She looked up at Henry. Maybe he was right. Maybe there was a way to stop her father-in-law. "Remember the stairs? The basement stairs? My injured back? The disc? You thought I had fallen? I hadn't fallen. He pushed me. He was the one. Me, pregnant with Susie, my little girl! When Bobby found me, he thought I was dead. Poor kid! It must have scared him to death!"

"Why didn't you tell me? Why didn't Bobby tell me?"

"He ran out just as Bobby came home from school. I was lying at the bottom of the stairs. He threatened Bobby not to tell anyone that he'd been here!"

Henry shook his head. She could tell that it was difficult for him. His own father!

"Was this the first time that he threatened you?"

"No, it wasn't."

Somehow Kitty wasn't afraid any longer. Maybe she had never been that afraid of her father-in-law's threats. Maybe it had been more her fear that Henry wouldn't believe her, wouldn't believe that his own father was capable of such violence, such depravity. Maybe it was also shame, her great shame for not having defended herself more vigorously.

Be that as it may, over the next few weeks her words spilled like throbbing, black lava from an erupting volcano. "He put a knife to my throat!" She clutched her throat to show Henry how he did it. "You're going to die, he said, if you speak one more word to Henry, to anybody!"

Henry stared past her.

"That was his usual way. That's how it all started years ago. Before you had any idea." She turned away from Henry, shaking her head, only half-believing her recall. "Sometimes—"

"What?"

"He rammed a knife into my . . ."

Henry's cheeks were glowing. "Vagina?"

Kitty nodded, biting her lip. "It was awful! I can still feel the blade! Right here, inside of me!"

"What was it that he didn't want you to talk about?"

It was at this point that Kitty began telling Henry everything about visiting his parents over the long weekends when he was overseas, about her abduction to Wisconsin, the rape by his father, the continuing sexual terror, Dr. Martin, the hospital and, finally, the abortion.

Henry could only shake his head. Was all of this really possible? Was it really possible that this man, who had brought life to him, who had raised him, who had sheltered him, was the same man that Kitty was talking about? Could it be that this man, who had always been so self-assured, who had always placed himself beyond criticism, had so completely misused the prerogatives of fatherhood? Could it be that this man, his father, had been so drunk with carnal passion that he had indulged his most barbaric instincts—so much like the Nazis' vilest savageries—to defile and maim his son's bride?

There were weeks and months of questioning, of recall, of detailing, until all of the incidents were laid bare. Only then did

Henry stop his questioning. Only then did he begin to think about ways to punish his father for the rape of his wife, for all the atrocities he had committed to keep her from talking and, at the same time, find ways of protecting Kitty from any further trauma.

Chapter 21

December 1957

Still Henry asked himself, How could this all have been possible? How could his father, any father, have committed such atrocities while his son was fighting for his country?

To dispel any doubts (there are many who question revelations arrived at from so-called repressed or unconscious impulses and anxieties that are used to protect the ego from shame or other unacceptable feelings), Henry made arrangements for Kitty to take a detailed polygraph examination. The polygraph focused on two basic questions: Did his father sexually assault Kitty during the war years? Had he threatened to kill her if she talked about it?

The results were conclusive and dispelled any doubts about what had happened. For Henry it was the final confirmation he needed to confront his father, to try to awaken his conscience to what he had done to Kitty and his son.

"Why, Henry," his father smiled at him auspiciously, "how nice of you to come to see me." He seemed not at all surprised. "Sit down." He pointed to an armchair right across from him and, sitting down himself, he lit a cigar. "How's Kitty?"

"Fine."

"And the kids?"

"They're fine too."

He leaned toward Henry, an earnest look on his face. "You know, in a way, I'm really glad you came. I've been wanting to talk to you, anyway."

"Oh?" His father had wanted to talk to him? "What about?"

"Your wife, Kitty."

"Who? Kitty?" Henry frowned. He had been caught off guard.

"Yes, *your* Kitty!"

Hermann bit his lip, nodding deliberately, even pensively, passing it off for the great distress he felt about what he was going to say. "Even though I haven't seen you for a while—and, by the way, that hasn't been my fault—I've been deeply worried about Kitty. I understand she hasn't been well lately?"

Henry nodded.

"You've had your share of troubles, son."

"What do you mean?"

"I think you know what I mean!"

"I do?"

"To put it bluntly, I think she needs help."

"Help?"

"I don't want you to think of me as interfering in your life, but, after all, you're my son. My only son. Who else do I have to be concerned about," he leaned forward and patted Henry's knee, "if not you?" His sidelong glance was almost benign.

"What do you mean?" Henry repeated.

"What I mean is, simply, that Kitty . . ." He hesitated and, with his lips pursed, simulated great reluctance about what he was about to say. "That Kitty needs a good doctor."

He waited for Henry's reaction. When it didn't come, he continued. "Of course, I understand full well that all of that costs a lot of money."

To Henry, the delight in his father's eyes at making so generous an offer, using his money like a tool to fix things, all things, no matter how troubling the carnage, trying to seduce his son, was really mocking the misery he had caused.

He wanted to hear the rest. "What for?"

"To talk to her."

"What about?"

"Her fabrications."

"Her fabrications?"

"In case you don't know—and apparently you don't—she's been calling me off and on for a long time, asking me to meet her."

"Really? When was that?"

"Well, at least over the last three or four months."

"Why in the world would she want to meet with you?"

He shook his head, raising his eyebrows, feigning surprise at his son's ignorance. "You mean you don't know? You don't know what your wife has been up to?"

"No. Of course not. Why would she call you?"

"To threaten me, of course." He frowned, mirroring total amazement. "What else do you think? Threaten me with the same things that she's been telling you about."

"Who? Kitty?"

"Yes, your Kitty."

"Threaten you with what?"

"Of course, you must know. The same old story. That I attacked her." He raised his eyebrows, incredulous. "Sexually!" He waited. "While you were gone. During the war."

"Really?"

"She called me again. Only a few days ago. That's when I finally decided to get this thing straightened out once and for all."

"And what happened?"

"I went to see her."

"You went to see her?"

"Yes!" He nodded slowly, agonizing over what he was going to say, but also saddened. "She accused me again." He shook his head. "It's really unbelievable." He stared at his son, waiting for him to register equal shock at his words. "She even screamed at me. I must tell you that I think she's gone crazy!" He waited for Henry's reaction. "I didn't want to tell you all this before."

"Oh! I really don't mind." Henry's voice was icy.

"Well," Hermann looked down, trying to gather up his resolve, "and now I must tell you the most shocking part of it all. She told me that it would cost me plenty." He gazed at Henry, his face grim.

"What would cost you plenty?"

"For her to forget." His voice was choking.

"And what did you tell her?"

He took a deep breath. Suddenly, his face reflected a new, steely determination. "Of course I laughed at her. This is all just too ridiculous." He cut his grin short.

"It is?"

"Think about it! If you think about it, you realize how ridiculous it all is." He frowned, cocking his bushy eyebrows. "While you were gone, she was only too happy to see us, both your late mother and me, over the weekends. I was like a father to her. Yes, I was like her own father." He shrugged with disappointment. "The father she never had. As a matter of fact, that's exactly what she told me. Can you believe that? I was like her father! And now," he frowned again, sniffling, holding back emotions, "and now . . ." Suddenly he turned stern, pursing his lips. "After all these years, she has the nerve to accuse me like that? If anything—if there ever was anything wrong—it was *she* who played up to me! Yes, that's right!" He nodded, waiting.

"She did?"

"That's no innocent babe you've got yourself there."

"Really?" What a twist! What a goddam, clever twist, Henry thought. For somebody who didn't know the facts, this could be a damned believable story. He wanted to hear the rest of his father's concoctions. "Why would she play up to you?"

"Money, of course." He nodded. "Money! That's all that she and her mother ever had on their minds."

Henry leaned back. His father, as always, was on the attack. How plausible he made it all sound. Trying to control the world by keeping others on the defensive, off balance.

"What would you say if I told you that Kitty told me her version of this, and I believe *her*?"

"Then you're not well, either." Hermann shook his head. "As your father, I must tell you that you must get her to a doctor before it's too late."

"I see."

"You're taking your chances. I know her family. I know all the circumstances. How she grew up. Her mother's wild parties. The famous 'Merry Widow of Cologne!' Going on vacations with her boyfriends. In those times. In Germany. Taking her young daughters along. What kind of morals do you call that?"

"I see."

"Get her to a doctor. Of course, I understand that costs money. So, if not a doctor . . ."

"What?"

"I hate to tell you this."

"Tell me anyhow!"

"Put her into an institution. It's best for her. It's best for everybody. For you, the kids . . ."

"Really?" These were Reggie's words. Goddamn! Her exact words.

"Yes and, deep down, deep inside of you, you know that I'm right," he continued. "But, of course, I fully understand your predicament, Henry. I know this is not an easy matter for you to consider. After all, she is your wife. If you need any help . . ."

"I don't need your help." He gazed at his father. Their eyes locked. "Kitty is sick all right, and you and I know why!" Henry nodded grimly. "There's no point feeding me all those lies." He watched as his father took another puff on his cigar and smiled at him with that silent, contrived benevolence of his. He needed to confront his father. "You and I know what your intentions were. You know the difference between right and wrong. We both know what you did!" A new assertiveness had grown within him. "If she's sick now, she's sick on account of you. On account of what you did! You're the one who's to blame!"

"Really?"

"Look," suddenly his eyes were hard and full of anger, "let me make something crystal clear. If I ever catch you at my home, or anywhere near it, if I ever catch you threatening Kitty again, I'll beat your brains in!"

The moment he made the threat, he realized how absurd it really was. It was foolish to make a threat he knew he would never carry out! He was not a violent man.

He looked away. He couldn't stand looking at his father any longer. This man who looked like his father but really wasn't. For he had nothing in common with this man sitting across from him! Nothing at all! "I'm not your son! I never was your son! You have no son!" He shook his head but then, suddenly, he looked up and stared at his father, his lips pursed, his eyes blazing. "Just stay away from Kitty! I warn you!"

"Believe me, I have no intentions of ever seeing her again." Then suddenly, with his mien darkening, his chin jutting, he added, "As a matter of fact, I don't want to see you ever again. You just stay away from here, from me."

He had had enough. He was ordering his son out of his house, out of his life. He was, as he had always been, in charge, in control, dealing out punishment like a harsh judge, directing the end of the scene by closing the curtain.

Henry sensed his failure. This wasn't the way to make his father accept responsibility for what he had done. To make amends for threatening Kitty. To make her feel safe. All it earned him was more of his father's scorn and derision. "This is not over yet!" he said.

But it was.

Hermann simply walked out of the room. He had finished with his son and that was that.

Henry should have known. Did he really think that his father's conscience could be awakened?

But Henry, at this point, was much more an emotional animal than a rational one, and where reason argues for one course of action and emotions for another, invariably emotions carry the day. He walked toward the back of the room, where his father had disappeared. "The day you were at my house, I missed you by just one moment," he screamed into the silence. "I promise, I won't miss you again."

He waited. There was no response. Yes, the visit was over.

Chapter 22

March 1958

Yes, he had been naive. He had been the butt of his father's contempt. He should have known better. Known better than to believe he could kindle Hermann's finer feelings. Feelings of moral anguish, of remorse.

What nonsense! What utter nonsense!

Still, his anger controlled him. He couldn't let go of it. He couldn't let his father get away with his lies, his distortions. He must make him face up to them. If he could not make him face up to them in his own court, in his home, he had to find another arena where they would stand as equals.

His next delusion was the belief that if he confronted Hermann in Kitty's presence, his father would have to confess his venality. Which was, of course, totally naive!

For weeks Henry cased his father's movements until, just like a burglar, he was able to pinpoint a suitable moment.

It was raining heavily, which made it easy for Henry to follow his father's car. When Hermann stopped for a red light at the intersection of Pratt and Western, Henry jumped out of his car and before his father realized what was happening, he was sitting next to him. "Pull over," he commanded, "right around the corner!"

The light changed and his father parked the car. "What do you want?" he demanded.

"I want to talk! The three of us, Kitty, you, and me." Kitty was parking just ahead.

"I don't want to hear any more of your asinine accusations." He pulled the keys from the ignition. "I've had enough of them!"

As Hermann opened the door, scrambling to get out, Henry held on to the collar of his jacket. But Hermann yanked so forcefully that he ripped the jacket all the way down the back, freeing himself and leaving Henry holding the empty, torn coat.

Henry jumped out after him, the hard rain soaking him, determined not to be defeated again. "Get back here," he screamed at his father. "I want to talk to you!" When he finally caught up to him, he held him by his arm. Trying to twist himself free, Hermann lost his balance and slipped on the slick pavement, stumbling to his knees.

"Stop it," Kitty screamed as she came running after Henry. "Let him be!"

He stared at the old man kneeling on the sidewalk, drenched from the rain, hoping to escape certain humiliation. He stood there right above him, watching him. He was still watching him when he ran into the street and hailed a taxi. When the door slammed shut and he was gone. When it was all over. When he knew that he had failed again.

Kitty shook her head. "Let him be," she repeated. "It's no good this way."

Henry nodded. She was right. She was saying things that he had known all along. It was no good this way. As he put his arm around Kitty, they slowly walked back to the car.

In the cold light of the next day Henry clearly saw that this sort of senseless, irrational behavior created more problems than it solved. Had he harmed his father, he would have handed him a weapon with which he could have muddied up the accusations

Kitty had made against him and completely changed the terms of the conflict.

Yes, his first task was to act as an advocate for Kitty. After all, she was the one who had paid the highest price for his father's brutality. And Kitty was not ready for a dead-on confrontation with her tormentor.

The most obvious answer came to him: he would bring his father before the bar of justice and force him to answer publicly for what he had done.

Cook County Criminal Court, at 26th Street and California, a huge complex serving the busy Chicago metropolitan area, also housed the State's attorneys' offices, located temporarily in the basement of the main building. With its grimy, flaking walls, with the clanking columns of chained prisoners tramping by and the staff's booming voices shrieking questions and answers across the room, Kitty and Henry, waiting to be called, felt as if they had been thrown into a raucous, chaotic chicken coop.

When they were finally summoned, the elderly attorney barely looked up from his desk. "Make it short," he demanded.

How short? Henry wondered. What few words would be appropriate to explain what his father had done? The pain it had caused. What should be included, what left out, to keep this man listening?

But the lawyer did listen.

"I'll give him a call," he said when Henry and Kitty had finished.

"I want him kept away from my wife, my home."

"I'll call."

"A call won't do it."

"That is the best I can do."

"How about a restraining order?"

"Come on, man, your own father?"

He had not understood. He had not understood anything. Henry shook his head. "Yes, my own father."

Kitty looked at Henry. Give up Henry, she seemed to say.

"What do you want me to do? Maybe you want me to put him in jail? Come on, man, you wouldn't do that to your own father?" the attorney asked.

Yes, of course, this man was a father himself. This case was inconceivable to him. "I guess you didn't understand."

"I understood all right. You want your father put away." He shook his head. "No way!"

Kitty rose. "That's not at all what we wanted." She walked toward the door, then, momentarily she stopped and glanced back at the attorney. "Thank you for listening. Thank you very much, sir." She spoke in a low voice, as always respectful of authority.

Henry followed her out.

There were other lawyers. Their eyes glazed over as Kitty and Henry explained. The rabbi, who talked about God and God's inscrutable ways. The police detective, who only leered at Kitty. Precious months passed. Kitty still lived in daily fear of her father-in-law, that he'd catch her alone, sooner or later, somewhere, somehow, even though Henry had hired a housekeeper and had instructed the neighbors to come to Kitty's aid if the DeSoto appeared.

And so it went until Henry called Leo Leavitt. This publisher of a major chain of metropolitan newspapers, a civic leader in Chicago, was willing to listen.

Kitty told her story. The rape, the threats, her despair. His denials, his countercharges, the polygraph. Their failed attempts at finding a legal remedy.

Her voice quivered with all the telling. She feared, as always, that she wouldn't be believed.

But he believed her. He asked but a few questions. Then, leaning back in his chair, he picked up the phone. "I'm calling a friend of mine, a police sergeant. Sex Offense Investigation Unit," he said.

Kitty lit a cigarette. She leaned back. She sighed. It was a deep, releasing sigh. Suddenly it seemed that the whole world was changing. She could feel it in the pit of her stomach. There were strange, sensuous stirrings as if she were playing Chopin. Yes, that's what she felt: that same delicate tenderness.

She closed her eyes.

Finally, after all these months, after all these disappointments, someone was going to speak, was going to act on her behalf. Someone who believed in the weight, yes, one could even say in the nobility, of truth. Someone who believed in the truth she was speaking. Someone who was willing to stand up to the corrupt and distorting lies of her father-in-law.

Reggie and Eric had come to talk to him. Henry hadn't wanted to meet with them, but they had insisted. Of course, they would talk about Kitty. What could he tell them?

The waitress waited for their orders. They all ordered coffee.

Reggie spoke first. "We hesitated for a long time before we decided to call you." She hadn't changed much. A little fuller, the furrows above her mouth a little deeper, but her lips were still firm and her blue eyes as penetrating and relentless as ever.

Eric shrugged, raised his eyebrows. "I told her repeatedly to leave you alone," he said. "It's none of our business."

"Well, I'm not so sure about that," Reggie continued grimly, turning to Eric. "I'm Kitty's mother and you don't see her the way I do. You really cannot have an opinion."

Henry kept his silence.

"I called Kitty the day before yesterday," she continued. "About noon. She sounded funny. I mean, different. I couldn't tell why at first. It was difficult to understand her. I would have suspected she had been drinking, but I've never known her to drink. She said something about your father. Whatever she said, it wasn't very clear. Something about being terribly scared. She started to cry. She poured forth about 'her poor kids,' who were suffering on account of her. Of course, we all know that! But, mind you, all the time she spoke, I had to keep asking her to repeat herself. Her speech was so slurred. She mumbled her words. It was nearly impossible to understand her."

Henry nodded. Yes, of course, he knew all that. Kitty was scared to death about going to court, the day when she'd have to confront his father. She had misgivings for no other reasons than that they might lose. "What then?" she had demanded of Henry.

"I told her that I'd come over," she continued. "She seemed in such a terrible state. She was very pleased that I would come to see her. Maybe I should have called you first and told you how bad she was. But I didn't want to trouble you. I'm sure you were busy. Besides, what is a mother for?" Again she paused, as if waiting for Henry's permission to go on.

Henry nodded once more. Of course Reggie had to stick her nose into it.

"Anyway, when I arrived at your home and saw Kitty, I nearly fell over. God in heaven, I couldn't believe my own eyes. Maybe it's because I have never seen Kitty in this sort of state. Believe me, I'll never forget that moment when I first saw her. She was still in bed, her hair a mess, hanging in long strands, her eyes out of focus, her jaw drooping, saliva drooling from her mouth. What a sight! What a sight for a mother to see! I hope I'm not shocking you, Henry. But I'm certain you must have seen her like this." She waited for someone to say something.

"Go on," Henry said, flinching at her graphic description, wanting to get it over with.

"She had a difficult time focusing her eyes. She trembled. I asked her whether she was cold, but she said she wasn't. Well," Reggie said, shaking her head, "all I can tell you is that I have never seen my Kitty like this! Of course, I've been familiar with all those sicknesses of hers. She was sick lots of times. And lots of times—and I hate to say this to you again—she concocted her own symptoms. But in all the years I've known my daughter, I never dreamt that anything could be as bad as this." She paused once more, shaking her head.

"I looked for the housekeeper. Apparently she didn't bother with Kitty. That wasn't her job. I can understand that. But I couldn't leave Kitty like that. She had wetted herself. I changed her. It wasn't easy to move her around. She was limp and heavy to lift. She thanked me more than once. She wanted to give me a hug. I let her. All along, she acted like a child. I really don't know what's wrong with her. In all the years, I've never seen her like this."

Reggie started to cry, which wasn't at all like Reggie. She even looked away. Henry felt embarrassed. After all, he felt responsible for Kitty and the way she was. Maybe he should have kept a nurse with her. Maybe going to court was too much for her.

Reggie collected herself and looked up at Henry once more. "You're doing very wrong, Henry," she said. "Kitty does not belong at home. She cannot take care of herself, and certainly she cannot take care of the kids."

"That's why I hired the housekeeper."

"The housekeeper? Is that what she does? Ignore Kitty?"

"I'm doing the best I can. She cooks and she's good to the kids."

"And Kitty?"

"I can't afford a nurse."

Reggie nodded slowly, wistfully. "She might harm herself in this condition. Do you know that?"

"I don't think so," he said. "She's just scared."

"But tell me, what's this about your father? Kitty said that you are going to court against him?"

Henry hadn't expected this turn. Kitty had talked to her mother. "It is difficult to explain." He couldn't make up his mind as to whether he should divulge all that had occurred. And anything less than the whole story could never justify his taking his own father to court. "It's a long story. All I can say is that part of the reason why Kitty is the way she is has to do with my father. But I'd rather tell you some other time."

"Well, whatever it is, I never heard of such a business." Reggie shook her head. "I really don't understand. I don't understand how you could put my daughter through such an ordeal. Going to court against your own father and seeing her in a state like this."

"It will have to be." Henry nodded. Yes, she was blaming him.

"I think you're doing wrong, very wrong." Apparently, she had made up her mind to say whatever she had to say. "I think that you have a responsibility toward your children. They are suffering. Whatever you have against your father, forget it. You're going to kill Kitty by doing what you're doing. It can't be all that important. Sometimes it's better to leave things alone."

"I can't." He looked directly at Reggie. Something in him took offense at the certainty with which she presumed to tell him what was right for his family and, without proper reflection on what he was going to say, he spit out the words. "What would you say if I told you that my father attacked Kitty sexually?"

"I'd say that you're crazy! Do you really believe that? An old man like your father attacking Kitty? You're out of your mind. Is that what you're going to court for?"

"There's more to it," he said, but he knew that he had made a mistake and that to try to explain these matters to Reggie would be hopeless.

"I can just imagine. I bet you have a real good story."

He had to contain his anger. "Well, I'm going to do something about this *real good story*. I'm not going to sit back and let someone threaten Kitty without fighting back. That's the way I am. He is evil, and if I don't fight back, his evil will consume both Kitty and me. This is not only my right but also my obligation."

Eric shook his head. "It's really none of our business."

"Maybe it's none of our business," Reggie agreed, "even though we're Kitty's parents. But let me tell you something. You're doing wrong! You're doing very wrong! You'll find out. You'll find out when it's too late. I know what I'm talking about."

"What do you want me to do?" His curiosity made him ask the question.

"With Kitty?"

"Yes, with Kitty."

"*Put her away!*"

"So you really still think that I should put Kitty away?" Henry asked, challenging Reggie.

"I think it might be the best solution. Think about it. You know that we mean well. Isn't that right, Eric?"

Eric nodded.

"Put her away! How many times have I heard that?" Henry shook his head. "Let's agree that you mean well. I understand how you feel," he conceded. "But I'm not changing my mind about going to court. Too much harm has been done already. I cannot permit my father to prevail. Going to court is the only thing that will heal Kitty, bring her deliverance." He nodded pensively. "I know that it's going to be an ordeal for Kitty, but she's committed to it. All I can ask of you is that you stand by her, no matter what you may think. She needs your support more than ever right now."

Reggie had a blank expression on her face. "I don't know what this is all about. But I had to say what I did. I will not change my mind about it. I don't know what you're doing, but I'll try my best to give you the benefit of the doubt. That's all I can say."

Eric got hold of her elbow. "Let's go," he said.

"All right." Reggie got up and looked at Henry earnestly. "Don't tell Kitty about what I said."

"I won't."

After they left, Henry just sat there and finished his coffee. He wondered if he should have explained more. Or had he already explained too much?

Chapter 23

February 1960

After many delays, the trial was set for 13 February 1960.

When Henry and Kitty arrived on the fifth floor of the Family Court of Cook County on South State Street, it was still early. The frosted, pear-shaped lamps hanging from the tall ceiling threw a pale, somber cast on the few people already in the courtroom. Neither Henry's father nor the lawyers had arrived yet. The clerk was still busy sorting the cases to be called when they sat down on the straight-backed wooden bench, Bobby, their son, between them.

Kitty stared vacantly at the dusky, grayish morning that tinted the lofty windows in drab, dismal hues. What would happen today? Would the turmoil ever end? Would she ever be able to deal with the cloud of uncertainty that was hanging over her? Nothing had ever held together. Everything had always fallen apart. Fallen apart like a house of cards.

She closed her eyes. She was trying to escape the agitation that churned deep inside of her. If she were only able to bring back those beautiful days with Papa! Way back! When she was young. When she felt so safe, so snug, so sheltered. So carefree. When Papa was still with her. When he held her hand. Guided her. Along that river bank. God, where was it again? She shook her head. It was all so familiar. Yes, of course, she remembered, it was at the spa: Bad Ems. Strolling beneath those *Linden* trees. Along the clear, rippling waters of the River Ahr. On that beautiful, sparkling day in summer.

But then, abruptly, the daydream ended. As always, she was left standing alone. She was left standing alone on the path, beneath those *Linden* trees. The Ahr still rushing by. Papa's face slowly fading into the distance. She, standing there, a little girl. Frightened. Looking for her Papa. Everywhere. Left and right, up and down. Trying not to cry. Trying not to let anyone know about her mortal fears.

She opened her eyes. For a moment she didn't remember where she was. Yes, she was in court. She was holding on to Bobby's hand. At once, she gazed at her son, squeezed his hand, and put on a small smile. Oh, my God, why did he have to be here? So young! Much too young! Only twelve! Clutching her hand, sitting next to her, so silent, so bewildered. Holding on to her just like she had held on to Papa's hand.

What would he think of her in years to come? What could she ever say to him? Taking him to court to bear witness against his grandfather?

Within the labyrinth of her mind, within her agitated, desolate heart, she listened to the whispers coming from deep inside of her. What will happen to me? To my family?

She was certain that Henry was as shaken as she, feeling as inadequate as she, for they were risking the disapproval of their friends, their elders. What if the court didn't rule in their favor?

"We shouldn't have come," she murmured, biting her lips, shaking her head, staring out the window.

Henry didn't answer.

She turned to him. "Say something, please!" Her voice was aquiver with all of her deep doubts. "Don't you agree that we've done wrong?"

"No, we haven't." Henry looked away from her. For him, this was not the time to doubt. The words only reminded him of

Reggie's warnings. Wouldn't these proceedings prove too much for Kitty? The court, her son, her recollections?

They arrived slowly. First, there was Henry's father. Then his lawyer. Then some of his friends. One of Henry's cousins.
What were they all doing here?
When Jayson Burroughs, their lawyer, arrived, he sat down next to Kitty. "How are you doing?" he asked.
"Fine," she lied.
"And Bobby?"
She looked at Bobby. "Okay."
"We won't need him." He patted Bobby's knee.
"No?"
"He did well. The judge read the transcripts of the pretrial consultations and he is satisfied. There won't be any problems."
"You mean we didn't have to bring Bobby?"
"No. They take great stock in their psychological services here in family court." He shrugged. "I'm sorry, but I didn't know till just a few minutes ago."
She stroked Bobby's head, holding back her tears. "It hasn't been easy," she said.
Jayson looked at Hermann. "See that! All his friends. Witnesses to his character!"
"His character?"
"It won't mean a thing."
"What?"
"His friends. The relatives. It's all cut and dried." He nodded.
Suddenly, Jayson's words brought forth a cathartic clarity to Kitty's raging ambivalence: this powerful, seemingly omnipotent man, her father-in-law, who had abused her with apparent impunity, couldn't face her by himself. That's why he had brought all of his friends. *He actually feared her!* He feared her accusations! He feared the truth of her words!
She glanced around the courtroom and, suddenly, everything seemed different. She stared at her father-in-law, his

new wife, all of his friends, sitting right there in front of her, close to the judge's bench, and dared them to turn around and look at her. She *knew* that the truth was with her and that her father-in-law would fail, in spite of all his friends!

For a moment she could barely suppress a smile, believing, as she had never believed before, that maybe this was going to be the end! That maybe she would never again be in terror at the sound of his car, at the sound of his voice. That maybe she would never again have to live in fear of him.

But, of course, no one turned to look at her.

Finally, the case was called. Loud and clear. "State of Illinois, Plaintiff, versus Hermann Morgenthal, Defendant."

He was there first, in front of the judge, with his wife, four of his friends, and his lawyer. Kitty and Henry came up on the left, slightly to the rear of Jayson Burroughs.

Kitty was sworn in by the clerk. Her father-in-law was sworn in. This was for real.

The clerk retired. The judge looked up from the papers he had just been reading. Kitty watched closely as he addressed himself to her father-in-law's lawyer. "Who are all these people?"

"Witnesses, your Honor."

"To the facts?"

"To the accused's character."

"We don't need them." The judge looked down at his papers to avoid any further dialogue with the defendant's lawyer.

The witnesses went back to their seats.

"Will the counselors please step to the bench!" He glanced at the two lawyers in turn. They stepped forward. He leaned over to be at eye level with them. They all talked for a minute. Then the lawyers stepped back, nodding.

"In view of the nature of this case and in light of precedents I have cited to the attorneys, I would like the two parties to agree to a psychological evaluation of themselves by the court's Psychiatric Department."

The judge turned to Kitty, then to Jayson Burroughs. He nodded. Kitty nodded. Then he looked at the defendant, who turned to his lawyer. They whispered. His lawyer nodded. "We will continue . . ."

The defendant's lawyer stepped up to the bench. "Your Honor, may I address the court?"

"Go ahead," the judge nodded.

"Your Honor, my client feels that due to the false allegations made against him by his son and daughter-in-law, allegations which by their very nature impugn his character as both a father and as a respected citizen of this community, the psychiatric examination should include his son. Clearly, when such grave accusations are made by a son, whom my client nurtured and sheltered for most of his life, the basis of these accusations should be questioned and tested by an equally thorough evaluation of his character, such as is being asked of the father. May I submit this to the court for consideration?"

There was silence. Conceivably this was a maneuver for dismissal, based on an expectation that Henry would refuse. It could also be an effort to change the terms of the conflict, from one in which an older man is accused of having taken advantage of his daughter-in-law to one between a giving father and an ingrate son.

"May I remind counselor that the charges have been brought not by the son but by the daughter-in-law."

"I am fully aware of that, your Honor. Yet, may I suggest that it was upon the son's insistence that these charges were entered. I would also like to point out that he was fully aware of his wife's mental state, her confinement to a hospital for a nervous collapse, her continuous psychiatric treatment, which has been going on for many years, her fabrications that on many occasions even he was aware of, and the previous accusations against his father, which were admittedly false."

They're trying hard, Henry thought. Even engaging in exaggerations and clear falsehoods.

"Your Honor," his lawyer continued, "I could go on and on. This is an obvious attempt by the son to discredit his father. I'm not clear for what reasons. It is inconceivable to permit these charges to go forward based only on the word of such a mentally disturbed complainant. If you will agree, I strongly urge that your Honor dismiss them, considering the mental state of the complainant. For I believe that the psychiatric examination will reveal that the real conflict here is between father and son, and that the daughter-in-law is only the instrument of revenge."

The judge turned directly to Henry's father, the defendant. "I do not understand your objections to the evaluations the court has proposed. If the contentions of your counselor are true, certainly the evaluations will bear him out. If they are not true, the state and the complainant are fully entitled to file these charges and be heard." Now the judge bent his gaze on the attorney. "Certainly, any charges made by the defendant's son, or any influence that he exerted on his wife, however decisive this influence may have been in inducing her to file the complaint, are irrelevant to a determination on the merits of the complaint. Motion denied."

The judge turned to the clerk and consulted with him on the date of the continuance. Then he checked with the two lawyers. They all agreed on a date.

The clerk called the next case. It was all over, at least for the time being. Kitty took a deep breath and held it. The expected sigh did not come.

Two months later Kitty stood once again before the same judge. Jayson Burroughs had already indicated that the psychological report on her father-in-law had been affirmative: subliminal sexual preoccupation with strong perversive tendencies, enough to convict him. But, he pointed out, that in light of his age and of the fact that he had no criminal record, most likely he would not be incarcerated.

The judge pronounced the sentence: "Hermann Morgenthal, defendant, you are placed under the court's supervision for a period of one year." Then he addressed Kitty: "If, at any time during the period of one year, you are molested or threatened by the defendant, Hermann Morgenthal, you are to report to the court immediately. Do you understand?"

She nodded to the judge.

When Kitty turned away, her eyes were watery and, locking her arms around Henry's neck, she drew him close to her. "We've done it!" she said to him.

Downstairs, outside in front of the courthouse, Kitty looked up at the overcast sky. She shook her head. She still could not quite believe her good fortune. It had happened. The impossible had happened. They had won! She needn't fear her father-in-law any longer.

All at once, as the sun spun free from behind the fast-moving clouds, Kitty grasped Henry's hand and, with tears streaming down her cheeks, she shouted out loud for all the world to hear. "Everything has an ending! Thank you, God!"

Chapter 24

April 1962

It was now a little over two years since Kitty had been in court. Court supervision had worked. No one had bothered her, no one had threatened her, and gradually, over the course of the two years, she became confident that no one would.

The extent of the change that had come over her was really amazing. Her brittle smile had turned into hearty laughter, her hesitant gait had grown into a resolute stride, and her timid, characterless glance had changed into a steady, fixed gaze. Her friends could hardly believe that this was the same Kitty they had known all along.

Henry was delighted to hear outside confirmation of this transition, even though, in his own mind, knowing Kitty the way he did, he wasn't at all certain that her recalls had been completed, that her past had been conquered. He still wondered about Reggie and Kitty's sister, Ruth. How much of Kitty's past had been written by them?

He asked her anyhow. "Now that you've erased your great fears, what do you want to do with the rest of your life?"

Kitty hesitated. "My kids! I want to get to know my kids." Her eyes watered. "They've only known their mother as a sick person."

Henry nodded. "What else?"

"I want to have friends. Lots of friends," she replied, shaking her head. "I don't want to be alone any longer." Tears started to flow, but she quickly shrouded her feelings. "I want to forget. I never want to think of my past again." She bit her lips. "That horrible, lonely past of mine." She turned away from Henry, tears running now down her cheeks. After a while she turned back. "I want to help others. Others that are like I was: trusting, unsuspecting, so vulnerable." Her voice quivered. "I must tell them. Tell them about my life. Tell them about hope. Tell them that they too can make it. That as badly as they might feel about themselves, things *can* get better."

Each week Kitty volunteered a day at Dunning State Hospital at Irving Park Road and Narragansett, an asylum made up of a dozen red brick buildings dating from the turn of the century, housing thousands of mentally ill, held there with minimal care for most of their lives. It was her turn to help.

Nora couldn't be more than seventeen, maybe eighteen at most, not pretty, but at the same time, with no distorting features. A plain girl. Could have been a farm girl of the twenties.

Nora came up to Kitty, her hair uncombed, her lower lip hanging, her eyes unfocused. "Ma!"

Kitty embraced the young girl with much passion, held her close, stroked her hair. "It's all right, Nora."

Kitty's heart overflowed with compassion. Yes, it could have been her. How hopeless it was for Nora. Dunning! To be at Dunning was like giving up. Just like herself! "Put me away," she had said. How often had she said it! Yes, of course, she had been ready to give up, too. If only she could help Nora understand. Help her understand that things can get better! A lot better! That one must try. In spite of everything.

They sat down at a table, across from each other. "How've you been doing, Nora?"

Nora tossed her head to the side and gave a broad grin, which seemed rather odd. It was more like a grimace. There was a ghost lurking behind her facade. "All right."

Nora was catatonic. A hopeless case, they had said. "What have you been doing?"

Nora slowly turned her head away from Kitty, as if she were taking no interest in being talked to. She looked toward the wall. "Nothing."

Kitty grasped Nora's hands and held on to them, shaking her head. "Nora, you must try."

Nora looked down, her head not moving.

Lowering her own head, Kitty tried to meet Nora's eyes. "Nora, please, you must try!"

Nora did not respond. She kept on staring at the ground. She was spiritless, sullen.

Oh God, why doesn't someone do something! Nora was shutting herself off from everyone. "Does anyone come see you?" Nora had a mother.

Nora shook her head stolidly.

"No one?"

She shook her head once more.

Kitty looked away. What could she do with the girl? Nora was in her own prison. She was cut off from the world, stricken with despair. Yes, of course, she was catatonic.

Standing up, she took Nora's hand. "Come on, Nora, let's take a walk. Let's get your coat."

She walked over to Nora's bunk and helped her with her coat. Then she put on her own coat.

Outside, the sun was bright but the air was chilled. They walked along the wide path that twisted between the red brick buildings, Kitty holding on to Nora's hand. Every so often her head turned to the girl. She didn't know what to say to her to bring her out. To break that shell and open her up.

All along, the stoic expression on Nora's face did not change. Of course, she thought, Nora was afraid! She was closing it all in. Afraid to find out about her hidden secrets! Like she had been. Yes, it was all so familiar.

God, how lucky she was.

When they returned to the quarters, she gave Nora another hug. She held on to her for a long time. For an instant she felt her shriveling, shrinking. It was something. Nora had felt something. Then, suddenly, Nora turned and, dragging her feet, with her eyes riveted to the floor, she snuck away from her, not saying anything.

"Bye, Nora," she called after her.

But Nora did not hear her.

Kitty stood there. She was waiting for something more to happen. She had felt Nora's deep isolation, her unvoiced pain. She had also felt her own helplessness in the face of it.

Finally, she buttoned her coat, put on her gloves, and turned up the collar. She looked out into the distance, puzzled, shaking her head. What was it all about? What was this world all about?

As she trod along the path that wound between the red brick buildings, she could still feel herself shaking her head. She was so mixed up. She did not know where she was going. Nothing made sense any more.

Then, suddenly, her mind cleared. No matter what, one must try. She knew that. One must try one's best. Otherwise, there was no hope. There was no hope at all.

Kitty became involved in the Peace Movement at the time when the Cuban Missile Crisis nearly brought the Soviet Union and the United States to war. It was only natural that she would work for peace. Well aware of the capacity for hatred and violence among her fellow humans, she was convinced that a better world could be forged only if people of good will stood together.

She had become a woman with a mission. She stood on street corners handing out leaflets, she joined in protest marches, arm-in-arm with her fellow dissenters, she argued the cause of peace, even though her convictions were often ridiculed. Nothing and no one could hold her back. She continued even though her efforts were often characterized as naive, her ardor mocked, and "peaceniks" became the butt of comedians' jokes.

In late October 1962, Kitty was asked to give a recital at a large peace rally at Chicago's McCormick Place. The hall was filled to capacity that night. Nearly two thousand people, the Voters for Peace, had gathered to promote their candidates in the upcoming elections.

That night, when she walked onstage in her black, tight-waisted, bell-shaped taffeta dress, a lonely strand of pearls dangling from her neck, her hair up in a French twist, there was an overflowing, exuberant intensity in her face. She looked strikingly fit. She didn't look like a woman who had once been severely disabled by mental illness.

When she sat down at the grand, she turned to the audience and smiled. Then, looking to the ceiling, collecting herself, she waited for the deepening silence. After a few moments, one could hear a pin drop. She began to play Schubert's "Impromptu," his Opus 90, No. 4.

On that night, her touch was so light, so easy, and she played with such effervescence that the scales cascaded like waterfalls. On that night her music was like a joyous celebration, a conquest of sorts, not of anything tangible, but of the spirit, her own spirit. Yes, she had finally come home again. She had come home to what she once was and had been all along.

When she finished, the audience broke into wild applause, so deeply felt was the consonance between this artist and her audience. For she was one of them, a kindred spirit. But it was also clear to all that here was a talent well beyond what they had expected.

She encored with a waltz, a waltz from her past. Lehar's "Merry Widow Waltz." She closed her eyes and her head swayed ever so slightly with the joyful rhythm of the music, the delirious three-quarter beat of the waltz. It was so much fun. It was so much fun to be what she had always wanted to be and now was.

When she finished and curtsied, her face was flushed. Norman Thomas, the old-time Socialist, a tall, gaunt man, came over to greet her. "I want to thank you for all of us. It was a marvelous performance." He held her hand. She blushed deeply, unaccustomed to accolades. For a moment, she thought of Henry Woods. He had the same kind eyes. She was barely able to voice a "Thank you, Sir."

It was an evening she would never forget. She said later that it was the happiest day of her life. As she would put it, she took that evening as her "welcome back."

"It was a marvelous performance, and I'm so very happy for you," Henry said later on. "Please, tell me, why did you choose a piece so much associated with your mother for an encore?"

"I don't care. It doesn't matter any longer. I've always loved that waltz."

Chapter 25

July 1964

In spite of her flirtation with happiness on that wonderful night, little by little Kitty's health gave way. She was not yet ready for the vigorous life she had chosen for herself, the pressing effort, the total commitment. Little by little, she turned to doctors and drugs. She tried to do for her body what a little more common sense about her obvious limits might have accomplished more easily.

"Why are you pushing yourself so hard?" Henry reproached her.

"Because I must."

"Why, in the name of God, can't you take a break from it all?"

She looked away from him.

"Why is it necessary to outdo yourself? Didn't we have enough trouble? Do you have to bring about more?"

Old patterns of recrimination triggered old responses. "Why don't you just get rid of me," she answered bitterly. "I'm no good for anybody. I'll only cause you more trouble. I've always caused trouble. For everybody. Why don't you put me away? I know where I belong."

Oh, how familiar these words were. Kitty lapsing into her former mode. Surrendering, defusing any criticism by deprecating herself.

Henry tried to resist her attempt to obscure the issue by imposing cold reason on her impulsive excesses. "Just slow it!" he said. "I'm not asking you to give up on your tasks. Slow down. You can do more by doing less. By conserving your strength you can choose what really needs to be done, and do these things more consistently, over a longer period of time."

"I can't slow down. There isn't enough time. I can't stop myself. What am I to do?" She hung her head. It was all too much. The pain, her disappointment. His harsh censure. "If I can't live the way I want to live, if I have to treat myself like an invalid, then life is hardly worth it."

"All I ask of you is that you slow down."

"Go ahead and criticize me. You have every right to do it. I deserve it. I don't take care of anything. I don't take care of you. I don't take care of the kids. I don't deserve to live."

"I'm sorry," was all Henry could say. Though he recognized that he might have gone too far in his criticism, he remained certain that he had not been altogether wrong to raise the issue. To simply protect her feelings at this time would have been dishonest. He had to try to get her to understand what she was putting at risk.

Finally Kitty turned to Henry, her eyes tearing. "I don't know what's the matter with me," she said to him quietly. "It's just that I want to live so badly right now. I can't stop myself. I can't go back to lying around waiting for something to happen." She bit her lip and shook her head. "If I can't live a real life, I'd rather die."

She was being dramatic. But was she also being prophetic?

It all started so suddenly. The 107-degree fever continued for three days. There had been no prior complaints, no accompanying symptoms. As Kitty remained delirious, beyond their reach, the doctors were mystified. She was too sick to be taken to a hospital in the frigid Chicago winter. All that could be done was to wrap her in ice packs, give her alcohol rubs, and feed her saltwater.

All this brought no response from Kitty. Her condition seemed hopeless.

Then the fever broke as suddenly as it had begun. The end of the fever did not mean the end of Kitty's illness. When she was finally taken to the hospital, she began to shiver with severe chills as one does with malaria, though she did not have malaria. In fact, there were no causes for the fever or the shivering that the assembled doctors could identify.

Henry sat at her bedside. Kitty, her face ashen, her eyes leaden, blankets up to her chin, stared vacantly at the ceiling.

He grasped her hand. "You had us worried."

She kept a stoic silence.

"I'm glad you're feeling better."

She turned her head away. She was in no mood to talk.

"I'll be quiet," he relented.

After a while, her head turned back and she stared at the ceiling once more. She was clearly upset. Henry studied her face for some sign of recognition. But there was no response.

When the nurse came into the room, she greeted Henry. "You're her husband?"

Henry nodded.

She felt Kitty's pulse, took her temperature, checked her breathing. Then she placed her hand on Kitty's forehead as if she hadn't trusted the thermometer. "You're doing fine," she said, "much better."

As she left the room, she beckoned Henry toward the door. "Outside," she whispered.

He followed her.

"Is your wife German?" she asked.

"Yes."

"I don't know what's wrong with her."

"Yes?"

"She screamed a lot in German."

"When was this?"

"Early this morning, after we changed shifts. I understand that she screamed all night. Even with the sedation. She's quiet now. I guess she's exhausted. Something's upsetting her."

"What did she scream?"

"She kept throwing her head back and forth, and screamed 'Nein . . . nein . . . nein!' over and over again."

Henry shook his head.

"She flailed her arms as if she were trying to ward off somebody."

"She did?"

"Yes."

"Anything else?"

"I tried to figure it out. She cowered in the corner of the bed, quaking, shaking like a leaf. Tossing her head wildly, fighting off something or somebody. I can't imagine what or whom. She seemed terribly frightened. She screamed hysterically like a little girl. It was difficult to understand. She screamed something that sounded like 'Gay vek!'"

"You mean *Geh weg!* (Go away!)"

"Yes, that's what it sounded like. Oh, it was so awful to hear her and not to be able to do anything."

"I know."

"At least her chills have stopped now. She's quiet. I'm so sorry. I feel so sorry for her. She must have had a bad time of it."

Henry nodded. "Yes."

"You'd never know."

He nodded.

"Such a pretty woman."

"I really appreciate your help."

"It was nothing. I'm only too glad to be of some help." She shook her head. "I wish I could have done more."

"Thank you so much."

As if standing at the shore of Loch Ness, waiting for the mysterious sea monster to come into view, Henry, his heart pounding with dire forebodings, wondered what was next in the endless sequence of Kitty's dark secrets.

He didn't have to wait long. The high fever, like a sudden spring thaw, had melted the cryogenic tomb of Kitty's unconscious. Over the next several months, after she had recovered from her puzzling illness, Kitty was able to recall her wretched days in Dachau.

For a long twenty-seven years, Dachau had remained repressed within the deep, unfathomable corridors of her mind. The legacy of her release, her mother's specious recriminations upon her return to Cologne, had served to silence Kitty. It had not produced the healing catharsis that most survivors went through upon their return: the telling of the cruelty and violence committed in the camps. Instead, she had experienced only greater disapproval, causing her to drift ever farther away from what should have been a supportive family.

"I should have left and let you worry about yourself." How well she remembered her mother's words.

During long months of analysis, Kitty retraced the abuse by the SS, the gang rapes and penile mutilation at Dachau, the brutal killing of Lore and later of Margot, her constant fear of abandonment, the lonely struggle to reach home—bringing back all of the old terrors. Detail by detail, with the reliving of each event, she was able to unburden herself of these fearful memories and find a cathartic easing within herself.

Once more, Kitty tried to resume her place in the world, as a mother, as a wife, and as a friend. Yet, like an apple hanging too long on a tree and gone bad, finally falling to earth, Kitty was shunned after her recovery from her lengthy, puzzling ailment. Her "apparent" recovery seemed doubtful considering her frequent relapses, and the subject of her disturbance seemed too far removed in time to evoke much compassion. More and more, she found herself an outsider and, rejected by her former friends, her disposition grew more sullen and despairing.

Wearing a tailored, gold-embroidered jacket, Kitty moved around the ballroom, held securely in Henry's arms. She hadn't danced for such a long time. With her face still ashen, her lips painted a deep plumrose red, her vacant smile pretended a gaiety that was far beyond her reach.

"Didn't the bride look beautiful?" she whispered into Henry's ear, eager to engage him in light-minded conversation.

"Yes, she did," he replied.

"It was good of Annette to invite us."

"Yes, it was."

There hadn't been many invitations. It had been a long time since they had danced at a party, especially at a wedding.

Someone called out. "Hey, Kitty!"

Kitty turned her head.

"How are ya', Kitty?"

"Fine." Kitty stopped dancing. "How are you, Bea?"

"All right." Bea gaped at Kitty, frowning. "Haven't seen you around much lately."

"I haven't felt too well."

"Really?" Bea acted surprised. "What's the matter with you?"

Bea's question shook her up. She'd have to explain. She'd have to explain about her past. There were always questions, questions that deserved answers. It was like going on trial. Jurors gaping at her, judging her. Jurors not believing her, thinking she was delusional, crazy, her memory false.

She took a small step backward. "Back trouble." It was an easy answer.

"Oh?" For some reason Bea suddenly turned to Henry. "So, why don't you see a doctor?"

"I have." Damn it, Bea, shut up already! Stop asking your stupid questions! Go away!

"So? What does he do for you?"

"Tells me to get off my feet."

"He does? Is that all? Is that all he does for you?" Raising her eyebrows, she waited for Kitty's answer. Then she continued anyway. "You should go and see a specialist, an orthopedic man. There might be something wrong with one of your discs. Don't you think so?" Her glance shifted again to Henry, but she didn't wait for an answer before turning back to Kitty. "I have a good friend who had a slipped disc. Mind you, she carried on for months, not knowing what was wrong with her. Just laid there in bed all the time, crying her heart out. Then, finally, she went to a specialist, a top man, you'd know him if I told you his name . . ." She turned to her husband. "Art, what's his name?" But she did not wait for his answer. "Never mind. Anyway, this man put her into traction for ten days, or—I don't remember, it might have been longer—very painful, I mean the stretching—and then he put her in a plaster cast. It sounds horrible, I know, but she's as good as new. We played bridge the other day and she told me that she never felt this good in all her life. It's marvelous what those doctors can do today."

"Yes." Kitty nodded, leaning against Henry.

"Anyway, I wish you would see this man, Kitty. I'll remember his name. For sure. I'll let you know. By the way, how are the kids? We loved having them over for supper last week. They're growing up so fast."

"Oh, thank you," Kitty smiled, lost for an answer. "They really should have told me."

"Oh, never mind. They're welcome anytime. They're so well-behaved. Anyway, have a good time tonight. Don't overdo it. Show yourself sometime, Kitty. Okay?"

"Yes," Kitty nodded.

When Bea was gone, Kitty sighed deeply. "Oh, honey," she said to Henry, "sometimes I just can't take it any longer. I wish the world would go away. God, how I wish it would go away forever."

But for Kitty, the world didn't go away.

Chapter 26

January 1965

One late afternoon in January 1965, Kitty, resting in bed, asked for Susie, her youngest child, now eight years old. Susie was a quiet young girl, who mostly knew her mother as a bedridden invalid who rarely functioned as a caring parent.

"I want to hold her," Kitty said to Henry. "Please, let me hold my little girl."

When Susie lay down next to her mother, with her back toward her, Kitty reached around the child with her meager arms and held on to her with all her might. Susie gazed up at Henry, who was standing at the side of the bed, her wide-open eyes apprehensive. Kitty must have seemed incoherent, maybe even delirious, and Susie was clearly frightened.

Suddenly, Kitty broke into deep sobs, squeezing Susie with so much might, unaware that she might hurt the child, that Henry couldn't help but free the frightened girl from her mother's grip. As soon as he did, the child fled the room.

It was at that moment that an all too obvious thought passed through Kitty's mind. Here was Susie, her young daughter, at the very age at which she had suffered one of her greatest adversities: the tragic death of her father. Abandoned by her own mother, Kitty now saw herself as an equally inadequate mother, unable to fulfill even the minimum needs of her own daughter.

Copious tears started to pour down her cheeks. She shook her head in disbelief and finally slumped onto her back. "I've lost her! I've lost her, too! I've lost her like I've lost everything else!"

Henry sat down next to her. "No, you haven't." He took the corner of the sheet and wiped her tears. "She's too young. She doesn't yet understand."

"She does! She understands too well! My God, what have I done?"

Henry stared ahead. "You expect too much."

"What I wanted most in my life was not to fail my own child."

"I know."

"I want my little girl!" It was a thin whimper, like that of a child.

"Yes, I know."

"I want her!" She stared at Henry, her eyes pleading. "Please!"

"Of course you want her."

"Give her to me!"

He sighed. "Susie doesn't understand."

"Why can't I have her?"

"She's too young."

"Oh God, I know!" She started to sob again, turning away from Henry, nodding. "I know so well! I've failed her, just like my mother failed me."

"That's not true."

Her child had been torn away from her. Didn't anybody understand what this meant? She didn't know her own mother. Too frightened to be with her. She was a mother, and this was her child!

"I was her age."

"Yes."

"I was her age once."

He nodded.

"I had a mother." Suddenly, she held her breath and, shaking her head wildly, her eyes popped wide open. *"Oh, my God!"*

"What?"

"Oh, my God!" She tried to lift her head, but try as she might, she couldn't. "Please, I must go!" But something was holding her back.

"What?"

"Oh, my God!"

"What is it?"

"Why can't they ever leave me in peace?" Her breathing came in staccato gulps.

"They?"

"All of them."

"All of them?"

"I want to end it all." She held her mouth.

"End what?"

"Please, God in heaven, please, I want to die."

Henry grasped her hand, but she tore it away from him.

"Why won't it ever end?"

He could only shake his head. He didn't know anymore what was going on.

"Why can't they leave me alone?" Her breathing finally slowed.

"Who?"

"They!" She looked away from Henry.

"Who are they?"

"Why can't they let me be?" Her voice slowly faded.

He stroked her forehead. "They?"

Suddenly, her sobbing stopped. Her face relaxed and saddened. Her eyes opened wide. She was confronted by the truth. The truth that had been so long in hiding. *"She killed him!"*

"What are you talking about?"

"Yes, she killed him!"

"Who?"

"Papa!" She was revisiting a moment she had long forgotten.

"Your father?"

"Yes!"

He shook his head. "I know you saw her strike him, and I know you believe he died from that blow."

"No!" She looked up at Henry. "Don't you hear me?" She shook her head. "She killed him! She did! Not with that blow. Later on, while he was in bed."

"What do you mean?"

Suddenly Kitty's jaw dropped, her cheeks collapsed. She covered her mouth and stared ahead vacantly. She couldn't believe her own words.

Finally, she spoke again. "I watched it all. I watched everything." She sighed, shaking her head. "How could I have ever forgotten it? I can see her face. It's all so clear now. I have no doubt about it. I can see it all as if it happened yesterday. As if I were there again."

"You can?"

She shook her head slowly. "I didn't do anything."

"What?"

"I let her do it!" She gave a deep sigh.

"Do what?"

She bit her lips. "I heard his loud, hoarse moan. It sounded like . . . like what? . . . yes, like a cow mooing. I heard it all the way up in my bedroom. God, I was so young. I was so scared. I didn't know what it meant. I tiptoed down the stairs all the way to his bedroom. It was so dark in the big house. I waited by the door. That's when I heard the moaning again. It was not as loud this time. It came from inside—inside his bedroom. I waited some more. There, there I heard it again. I pressed down on the handle and pushed the door open just a little bit. I couldn't see anything. Then, all of a sudden, I heard the moaning again. This time much louder. Much clearer. Much worse. But I still couldn't see anything. Only the night light by the bed. Then, all at once, I stuck my head through the door."

"Oh, no! My God!"

Kitty held her breath, her hand covering her mouth. She could see it all so clearly. *"Get away from him!"* Suddenly, her voice shrunk, turned timid, like that of a little girl. *"What are you doing, Mama? What are you doing to Papa?"*

"What was she doing?"

"The pillow . . ." she said, swallowing hard. "It's the pillow. She presses down on the pillow."

"What?"

"His arms . . . his arms are beating the air." Kitty looked away from Henry and sighed.

Even though thirty-three years had passed, Kitty's recall was as graphic as if it had only happened yesterday.

"I didn't say anything. I didn't do anything. I just stood there watching it all happen." She shook her head, staring ahead. "I'm such a coward. I'm such a damned coward." She kept on shaking her head. "I never said anything! I never did anything! Nothing! I did nothing at all!"

Henry sat there, totally stunned, hearing all about the murder of Kitty's father.

Finally, Kitty spoke again. "I didn't say anything. I didn't do anything. I just stood there, my head through the door, watching, letting it all happen."

"But you were so young! You were only a child! There was nothing you could have done. Nothing in the world."

"I could have tried. I could have tried to save him." She pounded the bed, crying out loud. *"Papa! Oh, Papa, I let you die!"*

"No, that's not true."

"I'm so ashamed of myself."

"You were so young."

"I let him die!" Kitty shook her head. "Why didn't I say something? I just stood there at the door, watching it all happen." She bit her lips. "I was still standing at the door when the moaning stopped. When there were no more sounds. When Mama placed his head back on the pillow. His face was ashen-white. His eyes so big. His lips so pale."

"But you were only eight."

"She finally turned around and saw me."

"She did?"

"Yes."

"And?"

"I can see her face again. Her face was full of rage."

"Yes?"

"I still see that face. It is the same face that I've seen all these years."

"Her face?"

"Yes! That was the time when I first saw that rage in her face, that hate. She was furious with me! Why didn't I recognize it? Why didn't I remember what that face was saying to me?" Suddenly, Kitty held on to her breath. With her eyes wide open, her mouth ajar, she stared at Henry. "Do you know what it was saying to me?"

Henry shook his head.

"Shut your mouth, if you know what's good for you! That was the message on her face. That was the message it always had for me."

Henry nodded.

"Oh God, that horrible face of hers! Whenever she looked at me, I became so frightened. I always did. All those years. I didn't understand it until right now." Kitty nodded, her fingers to her lips. "Yes, it's true. It was that face that should have reminded me."

"Reminded you?"

"All those years I never knew what it meant." She understood so much more. "All those years she terrorized me for the secret I kept! It was her whose evil secret festered in me."

Henry could only shake his head.

"It was her rage that consumed me."

"It did?"

"Yes." She nodded and closed her eyes. "Oh God, what do I do now?"

"What happened after this?"

Kitty took a deep breath. "I ran to my room. I locked the door."

"That was good."

Kitty gave out with a deep sigh. She had finally unloaded the unbearable burden of her mother's tyranny. "She never came."

Henry shook his head.

Suddenly she looked into the distance. "I'm no better than her."

"What?"

"I've failed my own child. I've failed Susie."

"Failed Susie?"

"I've failed my own daughter."

Henry could only shake his head.

"Just like my mother failed me."

"That's not true."

Her breathing became heavy and labored. "I failed her!"

"That's not true. I know that you love Susie."

"Yes, I do." She looked away, burying her head in the pillow. "Oh God in heaven, will you please forgive me for what I've done to my child?"

Her heart was breaking. She gave out completely. Suddenly, Kitty crumpled into a yielding heap of flesh. It was true: *she had failed Susie.* Just like her mother had failed her. History had repeated itself.

Chapter 27

March 1965

In March 1965, Reggie, now sixty-nine years old, having suffered a stroke, was laid up in a hospital, critically ill.

Kitty came to an abrupt halt outside the hospital room. She gave out a deep, aching sigh. Yes, right inside that room, right beyond that door, was her mother, the mother who had been so much a part of her yesterdays. The mother she had really never known. The mother who had always preferred her sister Ruth. The mother . . . she really didn't want to think about it.

Taking courage, she pushed the door open, walked over to the bed, and stared at the old woman lying there. She stared at her hollowed eyes, the sunken cheeks, the pale unmoving lips hidden under the oxygen mask. "Mother?" she whispered.

Reggie did not stir.

"Mother?" she repeated, her voice a bit more urgent.

Her eyelashes flickered only feebly. She had heard her.

"It's me, Kitty!"

Reggie's jaw dropped ever so slightly and her eyes, which had been unfocused, suddenly stared straight ahead.

"How're you doing, Mother?"

There was a faint tremor on Reggie's lips, an irresolute wavering. Kitty grasped her hand. "It's all right, Mother," she whispered.

It was at this moment, at the very moment that she observed the tremor on her mother's lips and clasped her lax hand that an amazing, one could even say crazy, thought crossed Kitty's mind. This old woman lying there, who looked like her mother, wasn't really her mother, the mother she had feared all of her life. For this old woman lying there appeared neither angry nor hateful. Instead, she seemed surrounded by a surprising calm, even, one could say, great serenity.

How wonderful it would be to kiss those pallid cheeks just once! How wonderful it would be to slip her fingers through that silky gray hair!

God, she was so mixed up.

In the end, she did nothing. She did nothing at all. Even though she knew that her mother's roar would be but a whimper.

Even though she knew that her mother's smirk would be but a grimace.

She squeezed her hand. "You're all right, Mother?"

Reggie withdrew her hand and, wiping the mask off her face, stared at her daughter. She took a deep breath, but with her muscles partially paralyzed, the left side of her face contracted, making her tortuous lips appear lopsided. "Of course I'm not all right." Even though her voice was barely audible, it was firm like it had always been. "Can't you see that?"

Her words struck Kitty like a bolt of lightning. The same biting words of old. Whatever stupid hope had she nurtured?

All at once, there was a timid whimper. "Kitty?"

She turned back to her. "Yes, Mother?"

She was gasping for air. At once, Kitty grabbed the oxygen mask and held it to her face. Little by little, Reggie got over the spell. Her breathing relaxed and she calmed.

After a while, Reggie removed the mask once more and spoke in a silvery voice, not at all like her own. "Thank you so much, Kitty."

"It's all right, Mother."

She looked up at her daughter, shaking her head. "I'm so sorry, Kitty."

"What is it, Mother?"

"I'm so sorry . . ." Momentarily Reggie looked away from Kitty, waited, put on the mask for a few seconds to catch more oxygen, and went on. "I'm so sorry that I didn't tell you."

"Tell me what?" What was her mother talking about?

Reggie stared at her daughter. "That I never warned you."

"About what, Mother?"

"About him."

"About whom, Mother?"

"About . . ." She stared at the ceiling, breathing laboriously, shaking her head. "*About him!*"

"Please, Mother!" Kitty placed her hand on Reggie's forehead, trying to calm her. Then she placed the mask over her face to let her breath. "Please, not now! Try to relax."

Reggie, pursing her lips, removed the mask once more. "*The bastard!*"

"What do you mean?"

Reggie's face had suddenly grown vivid. In spite of her sunken cheeks, in spite of the pale complexion, her eyes were sparking with fire and her tone had become razor-sharp. Just like in the olden days. "The bastard did it," she said, having to catch her breath. "He did it . . . because I wouldn't let him!"

"What is it, Mother?"

"I should have . . . strangled the bastard!" She barely caught her breath.

"What in heaven are you talking about, Mother?"

"I'm telling you, they're all bastards." Her face had turned white with the strain. "They're bastards or they're total failures."

"Who?"

"All of them!" She was breathing fast. She had to wait. Every one of them!"

"For heaven's sake, Mother, what are you talking about?"

Reggie looked up at her daughter. "You mean, you don't know?"

"Know what?"

Reggie nodded pensively, raising her eyebrows. Finally she quieted. "That I knew about him?"

"Who?"

"The *Kegelklub*, of course." She closed her eyes again, letting her breathing ease. "Remember . . . the *Kegelklub*?"

"What are you talking about, Mother?" She could feel her mother's stare, her penetrating eyes.

"You didn't know . . . that I knew all these years!"

"Know about whom?" Kitty covered her mouth. She had a feeling about it all.

"Listen to me, Kitty!" She shook her head, her eyes glued on her daughter. "Knew about . . . Hermann . . . of course."

"Hermann?"

"Yes, Hermann."

"You knew about him?"

Reggie looked up at the ceiling, her mouth ajar, nodding. "Of course I did," she whispered.

"You mean my father-in-law?"

Reggie nodded again. "Yes! Him!"

She didn't know what to say. All those years! Her mother knew about him. What he was like. "What did you know?"

"Listen to me, Kitty!" She grabbed Kitty's sleeve. "Do you hear me?" Her eyes popped wide open. "Hermann . . . was after me."

"He was after you?"

"He gave me . . . money."

"What money?"

"The store . . . remember?"

"The millinery store?"

Reggie nodded. She had to catch her breath.

Kitty looked away. God, Almighty! Her mother had known. Her mother had known all along. She had known all those years, known what her father-in-law was like.

"It was . . . his money!"

Her mother had known all along. But she had said nothing. Nothing at all. Not during the war. Not when he threatened her. Not when they were going to court. She had only told her now. When it didn't matter. When it didn't matter any longer.

She had no words.

Finally, Reggie closed her eyes. "You won't have to pay back the rest . . . he said to me . . . but I paid him back every cent. The bastard!" She took the mask, held it over her face, and took a deep breath. "You know . . . they're all bastards!" she repeated.

Kitty looked away.

"I'm so sorry, Kitty." Reggie reached for her daughter with her good right hand.

Kitty looked out into the distance. She couldn't bear looking at her mother. "You knew him," she repeated, "all along."

Reggie nodded.

"You knew what he was like." She covered her mouth.

Reggie nodded once more.

"You said nothing to me even though you knew what he had done?"

Reggie only shook her head.

Her insides smarting as if she'd been bit by a thousand gnats, Kitty dressed her face in a tight-lipped, pensive cast. She couldn't lose control.

"Papa?" It was but a whisper.

Reggie looked up. "What?"

"Papa?"

"What do you mean?"

"What about Papa?"

"Your father?"

"Yes! Papa."

Reggie looked away. She held on to the mask. Her breathing was thin but regular.

"I'm asking you!"

Reggie held the mask to her face. She didn't say anything.

"Tell me about Papa!"

Reggie remained silent.

"Answer me! Tell me, what happened to Papa?" Reggie turned back and looked up at Kitty, frowning, her eyes uncertain. "Tell me, Mother, what happened to him?" Reggie shook her head feebly. "Tell me! I must know!"

Reggie looked at the ceiling. Her lips were firm and her eyes were cold.

Kitty bent over her. She tried to catch her eyes. "I've waited all of my life," she said, biting her lips. "I must know!"

Reggie shut her lips tightly.

"I want to know what you did to him."

She still didn't talk.

Holding her down by her shoulders, Kitty stared at her mother. "You must tell me!"

Reggie turned her head away.

Kitty was breathing heavily. Her insides were out of control, recklessly at cross-purposes with themselves, their impact multiplying as the causes disintegrated. Yes, she was talking about her life. She had to know. *"What did you do to him?"*

Suddenly, Reggie looked up at her daughter, her eyes turning steely blue, her narrow lips firming. "You go to hell!"

For the first time in her life, Kitty felt a venonous hatred for her mother, a hatred that she had suppressed for so long. She saw her for what she really was: a *murderer*. Yes, it was true. She had murdered her father. All at once, a million images flooded her mind. Voiceless, faceless, distorted images without a center, without coherence, yesterday and today existing as a confused jumble, different times and different spaces combining in a here and now that was everywhere at once.

When it was all over, she smoothed the pillow and gently placed her mother's head on it.

She left the hospital room without a word, without ever looking back.

On the other side of the door she stopped cold. A sour, pungent belch welled up from deep inside of her. She hurried to the washroom. Slamming the door, she knelt and, embracing the bowl, pressed her stomach hard against it. She heaved. She heaved again and again, until the burning vomit cleared her throat. Little by little, she brought it all up until her stomach emptied and she produced only green curd. Until the raw drought in her empty gut made her shiver all over.

Only then did she get up.

She closed the door to the stall. At the sink she stared at the wan cast of her face. She washed herself, combed her hair, and put on some makeup. Her mother was dead, and that was that. She had tried to forgive. Tried to forgive what could never be forgiven. Still, her readiness to forgive had been a parent to a curse. The curse of making her think. Think of things she had never wanted to think about. Think of things she had never wanted to remember.

At the funeral a few days later, Kitty stood next to Ruth. It was hard to tell what Ruth was thinking, if anything. The distance between two sisters, though only inches, was really like miles. The way it had always been. They had nothing to say to each other. Nothing about anything. Nothing about their feelings, about their reminiscences, about their mother.

But, most of all, there were no questions from Ruth. In a way, Kitty had hoped that there would be some questions. Questions about how her mother had died. Questions about her father. But there were none. Not one word.

When Ruth left after the funeral, she gave Kitty a hug. Their heads did not touch. They did not smile. Nor did they have tears. There was nothing at all. Not a goddamned thing happened between them.

"Why didn't she ever hold me?" Kitty, her eyes glistening, asked Henry later that evening. "She never held me. Not even once. In all those years." Kitty covered her mouth. "Like other mothers!" She stared into the distance, shaking her head. "I don't understand. I don't understand it at all."

"I know you don't."

Raising her eyebrows, her eyes suddenly riveted on Henry. "But I was her child!"

"You were."

"Wasn't she a mother? Wasn't I once a part of her? Once inside of her?"

"Of course you were."

She closed her eyes and nodded. "I know I was. I know it was so."

Henry nodded but he did not say anything.

Opening her eyes, she pursed her lips and stared away from Henry. "She never held me because of Papa. I know that now. I understand that." She nodded. "Because Papa loved me so much."

Suddenly, big, heavy tears rolled down her cheeks. "Yes, I know that now. She never held me because of him. Because of his music. Because I was more like him and not like her. Yes, I know it all now." She gave a deep sigh. "All I am today, I am because of her. That can never be changed. For, what I have become, I have become because of her bitterness, because of her disappointment in him, because of her disappointment in me."

Chapter 28

May 1965

In early May 1965, less than two months after her mother's death, only five months after the recall of her father's murder, Kitty became disoriented. She wandered off, not certain where she was or where she was going. She had dizzy spells. She was unable to stand unsupported. Finally, and most gravely, her conversation became incoherent and sometimes she'd hide in the closet, closing the door behind her, whimpering like a child.

Henry sat down next to the hospital bed and grasped her hand. "It's me, Kitty! I'm here!"

She didn't hear him.

He stared at her. He stared at her empty face, at her listless eyes. He stared at the fragile frame, the unstrung limbs. Like a barren tree standing grimly against the winter's sunset, stripped clean of its spring blossoms and summer greens, she seemed only a pale likeness of her former self.

"Kitty, it's me!" He waited.

The doctors only knew how to treat her physical illness: a coronary spasm, they had said. If there were a way to help Kitty, the whole person, no one had yet come up with it.

"I'll take you home soon."

Telling her untruths to shield her, so troubling at first, had become an easy habit with Henry, one might even say too easy.

Like the roar of an oncoming train at the far end of the tunnel, she heard the drone from a distance. Suddenly, Kitty's eyes and mouth jarred wide open, her shallow breathing surged. She raised her head, all along heaving copious sighs like an infant catching its breath between loud wailings.

"Mama!"

The word broke free of its inevitable torture, like a monstrous creature delivered from its eternal suffering. Abruptly, Kitty dropped her head and, exhaling slowly, her cheeks drained and her breathing quieted, while her eyes filled up with tears. "Mama! Where are you?" Shrinking back into an icy silence, she stared at the ceiling. "I need you, Mama!"

Her life was no longer hers. It belonged to the fevered images bursting all around her.

But then, all of a sudden, everything did end. The dizziness, the fast heartbeat, had run its course. So quiet was her present state that, in spite of the relief she felt, it alarmed her. She sighed. It was a strange sigh, like the sigh of a child. A child from way back in her memory. A child left alone in a cradle in the black of the night. A child afraid to cry, afraid to breathe. A child feeling a stoic numbness. Aware that its terror had turned into stone.

After a while, slowly, feebly, she turned her head to him. Yes, he was there. Henry! His fingers moistened her lips. They felt soft and gentle.

"You'll be better soon," he said.

Her breathing was still scanty, shallow. She gave out a deep sigh. "I'm so tired."

He squeezed her hand. "I know you are."

"I always see her face."

"The past is over. You must look ahead."

Please, oh God, please! Make him understand! Make him understand that I can't let go of it. It's always there. "It won't let me be."

"Why? Why in heaven can't you leave it alone already!"

Suddenly, all the dizziness in her head, the weakness in her stomach, had returned. Like the first drops of dew on the autumn landscape, chilling beads of sweat had gathered on her forehead. There was no escape. Like a ball of ice, her memory was inching its way back to her heart. There was no stopping it.

She shut her eyes.

Old images flashing by. Memories! From way back! When she was still so young! How old was she? Where was she? Was it only a dream? No, it was real. The *Linden* trees. The River Ahr. The sunshine. Of course, she remembered: Bad Ems. Holding on to Papa's hand! How clearly she could see him still. Stopping. Stopping to watch the old angler. "Oh, the little baby! The little *Forelle!*"

"What in heaven are you talking about?"

"Oh no! It's me! I'm the one caught in the net! He won't throw me back," she whimpered.

"What? What's that supposed to mean?"

"I'm too big now." She shook her head. "He won't throw me back."

"You got another chance. You are free to swim away from it all."

She closed her eyes, still shaking her head. Don't you understand anything, Henry? Nothing has changed. Nothing at all. They're all still here. They're here right now. They never left me. All those eyes! Those eyes staring at me. The same stern, lecherous—oh my God, why won't it ever stop—bestial eyes. Following me around! All the time!

Those voices! All those voices ringing in my ears. Like the refrain of a song, repeating over and over again, without interruption calling out to me. "Come here, little Jewgirl!"

"Jewgirl? God, isn't that over yet?"

She turned her head away from him, taking short convulsive breaths. *"Mama, oh Mama, don't you hear me?"* She bit her lip, her jaws trembling. *"Where are you, Mama?"*

Yes, she was a castoff, an offering laid out between walls and curtains. Alone. Helpless. Contemptible. Without feelings. Hardened to stone. "I can't stand it any longer!"

Henry shook his head. "It's all over. Don't you know that?"

She frowned. She couldn't hold back the tears. "It's too late."

"How about all the others? How about all the thousands of others who survived the camps? They made it. They went on living. They left their past behind."

But Kitty remained silent.

He wouldn't let go. "My father is out of your life. Your mother has paid for her sins."

She still did not speak.

"You have three wonderful children."

"Susie." She bit her lips and shook her head. "I've failed my child." She gazed at Henry, her eyes still moist. He had been good to her. "I'm so sorry. I know I've disappointed you." She shook her head. "I was so weak. I was just like Papa."

"We're not all made of the same stuff."

"But we all live in the same world." She looked away from him. Like a long, deep shadow crossing her path, it suddenly seemed that all of her fears had dissipated with its passing. "I'm no longer afraid," she said quietly. "I'm much stronger now."

Yes, finally, she understood. Finally, she understood everything. It seemed that the portals of heaven had opened up for her. It was a merciful, splendid sight. "It's over!" she said and her voice was strong. "I am finally free!" It seemed that a blinding beacon had lit up the net and, like a butterfly, she was winging her way to her new destiny. "I'm free of her!" Yes, her new freedom was a gift from heaven, from the God of her Fathers. "I'm free of all of them!" She looked up into the shiny light and she knew that it would all come right, that all the cruelty would end, and that peace and tranquillity would return.

Henry waited for something more. Some words, some hope. But there was nothing but silence. He waited and waited, the interminable silence throbbing in his veins, bringing back to life the pain of the years, the bitter moments. He waited for her eyes to open again. He wanted to look once more into their dark, gentle passion. But they remained closed.

In the end, he kissed her forehead, tasting those salty drops, something of her, so damned little, so close to nothing. He drew her head close to him. He wanted to hold on to her once more. "I love you, Kitty," he whispered. "I'll help you go on."

She shrank from him. "Go away!" Her face had no more strain in it. "You can't fix it this time."

That's all that Kitty said in the end. Not another word. "You can't fix it this time!"

Henry sat next to her for a long time. Like an endless chorus of breakers, her past was still rolling ashore, going on forever, into eternity. The story of a young girl, a child prodigy pianist who, inspired by her music, would but for a few brief moments come to realize that small part of kindness that should be everyone's birthright.

The next morning they found Kitty at the bottom of the stairwell, dressed only in her nightgown. Her head lay in a pool of blood. How she had gotten out of bed with no one seeing her was a puzzle to everyone. He had warned the nurses. But she had done it anyhow. She had made a decision, her own decision. No longer could anyone tell her what to do. For the first time in her life, Kitty, in leaving this world, had formed things in the shape of her own will.

Epilogue

"All she needs is an analysis," he had said. It had all sounded so simple. Too simple, in fact. Maybe he should have left things alone. But how could he have known? For each life has a hidden self, filling one paragraph or a whole book, and the need to reconcile ourselves with our hidden self is as strong as it is difficult. We search for ways all of our lives.

Yes, he had failed Kitty! The moment when he might have saved her—if there ever had been such a moment—had passed, and with it all the years to come. He had tried to lift her back into the world. But the wall beyond the past had been too high and its edge had been too thin.

Only Eric came to the funeral. Except for a few friends, no one else came from Kitty's or Henry's family. Ruth never arrived. Henry's family shunned him because of his court case against his father. Alone, as always, even in death, Kitty's secrets were buried with her.

On the way to the cemetery, Eric sat next to Henry. "I've let things happen." He shook his head, trying to hide the swelling tears. "I should have done something."

How easily the good take on the guilt of the evil, Henry thought. "What could you have done?"

"Not be silent. Not look the other way."

Henry shook his head. "By the time you married Reggie, Kitty was already all that she would be."

"No. I could have done something. I knew Reggie. I knew your father." He looked up at Henry and shook his head.

Henry only nodded.

"I'm such a weak man." Eric looked dejected. "Kitty could have been a great artist." Tears flooded his cheeks. "I just stood by and let things happen." He shook his head. "You cannot let evil go unnoticed. If you do, as I did, you become part of it and have to live with its shame."

Henry nodded again.

"Will you forgive me?"

Henry saw Eric for what he was: weak, old, and now filled with so much guilt. He wished to comfort him. "There is nothing to forgive," he said to Eric.

After the funeral, when he was ready to leave, Eric put his arms around Henry. "Take good care of the children," he said. "Make sure they always remember their mother."

And so Eric tried to assuage his own guilt. But other than in Henry's memory, Kitty's only legacy were a few scraps of DNA passed on to her children, bearing only mute witness to all that she could have been in her short and tormented life.

The End